序 言

　　教科書開放以後，各校採用的版本不一樣，光
課本的文章，不足以參加「英語能力檢定測驗」。本書
是針對教育部「中級英語檢定指標」，在 5000 字常用單
字範圍內，完全**依據教育部的「中級字彙」**題型編輯而
成。每份試題均有詳細解答，每題附有翻譯與註釋，同
學不需浪費時間查字典。

　　一本好書，要有好的版面，才看得下去，本書的試
題編排、版面，經過長時間的研究，使同學看了，就有
想做下去的衝動。書中的資料非常珍貴，取材自各大規
模的考試，出題才會客觀，學生練習後，**能輕鬆應付各
種詞彙試題**，並能同時增強克漏字、閱讀測驗的解題能
力，進而全面提升英文實力。

　　所有高中學生都將面臨「中級英語檢定測驗」，現
在在校高中學生，都應該提早準備，為學校爭光。本書
另附有「教學專用本」，適合高中老師教學使用。

劉 毅

TEST 1

Directions: Of the four words given after each sentence, choose the one most suitable for filling in the blank.

1. Everyone was asked to _____ suggestions for the party.
   - (A) relax
   - (B) contribute
   - (C) strive
   - (D) sacrifice   (   )

2. The _____ objective of this organization is to help the poor.
   - (A) academic
   - (B) local
   - (C) subject
   - (D) primary   (   )

3. Smoking is a leading _____ in lung diseases.
   - (A) favor
   - (B) factor
   - (C) labor
   - (D) grade   (   )

4. The cancer has spread to the surrounding _____ .
   - (A) organs
   - (B) centuries
   - (C) cases
   - (D) opinions   (   )

5. The energy of the sun can be used to _____ electricity.
   - (A) desert
   - (B) contain
   - (C) generate
   - (D) respond   (   )

6. The boys ⎯⎯⎯⎯ with each other for the prize.

   (A) protected
   (B) concluded
   (C) blamed
   (D) competed   (   )

7. I ⎯⎯⎯⎯ the decision be moved to another date.

   (A) attend
   (B) propose
   (C) accomplish
   (D) bother   (   )

8. ⎯⎯⎯⎯ is a very desirable trait in business.

   (A) Disease
   (B) Efficiency
   (C) Item
   (D) Amount   (   )

9. Before classes start you had better get ⎯⎯⎯⎯ with one another.

   (A) offered
   (B) doubted
   (C) acquainted
   (D) avoided   (   )

10. This university ⎯⎯⎯⎯ in engineering courses.

   (A) claims
   (B) excels
   (C) values
   (D) feeds   (   )

TEST 1 詳解

1. (**B**) Everyone was asked to <u>contribute</u> suggestions for the party.
   每個人都被要求針對這次的宴會提出建議。

   (A) relax〔rɪ'læks〕v. 放鬆
   (B) ***contribute***〔kən'trɪbjut〕v. 貢獻
   (C) strive〔straɪv〕v. 努力
   (D) sacrifice〔'sækrə,faɪs〕v. 犧牲

con	+ tribute
together	+ *bestow*（贈與）

2. (**D**) The <u>primary</u> objective of this organization is to help the poor. 這個組織的主要目標是救濟窮人。

   (A) academic〔,ækə'dɛmɪk〕adj. 學術的
   (B) local〔'lokḷ〕adj. 當地的
   (C) subject〔'sʌbdʒɪkt〕adj. 服從的
   (D) ***primary***〔'praɪ,mɛrɪ〕adj. 主要的

   * objective〔əb'dʒɛktɪv〕n. 目標

3. (**B**) Smoking is a leading <u>factor</u> in lung diseases.
   抽菸是造成肺病的主因。

   (A) favor〔'fevɚ〕n. 恩惠；偏愛　(B) ***factor***〔'fæktɚ〕n. 因素
   (C) labor〔'lebɚ〕n. 勞動　(D) grade〔gred〕n. 等級；分數

   * leading〔'lidɪŋ〕adj. 主要的

4. (**A**) The cancer has spread to the surrounding <u>organs</u>.
   癌症已擴散至附近的器官。

   (A) ***organ***〔'ɔrgən〕n. 器官　(B) century〔'sɛntʃərɪ〕n. 世紀
   (C) case〔kes〕n. 情況　(D) opinion〔ə'pɪnjən〕n. 意見

   * cancer〔'kænsɚ〕n. 癌症　surrounding〔sə'raʊndɪŋ〕adj. 附近的

5. (**C**) The energy of the sun can be used to <u>generate</u> electricity.
   太陽能可用來發電。

   (A) desert〔dɪ'zɜt〕v. 拋棄　(B) contain〔kən'ten〕v. 包含
   (C) ***generate***〔'dʒɛnə,ret〕v. 產生　(D) respond〔rɪ'spɑnd〕v. 回答

6. (**D**) The boys <u>competed</u> with each other for the prize.

男孩們爲了得獎彼此<u>競爭</u>。

(A) protect〔prə'tɛkt〕*v.* 保護

(B) conclude〔kən'klud〕*v.* 下結論

(C) blame〔blem〕*v.* 責備

(D) ***compete***〔kəm'pit〕*v.* 競爭

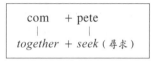

7. (**B**) I <u>propose</u> the decision be moved to another date.

我<u>提議</u>改天再做決定。

(A) attend〔ə'tɛnd〕*v.* 參加;上 (學)

(B) ***propose***〔prə'poz〕*v.* 提議

(C) accomplish〔ə'kɑmplɪʃ〕*v.* 完成

(D) bother〔'bɑðɚ〕*v.* 打擾;困擾

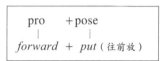

8. (**B**) <u>Efficiency</u> is a very desirable trait in business.

<u>效率</u>是商場上人人都想擁有的特點。

(A) disease〔dɪ'ziz〕*n.* 疾病

(B) ***efficiency***〔ə'fɪʃənsɪ〕*n.* 效率

(C) item〔'aɪtəm〕*n.* 項目

(D) amount〔ə'maʊnt〕*n.* 數量

* desirable〔dɪ'zaɪrəbl̩〕*adj.* 很想要的   trait〔tret〕*n.* 特點

9. (**C**) Before classes start you had better get <u>acquainted</u> with one another. 開學前,你們最好要先彼此<u>認識</u>。

(A) offer〔'ɔfɚ〕*v.* 提供　　(B) doubt〔daʊt〕*v.* 懷疑

(C) ***acquaint***〔ə'kwent〕*v.* 使認識　(D) avoid〔ə'vɔɪd〕*v.* 避免

* ***get acquainted with***~　認識~

10. (**B**) This university <u>excels</u> in engineering courses.

這所大學較<u>擅長</u>工程學方面的課程。

(A) claim〔klem〕*v.* 要求;宣稱　(B) ***excel***〔ɪk'sɛl〕*v.* 擅長;優越

(C) value〔'vælju〕*v.* 重視　　(D) feed〔fid〕*v.* 餵食

* engineering〔ˌɛndʒə'nɪrɪŋ〕*n.* 工程學

TEST 2

Directions: *Of the four words given after each sentence, choose the one most suitable for filling in the blank.*

1. Our _____ of smell is the least understood of all the five senses.
   - (A) sense
   - (B) status
   - (C) task
   - (D) chain ( )

2. The new subway system should _____ the traffic on the roads.
   - (A) refer
   - (B) reduce
   - (C) press
   - (D) resist ( )

3. Anderson's mother _____ a house for rent.
   - (A) persisted
   - (B) responded
   - (C) preceded
   - (D) advertised ( )

4. My officemates _____ me with a birthday cake.
   - (A) educated
   - (B) replied
   - (C) surprised
   - (D) imitated ( )

5. Old age has been the _____ cause of death.
   - (A) chemical
   - (B) plastic
   - (C) apparent
   - (D) savage ( )

6. I must perform the task that has been _____ upon me.

    (A) served
    (B) imposed
    (C) observed
    (D) researched   (   )

7. This machine can be _____ by remote control.

    (A) contained
    (B) respected
    (C) seemed
    (D) operated   (   )

8. Let us all _____ for the national anthem.

    (A) admire
    (B) rise
    (C) protect
    (D) delight   (   )

9. The people _____ the town in the wake of the flood.

    (A) deserted
    (B) chewed
    (C) disapproved
    (D) behaved   (   )

10. The _____ of rice is causing prices to rise.

    (A) scholar
    (B) spirit
    (C) culture
    (D) shortage   (   )

TEST 2 詳解

1. (**A**) Our <u>sense</u> of smell is the least understood of all the five senses. 在五種感官中,我們對嗅覺的了解最少。

    (A) ***sense*** 〔 sɛns 〕 *n.* 感官;感覺   (B) status 〔'stetəs 〕 *n.* 地位
    (C) task 〔 tæsk 〕 *n.* 任務;工作   (D) chain 〔 tʃen 〕 *n.* 鏈子

2. (**B**) The new subway system should <u>reduce</u> the traffic on the roads. 新的地下鐵系統應該可以<u>減少</u>道路上的交通流量。

    (A) refer 〔 rɪ'fɝ 〕 *v.* 提到
    (B) ***reduce*** 〔 rɪ'djus 〕 *v.* 減少
    (C) press 〔 prɛs 〕 *v.* 壓
    (D) resist 〔 rɪ'zɪst 〕 *v.* 抵抗

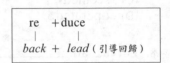

    * subway 〔'sʌb͵we 〕 *n.* 地下鐵

3. (**D**) Anderson's mother <u>advertised</u> a house for rent.
安德森的母親<u>刊登租屋廣告</u>。

    (A) persist 〔 pɚ'sɪst 〕 *v.* 堅持
    (B) respond 〔 rɪ'spɑnd 〕 *v.* 回答
    (C) precede 〔 prɪ'sid 〕 *v.* 在～之前
    (D) ***advertise*** 〔'ædvɚ͵taɪz 〕 *v.* 刊登廣告

4. (**C**) My officemates <u>surprised</u> me with a birthday cake.
我的同事買了生日蛋糕,<u>使我非常驚訝</u>。

    (A) educate 〔'ɛdʒə͵ket 〕 *v.* 教育   (B) reply 〔 rɪ'plaɪ 〕 *v.* 回答
    (C) ***surprise*** 〔 sə'praɪz 〕 *v.* 使驚訝   (D) imitate 〔'ɪmə͵tet 〕 *v.* 模仿

5. (**C**) Old age has been the <u>apparent</u> cause of death.
年老是死亡<u>明顯的</u>原因。

    (A) chemical 〔'kɛmɪkl̩ 〕 *adj.* 化學的
    (B) plastic 〔'plæstɪk 〕 *adj.* 塑膠的
    (C) ***apparent*** 〔 ə'pɛrənt 〕 *adj.* 明顯的
    (D) savage 〔'sævɪdʒ 〕 *adj.* 野蠻的

6.(**B**) I must perform the task that has been <u>imposed</u> upon me.
我必須執行<u>交付</u>給我的任務。

(A) serve〔sɝv〕*v.* 服務
(B) ***impose***〔ɪm'poz〕*v.* 加於～之上
(C) observe〔əb'zɝv〕*v.* 觀察；遵守
(D) research〔rɪ'sɝtʃ〕*v.* 研究

* perform〔pɚ'fɔrm〕*v.* 執行

```
im + pose
 |      |
on + place ( 置於其上 )
```

7.(**D**) This machine can be <u>operated</u> by remote control.
這部機器可用遙控來<u>操作</u>。

(A) contain〔kən'ten〕*v.* 包含
(B) respect〔rɪ'spɛkt〕*v.* 尊敬
(C) seem〔sim〕*v.* 似乎
(D) ***operate***〔'ɑpə,ret〕*v.* 操作

* ***remote control*** 遙控

8.(**B**) Let us all <u>rise</u> for the national anthem.
唱國歌時，請大家<u>起立</u>。

(A) admire〔əd'maɪr〕*v.* 欽佩
(B) ***rise***〔raɪz〕*v.* 起立
(C) protect〔prə'tɛkt〕*v.* 保護
(D) delight〔dɪ'laɪt〕*v.* 使高興

* ***national anthem*** 國歌

9.(**A**) The people <u>deserted</u> the town in the wake of the flood.
洪水過後，居民自城鎮<u>撤離</u>。

(A) ***desert***〔dɪ'zɝt〕*v.* 離開；拋棄
(B) chew〔tʃu〕*v.* 咀嚼
(C) disapprove〔,dɪsə'pruv〕*v.* 不贊成
(D) behave〔bɪ'hev〕*v.* 行為；舉止

* ***in the wake of***～ 在～之後

10.(**D**) The <u>shortage</u> of rice is causing prices to rise.
稻米的<u>短缺</u>造成價格上揚。

(A) scholar〔'skɑlɚ〕*n.* 學者
(B) spirit〔'spɪrɪt〕*n.* 精神
(C) culture〔'kʌltʃɚ〕*n.* 文化
(D) ***shortage***〔'ʃɔrtɪdʒ〕*n.* 缺乏

* rice〔raɪs〕*n.* 稻米

TEST 3

Directions: *Of the four words given after each sentence, choose the one most suitable for filling in the blank.*

1. Would you like to listen to some constructive _____ ?
   (A) criticism
   (B) root
   (C) source
   (D) religion   (   )

2. It is the _____ of every citizen to protect his/her country.
   (A) tension
   (B) duty
   (C) confidence
   (D) departure   (   )

3. Every male in the R.O.C. has to perform two years of _____ service.
   (A) military
   (B) false
   (C) familiar
   (D) potential   (   )

4. May gave a(n) _____ analysis of the play.
   (A) firm
   (B) temporary
   (C) bare
   (D) objective   (   )

5. Jane _____ her guests in the living room.
   (A) represented
   (B) entertained
   (C) attempted
   (D) intensified   (   )

6. The living standard of the people here in Taiwan _____ sharply with that of the people in Mainland China.

   (A) urges
   (B) rewards
   (C) contrasts
   (D) breeds   (   )

7. At the age of sixty, Sylvia decided to _____ from office.

   (A) appeal
   (B) approve
   (C) retire
   (D) select   (   )

8. The flight was _____ for two hours.

   (A) delayed
   (B) sacked
   (C) inspired
   (D) employed   (   )

9. Are you _____ that I am not telling the truth?

   (A) conquering
   (B) implying
   (C) withdrawing
   (D) nodding   (   )

10. After sitting for two hours, Lucy went out to _____ her legs.

   (A) alarm
   (B) flourish
   (C) import
   (D) stretch   (   )

TEST 3 詳解

1. (**A**) Would you like to listen to some constructive <u>criticism</u>?
你要不要聽一些有建設性的<u>批評</u>？

    (A) *criticism* ('krɪtə,sɪzəm) *n.* 批評   (B) root (rut) *n.* 根；根源
    (C) source (sors) *n.* 來源   (D) religion (rɪ'lɪdʒən) *n.* 宗教

    * constructive (kən'strʌktɪv) *adj.* 有建設性的

2. (**B**) It is the <u>duty</u> of every citizen to protect his / her country.
保衛國家是每位國民的<u>責任</u>。

    (A) tension ('tɛnʃən) *n.* 緊張   (B) *duty* ('djutɪ) *n.* 責任
    (C) confidence ('kɑnfədəns) *n.* 信心
    (D) departure (dɪ'pɑrtʃə) *n.* 離開

    * citizen ('sɪtɪzn̩) *n.* 國民；公民

3. (**A**) Every male in the R.O.C. has to perform two years of
<u>military</u> service. 中華民國的男性必須服二年<u>兵役</u>。

    (A) *military* ('mɪlə,tɛrɪ) *adj.* 軍事的   (B) false (fɔls) *adj.* 錯誤的
    (C) familiar (fə'mɪljə) *adj.* 熟悉的
    (D) potential (pə'tɛnʃəl) *adj.* 有潛力的

    * *military service* 兵役

4. (**D**) May gave an <u>objective</u> analysis of the play.
梅對這齣戲做了<u>客觀的</u>分析。

    (A) firm (fɜm) *adj.* 堅定的   (B) temporary ('tɛmpə,rɛrɪ) *adj.* 暫時的
    (C) bare (bɛr) *adj.* 赤裸的   (D) *objective* (əb'dʒɛktɪv) *adj.* 客觀的

    * play (ple) *n.* 戲劇

5. (**B**) Jane <u>entertained</u> her guests in the living room.
珍在客廳裡<u>招待</u>客人。

    (A) represent (,rɛprɪ'zɛnt) *v.* 代表
    (B) *entertain* (,ɛntə'ten) *v.* 招待
    (C) attempt (ə'tɛmpt) *v.* 企圖
    (D) intensify (ɪn'tɛnsə,faɪ) *v.* 加強

> enter ＋ tain
> | |
> *among* ＋*hold* (保持關係)

6. (**C**) The living standard of the people here in Taiwan <u>contrasts</u> sharply with that of the people in Mainland China.
台灣和大陸人民的生活水準，形成十分強烈的<u>對比</u>。

 (A) urge〔ɝdʒ〕v. 催促
 (B) reward〔rɪ'wɔrd〕v. 報酬；獎賞
 (C) ***contrast***〔kən'træst〕v. 與～形成對比
 (D) breed〔brid〕v. 養育

 ＊ ***living standard*** 生活水準 sharply〔'ʃɑrplɪ〕adv. 尖銳地；清晰地

7. (**C**) At the age of sixty, Sylvia decided to <u>retire</u> from office.
席維亞六十歲時決定<u>退休</u>。

 (A) appeal〔ə'pil〕v. 吸引 (B) approve〔ə'pruv〕v. 同意
 (C) ***retire***〔rɪ'taɪr〕v. 退休 (D) select〔sə'lɛkt〕v. 挑選

8. (**A**) The flight was <u>delayed</u> for two hours. 飛機<u>延誤</u>了兩個小時。

 (A) ***delay***〔dɪ'le〕v. 延誤
 (B) sack〔sæk〕v. 把～裝入袋中；解雇
 (C) inspire〔ɪn'spaɪr〕v. 激勵；給與靈感
 (D) employ〔ɪm'plɔɪ〕v. 雇用

 ＊ flight〔flaɪt〕n. 班機

9. (**B**) Are you <u>implying</u> that I am not telling the truth?
你在<u>暗示</u>我沒說實話嗎？

 (A) conquer〔'kɑŋkɚ〕v. 征服
 (B) ***imply***〔ɪm'plaɪ〕v. 暗示
 (C) withdraw〔wɪθ'drɔ〕v. 撤退
 (D) nod〔nɑd〕v. 點頭

         im + ply
          │ │
         in +*fold*（折疊於其中）

10. (**D**) After sitting for two hours, Lucy went out to <u>stretch</u> her legs. 連續坐了兩小時之後，露西到外頭<u>伸伸腿</u>。

 (A) alarm〔ə'lɑrm〕v. 使驚慌
 (B) flourish〔'flɝɪʃ〕v. 興盛；繁榮
 (C) import〔ɪm'port〕v. 進口
 (D) ***stretch***〔strɛtʃ〕v. 伸展

TEST 4

Directions: *Of the four words given after each sentence, choose the one most suitable for filling in the blank.*

1. His part-time job _____ with his classes.
   - (A) litters
   - (B) conflicts
   - (C) embarrasses
   - (D) reserves   (   )

2. Ultraviolet rays are _____ to the naked eye.
   - (A) gentle
   - (B) invisible
   - (C) anxious
   - (D) incredible   (   )

3. In the Bible, God _____ Adam by banishing him from the Garden of Eden.
   - (A) shared
   - (B) punished
   - (C) approached
   - (D) roared   (   )

4. Communist China possesses _____ weapons.
   - (A) facial
   - (B) nuclear
   - (C) prosperous
   - (D) loose   (   )

5. As far as I am concerned, my _____ is clear.
   - (A) perseverance
   - (B) irrigation
   - (C) conscience
   - (D) nerve   (   )

6. The _____ of this elevator is limited to ten people.

   (A) caution
   (B) concept
   (C) capacity
   (D) rigidity   (   )

7. You're as _____ as a mule.

   (A) coherent
   (B) fantastic
   (C) stubborn
   (D) illegal   (   )

8. Washington D.C. is the _____ city of the United States.

   (A) capital
   (B) solid
   (C) similar
   (D) accurate   (   )

9. Michelle _____ her father's business.

   (A) associated
   (B) descended
   (C) inherited
   (D) drowned   (   )

10. I have _____ my lawyers to act on my behalf.

   (A) reacted
   (B) authorized
   (C) predicted
   (D) attached   (   )

TEST 4 詳解

1. (**B**) His part-time job <u>conflicts</u> with his classes.
   他兼差的工作和課業相衝突。

   (A) litter〔'lɪtɚ〕v. 亂丟垃圾　　(B) ***conflict***〔kən'flɪkt〕v. 衝突
   (C) embarrass〔ɪm'bærəs〕v. 使困窘　(D) reserve〔rɪ'zɝv〕v. 預訂

2. (**B**) Ultraviolet rays are <u>invisible</u> to the naked eye.
   紫外線是肉眼<u>看不見的</u>。

   (A) gentle〔'dʒɛntḷ〕adj. 溫和的
   (B) ***invisible***〔ɪn'vɪzəbḷ〕adj. 看不見的
   (C) anxious〔'æŋkʃəs〕adj. 焦慮的
   (D) incredible〔ɪn'krɛdəbḷ〕adj. 不可思議的
   * ultraviolet〔͵ʌltrə'vaɪəlɪt〕adj. 紫外線的　　***the naked eye*** 肉眼

3. (**B**) In the Bible, God <u>punished</u> Adam by banishing him from the
   Garden of Eden. 根據聖經記載，上帝將亞當逐出伊甸園作為懲罰。

   (A) share〔ʃɛr〕v. 分享　　　　(B) ***punish***〔'pʌnɪʃ〕v. 處罰
   (C) approach〔ə'protʃ〕v. 接近　(D) roar〔ror〕v. 吼叫
   * Bible〔'baɪbḷ〕n. 聖經　　banish〔'bænɪʃ〕v. 驅逐
   the Garden of Eden 伊甸園

4. (**B**) Communist China possesses <u>nuclear</u> weapons.
   中共擁有<u>核子</u>武器。

   (A) facial〔'feʃəl〕adj. 臉部的
   (B) ***nuclear***〔'njuklɪɚ〕adj. 核子的
   (C) prosperous〔'prɑspərəs〕adj. 繁榮的
   (D) loose〔lus〕adj. 鬆的
   * communist〔'kɑmjʊnɪst〕n. 共產主義者　adj. 共產主義的
   possess〔pə'zɛs〕v. 擁有　　weapon〔'wɛpən〕n. 武器

5. (**C**) As far as I am concerned, my <u>conscience</u> is clear.
   就我而言，我的<u>良心</u>是清白的。

   (A) perseverance〔͵pɝsə'vɪrəns〕n. 毅力
   (B) irrigation〔͵ɪrə'geʃən〕n. 灌溉
   (C) ***conscience***〔'kɑnʃəns〕n. 良心　(D) nerve〔nɝv〕n. 神經

6. (**C**) The <u>capacity</u> of this elevator is limited to ten people.
這部電梯只能<u>容納</u>十個人。

(A) caution〔ˈkɔʃən〕 *n.* 小心；謹慎

(B) concept〔ˈkɑnsɛpt〕 *n.* 概念

(C) *capacity*〔kəˈpæsətɪ〕 *n.* 容量

(D) rigidity〔rɪˈdʒɪdətɪ〕 *n.* 堅硬

* elevator〔ˈɛləˌvetə〕 *n.* 電梯；升降機（escalator *n.* 手扶梯）

7. (**C**) You're as <u>stubborn</u> as a mule.
你像騾子一樣<u>頑固</u>。

(A) coherent〔koˈhɪrənt〕 *adj.* 有條理的

(B) fantastic〔fænˈtæstɪk〕 *adj.* 太棒了

(C) *stubborn*〔ˈstʌbən〕 *adj.* 頑固的

(D) illegal〔ɪˈligl̩〕 *adj.* 非法的

* mule〔mjul〕 *n.* 騾子；頑固的人

8. (**A**) Washington D.C. is the <u>capital</u> city of the United States.
華盛頓特區是美國的<u>首都</u>。

(A) *capital*〔ˈkæpətl̩〕 *adj.* 首都的 *n.* 首都

(B) solid〔ˈsɑlɪd〕 *adj.* 固體的

(C) similar〔ˈsɪmələ〕 *adj.* 相似的

(D) accurate〔ˈækjərɪt〕 *adj.* 準確的

9. (**C**) Michelle <u>inherited</u> her father's business.
蜜雪兒<u>繼承</u>了她父親的事業。

(A) associate〔əˈsoʃɪˌet〕 *v.* 聯想 (B) descend〔dɪˈsɛnd〕 *v.* 下降

(C) *inherit*〔ɪnˈhɛrɪt〕 *v.* 繼承 (D) drown〔draʊn〕 *v.* 淹死

10. (**B**) I have <u>authorized</u> my lawyers to act on my behalf.
我已<u>授權</u>給律師，代我處理一切事務。

(A) react〔rɪˈækt〕 *v.* 反應

(B) *authorize*〔ˈɔθəˌraɪz〕 *v.* 授權

(C) predict〔prɪˈdɪkt〕 *v.* 預測 (D) attach〔əˈtætʃ〕 *v.* 貼上

* *on* *one's* *behalf* 代替某人

TEST 5

Directions: *Of the four words given after each sentence, choose the one most suitable for filling in the blank.*

1. Thailand is a(n) _____ site for our new factory.
   - (A) ideal
   - (B) physical
   - (C) complex
   - (D) weak   (   )

2. Mel was a carpenter _____ to his job as an actor.
   - (A) terrible
   - (B) enormous
   - (C) prior
   - (D) private   (   )

3. Our encounter at the beach is still _____ in my mind.
   - (A) entire
   - (B) vivid
   - (C) honest
   - (D) average   (   )

4. She has undergone _____ three times to correct the deformity.
   - (A) diligence
   - (B) evolution
   - (C) cattle
   - (D) surgery   (   )

5. Napoleon's empire _____ of lands in Europe, Africa and Asia.
   - (A) transmitted
   - (B) instituted
   - (C) recycled
   - (D) consisted   (   )

6. The couple stayed together for the _____ of the children.

   (A) cave
   (B) sake
   (C) pessimism
   (D) field   (   )

7. It takes time to _____ a dictionary.

   (A) compile
   (B) exaggerate
   (C) abuse
   (D) port   (   )

8. Everyone's excited about the _____ of the test.

   (A) contempt
   (B) outcome
   (C) journal
   (D) industry   (   )

9. Nylon is a(n) _____ material.

   (A) wretch
   (B) synthetic
   (C) enthusiastic
   (D) precious   (   )

10. Mr. Lee is our _____ to South Africa.

   (A) ambassador
   (B) negotiation
   (C) paragraph
   (D) total   (   )

TEST 5 詳解

1. (**A**) Thailand is an <u>ideal</u> site for our new factory.
泰國是我們設立新工廠的<u>理想</u>地點。
  (A) ***ideal*** ﹝ aɪˈdiəl ﹞ *adj.* 理想的 (B) physical ﹝ˈfɪzɪkl̩﹞ *adj.* 身體的
  (C) complex ﹝ˈkɑmplɛks﹞ *adj.* 複雜的
  (D) weak ﹝ wik ﹞ *adj.* 虛弱的

2. (**C**) Mel was a carpenter <u>prior</u> to his job as an actor.
梅爾在當演員<u>之前</u>，是一位木匠。
  (A) terrible ﹝ˈtɛrəbl̩﹞ *adj.* 可怕的
  (B) enormous ﹝ ɪˈnɔrməs ﹞ *adj.* 巨大的
  (C) ***prior*** ﹝ˈpraɪɚ﹞ *adj.* 在～之前的 (D) private ﹝ˈpraɪvɪt﹞ *adj.* 私人的
  * carpenter ﹝ˈkɑrpəntɚ﹞ *n.* 木匠

3. (**B**) Our encounter at the beach is still <u>vivid</u> in my mind.
我們在海邊的相遇，至今仍很<u>清楚</u>地留在我的腦海中。
  (A) entire ﹝ ɪnˈtaɪr ﹞ *adj.* 全部的
  (B) ***vivid*** ﹝ˈvɪvɪd﹞ *adj.* 清楚的；生動的
  (C) honest ﹝ˈɑnɪst﹞ *adj.* 誠實的 (D) average ﹝ˈævərɪdʒ﹞ *adj.* 平均的

4. (**D**) She has undergone <u>surgery</u> three times to correct the deformity. 她為了矯正畸形，動過三次<u>外科手術</u>。
  (A) diligence ﹝ˈdɪlədʒəns﹞ *n.* 勤勉
  (B) evolution ﹝ˌɛvəˈluʃən﹞ *n.* 進化
  (C) cattle ﹝ˈkætl̩﹞ *n.* 牛（集合名詞）
  (D) ***surgery*** ﹝ˈsɝdʒərɪ﹞ *n.* 外科手術
  * undergo ﹝ˌʌndɚˈgo﹞ *v.* 動（手術） deformity ﹝ dɪˈfɔrmətɪ ﹞ *n.* 畸形

5. (**D**) Napoleon's empire <u>consisted</u> of lands in Europe, Africa and Asia. 拿破崙帝國是由歐、亞、非三大洲的土地所<u>組成</u>。
  (A) transmit ﹝ trænsˈmɪt ﹞ *v.* 傳送
  (B) institute ﹝ˈɪnstəˌtjut﹞ *v.* 設立
  (C) recycle ﹝ riˈsaɪkl̩﹞ *v.* 回收；再利用
  (D) ***consist*** ﹝ kənˈsɪst ﹞ *v.* 由～組成
   consist of~ 由～組成（= *be composed of* = *be made up of*）
  * empire ﹝ˈɛmpaɪr﹞ *n.* 帝國

```
con    +  sist
 |         |
together +stand （站在一起）
```

6. (**B**) The couple stayed together for the <u>sake</u> of the children.
這對夫妻爲了小孩的<u>緣故</u>，決定繼續在一起。

    (A) cave〔kev〕*n.* 洞穴

    (B) ***sake***〔sek〕*n.* 緣故   ***for the sake of***~ 爲了~的緣故

    (C) pessimism〔'pɛsə,mɪzəm〕*n.* 悲觀

    (D) field〔fild〕*n.* 田野；領域

    * couple〔'kʌpl̩〕*n.* 夫妻

7. (**A**) It takes time to <u>compile</u> a dictionary.
<u>編</u>字典需要很長的時間。

    (A) ***compile***〔kəm'paɪl〕*v.* 編輯

    (B) exaggerate〔ɪg'zædʒə,ret〕*v.* 誇大

    (C) abuse〔ə'bjuz〕*v.* 濫用；虐待

    (D) port〔port〕*v.* 端槍；使轉向左舷

8. (**B**) Everyone's excited about the <u>outcome</u> of the test.
測驗的<u>結果</u>，讓大家都很興奮。

    (A) contempt〔kən'tɛmpt〕*n.* 輕視   (B) ***outcome***〔'aʊt,kʌm〕*n.* 結果

    (C) journal〔'dʒɝnl̩〕*n.* 期刊；日誌   (D) industry〔'ɪndəstrɪ〕*n.* 工業

9. (**B**) Nylon is a <u>synthetic</u> material.
尼龍是一種<u>合成</u>的質料。

    (A) wretch〔rɛtʃ〕*n.* 可憐人

    (B) ***synthetic***〔sɪn'θɛtɪk〕*adj.* 合成的

    (C) enthusiastic〔ɪn,θjuzɪ'æstɪk〕*adj.* 熱心的

    (D) precious〔'prɛʃəs〕*adj.* 珍貴的

syn	+the	+ tic
together	+put	+adj.

10. (**A**) Mr. Lee is our <u>ambassador</u> to South Africa.
李先生是我國駐南非的<u>大使</u>。

    (A) ***ambassador***〔æm'bæsədɚ〕*n.* 大使

    (B) negotiation〔nɪ,goʃɪ'eʃən〕*n.* 談判；諮商

    (C) paragraph〔'pærə,græf〕*n.* 段落

    (D) total〔'totl̩〕*n.* 總數

    * ***South Africa*** 南非

TEST 6

Directions: *Of the four words given after each sentence, choose the one most suitable for filling in the blank.*

1. You've got a Mom who's really _____ about you.

    (A) ignored
    (B) created
    (C) concerned
    (D) wondered   (   )

2. Let me _____ the importance of your mission.

    (A) crowd
    (B) emphasize
    (C) deliver
    (D) pollute   (   )

3. The city has seen a(n) _____ increase in population in recent years.

    (A) steady
    (B) fresh
    (C) general
    (D) individual   (   )

4. Money laundering is a(n) _____ crime in the United States.

    (A) difficulty
    (B) public
    (C) serious
    (D) interest   (   )

5. Since no one _____ , the plan was approved.

    (A) harmed
    (B) defined
    (C) objected
    (D) gained   (   )

6. His _____ is to be a millionaire.

   (A) ambition
   (B) nation
   (C) evidence
   (D) herd   (   )

7. _____ studies show that green tea prevents cancer.

   (A) Worry
   (B) Moment
   (C) Indifference
   (D) Recent   (   )

8. Investigators have yet to _____ the cause of the crash.

   (A) measure
   (B) determine
   (C) refuse
   (D) memorize   (   )

9. The people could not _____ that military regime.

   (A) fit
   (B) tolerate
   (C) figure
   (D) differ   (   )

10. Most residents _____ the building of the nuclear plant.

   (A) oppose
   (B) manage
   (C) apply
   (D) promise   (   )

TEST 6 詳解

1. (**C**) You've got a Mom who's really <u>concerned</u> about you.
   你有一位非常關心你的母親。

   (A) ignore〔ɪg'nor〕v. 忽視　　(B) create〔krɪ'et〕v. 創造
   (C) **concern**〔kən'sɝn〕v. 關心　　(D) wonder〔'wʌndə〕v. 想知道

2. (**B**) Let me <u>emphasize</u> the importance of your mission.
   我要強調你這次任務的重要性。

   (A) crowd〔kraud〕v. 使擁擠　　(B) **emphasize**〔'ɛmfə,saɪz〕v. 強調
   (C) deliver〔dɪ'lɪvə〕v. 遞送　　(D) pollute〔pə'lut〕v. 污染
   * mission〔'mɪʃən〕n. 任務

3. (**A**) The city has seen a <u>steady</u> increase in population in
   recent years. 最近幾年，這城市的人口數有穩定的成長。

   (A) **steady**〔'stɛdɪ〕adj. 穩定的
   (B) fresh〔frɛʃ〕adj. 新鮮的
   (C) general〔'dʒɛnərəl〕adj. 一般的；普遍的
   (D) individual〔,ɪndə'vɪdʒuəl〕adj. 個別的

4. (**C**) Money laundering is a <u>serious</u> crime in the United States.
   在美國，洗錢是一項很嚴重的罪。

   (A) difficulty〔'dɪfə,kʌltɪ〕n. 困難
   (B) public〔'pʌblɪk〕adj. 公共的；公開的
   (C) **serious**〔'sɪrɪəs〕adj. 嚴重的
   (D) interest〔'ɪntrɪst〕n. 興趣；利息
   * laundering〔'lɔndərɪŋ〕n. 洗濯　　**money laundering** 洗錢

5. (**C**) Since no one <u>objected</u>, the plan was approved.
   既然沒有人反對，這項計畫就算通過了。

   (A) harm〔harm〕v. 傷害　　(B) define〔dɪ'faɪn〕v. 下定義
   (C) **object**〔əb'dʒɛkt〕v. 反對　　(D) gain〔gen〕v. 獲得
   * approve〔ə'pruv〕v. 批准；贊成

6. (**A**) His <u>ambition</u> is to be a millionaire.

他的<u>志願</u>是成為百萬富翁。

(A) ***ambition*** 〔æm'bɪʃən〕*n.* 志願；抱負

(B) nation〔'neʃən〕*n.* 國家

(C) evidence〔'ɛvədəns〕*n.* 證據

(D) herd〔hɜd〕*n.*(牛) 群

7. (**D**) <u>Recent</u> studies show that green tea prevents cancer.

<u>最近的</u>研究顯示，綠茶可預防癌症。

(A) worry〔'wɜɪ〕*n.* 擔心；憂慮

(B) moment〔'momənt〕*n.* 瞬間；片刻

(C) indifference〔ɪn'dɪfərəns〕*n.* 漠不關心

(D) ***recent***〔'risn̩t〕*adj.* 最近的

＊study〔'stʌdɪ〕*n.* 研究　　cancer〔'kænsə〕*n.* 癌症

8. (**B**) Investigators have yet to <u>determine</u> the cause of the crash.

調查人員必須<u>判定</u>這次飛機失事的原因。

(A) measure〔'mɛʒə〕*v.* 測量　　(B) ***determine***〔dɪ'tɜmɪn〕*v.* 決定

(C) refuse〔rɪ'fjuz〕*v.* 拒絕　　(D) memorize〔'mɛmə,raɪz〕*v.* 背誦

＊investigator〔ɪn'vɛstə,getə〕*n.* 調查人員

crash〔kræʃ〕*n.*(飛機) 失事；墜毀

9. (**B**) The people could not <u>tolerate</u> that military regime.

人民無法<u>忍受</u>軍權統治。

(A) fit〔fɪt〕*v.* 適合　　(B) ***tolerate***〔'talə,ret〕*v.* 忍受

(C) figure〔'fɪgjə〕*v.* 想；計算　　(D) differ〔'dɪfə〕*v.* 不同

＊regime〔rɪ'dʒim〕*n.* 政權；統治時期

10. (**A**) Most residents <u>oppose</u> the building of the nuclear plant.

大部份的居民<u>反對</u>興建核能發電廠。

(A) ***oppose***〔ə'poz〕*v.* 反對

(B) manage〔'mænɪdʒ〕*v.* 設法

(C) apply〔ə'plaɪ〕*v.* 申請

(D) promise〔'pramɪs〕*v.* 承諾；答應

op	+ pose
丨	丨
against	*+place*

＊resident〔'rɛzədənt〕*n.* 居民　　***nuclear plant*** 核能發電廠

TEST 7

Directions: *Of the four words given after each sentence, choose the one most suitable for filling in the blank.*

1. "There's no such thing as a free lunch" is his father's _____ .

   (A) philosophy
   (B) dormitory
   (C) purpose
   (D) progress   (   )

2. Without a witness, it'll be hard to _____ any wrongdoing on his part.

   (A) regard
   (B) produce
   (C) prove
   (D) unite   (   )

3. While driving, you must _____ on the road.

   (A) presume
   (B) obey
   (C) concentrate
   (D) affect   (   )

4. The case has been dismissed for lack of _____ .

   (A) evidence
   (B) term
   (C) matter
   (D) economy   (   )

5. Room service is _____ twenty-four hours a day.

   (A) previous
   (B) available
   (C) frank
   (D) probable   (   )

6. George has _____ for a patent for his invention.

   (A) involved
   (B) preferred
   (C) impressed
   (D) applied   (   )

7. You had better _____ the pros and cons of your move.

   (A) develop
   (B) weigh
   (C) excuse
   (D) obey   (   )

8. The _____ is always greener on the other side of the fence.

   (A) grass
   (B) strength
   (C) victim
   (D) control   (   )

9. I'm _____ that he's innocent.

   (A) convinced
   (B) succeeded
   (C) forced
   (D) obtained   (   )

10. Nineteen people were _____ in the accident.

   (A) participated
   (B) injured
   (C) conducted
   (D) instructed   (   )

TEST 7 詳解

1. (**A**) "There's no such thing as a free lunch" is his father's <u>philosophy</u>. 「天下沒有白吃的午餐。」是他父親的<u>人生觀</u>。

   (A) **philosophy**〔fə'lɑsəfɪ〕*n.* 人生觀；哲學
   (B) dormitory〔'dɔrmə,torɪ〕*n.* 宿舍
   (C) purpose〔'pɜpəs〕*n.* 目的
   (D) progress〔'progrɛs〕*n.* 進步

philo +	soph	+y
love +	wisdom	+ *n.*

2. (**C**) Without a witness, it'll be hard to <u>prove</u> any wrongdoing on his part. 如果沒有證人，就很難<u>證</u>明他有罪。

   (A) regard〔rɪ'gɑrd〕*v.* 認爲
   (B) produce〔prə'djus〕*v.* 生產
   (C) **prove**〔pruv〕*v.* 證明
   (D) unite〔ju'naɪt〕*v.* 聯合

   * witness〔'wɪtnɪs〕*n.* 證人　　wrongdoing〔'rɔŋ'duɪŋ〕*n.* 犯罪
   on *one's* **part** 在～方面；就～而言

3. (**C**) While driving, you must <u>concentrate</u> on the road.
   開車時，一定要<u>專心</u>注意路況。

   (A) presume〔prɪ'zum〕*v.* 假定
   (B) obey〔o'be〕*v.* 遵守
   (C) **concentrate**〔'kɑnsn̩,tret〕*v.* 專心
   (D) affect〔ə'fɛkt〕*v.* 影響

4. (**A**) The case has been dismissed for lack of <u>evidence</u>.
   這件案子因缺乏<u>證據</u>，不被受理。

   (A) **evidence**〔'ɛvədəns〕*n.* 證據
   (B) term〔tɜm〕*n.* 術語；期間
   (C) matter〔'mætə〕*n.* 事件；問題
   (D) economy〔ɪ'kɑnəmɪ〕*n.* 經濟

   * dismiss〔dɪs'mɪs〕*v.* 不受理　　lack〔læk〕*n.* 缺乏

5. (**B**) Room service is <u>available</u> twenty-four hours a day.
   客房服務是一天二十四小時都<u>有</u>。

   (A) previous〔'privɪəs〕*adj.* 先前的
   (B) **available**〔ə'veləbl̩〕*adj.* 可獲得的
   (C) frank〔fræŋk〕*adj.* 坦白的
   (D) probable〔'prɑbəbl̩〕*adj.* 可能的

   * **room service** 客房服務（旅館把膳食送到客房的服務）

6. (**D**) George has <u>applied</u> for a patent for his invention.

喬治已為他的發明<u>申請</u>了專利。

    (A) involve〔ɪn'vɑlv〕*v.* 牽涉

    (B) prefer〔prɪ'fɝ〕*v.* 較喜歡

    (C) impress〔ɪm'prɛs〕*v.* 使印象深刻

    (D) ***apply***〔ə'plaɪ〕*v.* 申請

    * patent〔'pætṇt〕*n.* 專利權

7. (**B**) You had better <u>weigh</u> the pros and cons of your move.

你最好<u>衡量</u>一下這次行動的利弊得失。

    (A) develop〔dɪ'vɛləp〕*v.* 發展   (B) ***weigh***〔we〕*v.* 衡量

    (C) excuse〔ɪk'skjuz〕*v.* 原諒   (D) obey〔o'be〕*v.* 遵守

    * ***the pros and cons*** 利弊得失;正反兩面

8. (**A**) The <u>grass</u> is always greener on the other side of the fence.

〔諺〕鄰家芳草綠;外國的月亮比較圓。

    (A) ***grass***〔græs〕*n.* 草   (B) strength〔strɛŋθ〕*n.* 力量

    (C) victim〔'vɪktɪm〕*n.* 受害者   (D) control〔kən'trol〕*n.* 控制

    * fence〔fɛns〕*n.* 籬笆

9. (**A**) I'm <u>convinced</u> that he's innocent.

我<u>相信</u>他是清白的。

    (A) ***convince***〔kən'vɪns〕*v.* 使相信

    (B) succeed〔sək'sid〕*v.* 成功

    (C) force〔fɔrs〕*v.* 強迫

    (D) obtain〔əb'ten〕*v.* 獲得

    * innocent〔'ɪnəsṇt〕*adj.* 清白的

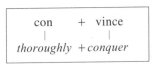

10. (**B**) Nineteen people were <u>injured</u> in the accident.

在這次意外中,有十九個人<u>受傷</u>。

    (A) participate〔par'tɪsəˌpet〕*v.* 參加

    (B) ***injure***〔'ɪndʒɚ〕*v.* 傷害

    (C) conduct〔kən'dʌkt〕*v.* 傳導;做(實驗)

    (D) instruct〔ɪn'strʌkt〕*v.* 教導

TEST 8

Directions: *Of the four words given after each sentence, choose the one most suitable for filling in the blank.*

1. What he _____ in intelligence he makes up with diligence.

   (A) expects
   (B) advances
   (C) packs
   (D) lacks   (   )

2. American Indians used smoke signals to _____ .

   (A) encourage
   (B) communicate
   (C) stick
   (D) beg   (   )

3. The students are _____ about the food.

   (A) affording
   (B) complaining
   (C) dismissing
   (D) civilizing   (   )

4. Archaeologists have _____ the ancient capital of the Aztecs.

   (A) discovered
   (B) dealt
   (C) reminded
   (D) supplied   (   )

5. It is illegal in Britain to park on _____ yellow lines.

   (A) pleasant
   (B) double
   (C) inevitable
   (D) proper   (   )

6. Milk is a(n) ———— ingredient in making ice cream.

   (A) essential
   (B) complete
   (C) scarce
   (D) worth   (   )

7. Of the seven only one ———— the accident.

   (A) collected
   (B) signed
   (C) suggested
   (D) survived   (   )

8. The consulate has ———— his visa application.

   (A) persuaded
   (B) rejected
   (C) tasted
   (D) presented   (   )

9. Earth is only a speck in the ————.

   (A) fellow
   (B) necessity
   (C) policy
   (D) universe   (   )

10. She ———— investigators into believing that he died
    of natural causes.

   (A) qualified
   (B) benefited
   (C) transported
   (D) misled   (   )

TEST 8 詳解

1. (**D**) What he <u>lacks</u> in intelligence he makes up with diligence.
   他以勤勞彌補智力的<u>不足</u>。
   (A) expect〔ɪkˈspɛkt〕v. 期待
   (B) advance〔ədˈvæns〕v. 前進；進步
   (C) pack〔pæk〕v. 打包　　　(D) *lack*〔læk〕v. 缺乏
   * intelligence〔ɪnˈtɛlədʒəns〕n. 智力　*make up* 彌補
     diligence〔ˈdɪlədʒəns〕n. 勤勉

2. (**B**) American Indians used smoke signals to <u>communicate</u>.
   印第安人使用煙霧信號來<u>聯絡</u>。
   (A) encourage〔ɪnˈkɝɪdʒ〕v. 鼓勵
   (B) *communicate*〔kəˈmjunəˌket〕v. 聯絡；溝通
   (C) stick〔stɪk〕v. 黏著；堅持 <to>
   (D) beg〔bɛg〕v. 乞求

3. (**B**) The students are <u>complaining</u> about the food.
   學生一直在<u>抱怨</u>食物。
   (A) afford〔əˈfɔrd〕v. 負擔得起　　(B) *complain*〔kəmˈplen〕v. 抱怨
   (C) dismiss〔dɪsˈmɪs〕v. 解散；下（課）
   (D) civilize〔ˈsɪvlˌaɪz〕v. 教化

4. (**A**) Archaeologists have <u>discovered</u> the ancient capital of the
   Aztecs. 考古學家<u>發現</u>了遠古時代阿茲特克人的首都。
   (A) *discover*〔dɪˈskʌvɚ〕v. 發現　(B) deal〔dil〕v. 處理
   (C) remind〔rɪˈmaɪnd〕v. 使想起　(D) supply〔səˈplaɪ〕v. 供給
   * archaeologist〔ˌɑrkɪˈɑlədʒɪst〕n. 考古學家
     Aztec〔ˈæztɛk〕n. 阿茲特克人

5. (**B**) It is illegal in Britain to park on <u>double</u> yellow lines.
   在英國，在雙黃線上停車是違法的。
   (A) pleasant〔ˈplɛznt〕adj. 愉快的　(B) *double*〔ˈdʌbl̩〕adj. 雙重的
   (C) inevitable〔ɪnˈɛvətəbl̩〕adj. 不可避免的
   (D) proper〔ˈprɑpɚ〕adj. 適當的
   * illegal〔ɪˈligl̩〕adj. 非法的

6. (**A**) Milk is an <u>essential</u> ingredient in making ice cream.
牛奶是製作冰淇淋的<u>必要</u>成份。

(A) ***essential*** 〔 ə'sɛnʃəl 〕 *adj.* 必要的
(B) complete 〔 kəm'plit 〕 *adj.* 完整的
(C) scarce 〔 skɛrs 〕 *adj.* 缺乏的；稀少的
(D) worth 〔 wɜθ 〕 *adj.* 值得的
  * ingredient 〔 ɪn'gridɪənt 〕 *n.* 成分

7. (**D**) Of the seven only one <u>survived</u> the accident.
七個人當中，只有一人在這次意外中<u>生還</u>。

(A) collect 〔 kə'lɛkt 〕 *v.* 收集   (B) sign 〔 saɪn 〕 *v.* 簽名
(C) suggest 〔 sə'dʒɛst 〕 *v.* 建議
(D) ***survive*** 〔 sə'vaɪv 〕 *v.* 自～中生還

8. (**B**) The consulate has <u>rejected</u> his visa application.
領事館已<u>拒絕</u>他的簽證申請。

(A) persuade 〔 pə'swed 〕 *v.* 說服
(B) ***reject*** 〔 rɪ'dʒɛkt 〕 *v.* 拒絕；退回
(C) taste 〔 test 〕 *v.* 嚐起來
(D) present 〔 prɪ'zɛnt 〕 *v.* 呈現

```
re  + ject
 |      |
back + throw（丟回來）
```

  * consulate 〔'kɑnslɪt 〕 *n.* 領事館   visa 〔'vɪzə 〕 *n.* 簽證

9. (**D**) Earth is only a speck in the <u>universe</u>.
地球只是<u>宇宙</u>中的一粒微塵。

(A) fellow 〔'fɛlo 〕 *n.* 傢伙   (B) necessity 〔 nə'sɛsətɪ 〕 *n.* 必要
(C) policy 〔'pɑləsɪ 〕 *n.* 政策   (D) ***universe*** 〔'junə,vɜs 〕 *n.* 宇宙
  * speck 〔 spɛk 〕 *n.* 微塵

10. (**D**) She <u>misled</u> investigators into believing that he died of
natural causes. 她<u>誤導</u>調查人員，讓他們以為他是自然死亡。

(A) qualify 〔'kwɑlə,faɪ 〕 *v.* 使夠資格
(B) benefit 〔'bɛnəfɪt 〕 *v.* 獲益
(C) transport 〔 træns'port 〕 *v.* 運送
(D) ***mislead*** 〔 mɪs'lid 〕 *v.* 誤導
  * investigator 〔 ɪn'vɛstə,getə 〕 *n.* 調查人員

TEST 9

Directions: *Of the four words given after each sentence, choose the one most suitable for filling in the blank.*

1. We are about to begin the _____ countdown.

   (A) foreign
   (B) final
   (C) extreme
   (D) certain   (   )

2. _____ the two mixtures in equal amounts.

   (A) Mention
   (B) Exist
   (C) Combine
   (D) Indicate   (   )

3. Had Jack _____ any kind of crime before?

   (A) absorbed
   (B) compared
   (C) committed
   (D) achieved   (   )

4. The results of these experiments _____ a secret.

   (A) accept
   (B) decide
   (C) remain
   (D) excite   (   )

5. His _____ with herbal medicine earned him a Nobel prize.

   (A) sorts
   (B) pilots
   (C) experiments
   (D) societies   (   )

6. His parents have long _____ his returning home.

    (A) calculated
    (B) reached
    (C) anticipated
    (D) handled   (   )

7. Ask the doctor about his _____.

    (A) addition
    (B) condition
    (C) effect
    (D) attention   (   )

8. The _____ in the city can go down as low as 10 degrees below 0.

    (A) technology
    (B) temperature
    (C) sincerity
    (D) health   (   )

9. This bag is made of _____ leather.

    (A) immediate
    (B) genuine
    (C) severe
    (D) straight   (   )

10. We'll be _____ our latest products at the show.

    (A) comforting
    (B) following
    (C) exhibiting
    (D) devoting   (   )

TEST 9 詳解

1. (**B**) We are about to begin the <u>final</u> countdown.
我們即將開始<u>最後的</u>倒數計時。

   (A) foreign〔'fɔrɪn〕*adj.* 國外的
   (B) ***final***〔'faɪnḷ〕*adj.* 最後的
   (C) extreme〔ɪk'strim〕*adj.* 極端的
   (D) certain〔'sɝtṇ〕*adj.* 確定的；某一

   * countdown〔'kaʊnt͵daʊn〕*n.* 倒數計時

2. (**C**) <u>Combine</u> the two mixtures in equal amounts.
將兩種等量的混合物<u>結合</u>在一起。

   (A) mention〔'mɛnʃən〕*v.* 提到   (B) exist〔ɪg'zɪst〕*v.* 存在
   (C) ***combine***〔kəm'baɪn〕*v.* 結合   (D) indicate〔'ɪndə͵ket〕*v.* 指出
   * mixture〔'mɪkstʃɚ〕*n.* 混合物   equal〔'ikwəl〕*adj.* 相等的

3. (**C**) Had Jack <u>committed</u> any kind of crime before?
傑克以前有<u>犯</u>過罪嗎？

   (A) absorb〔əb'sɔrb〕*v.* 吸收   (B) compare〔kəm'pɛr〕*v.* 比較
   (C) ***commit***〔kə'mɪt〕*v.* 犯（罪）   (D) achieve〔ə'tʃiv〕*v.* 達到

4. (**C**) The results of these experiments <u>remain</u> a secret.
這些實驗的結果<u>仍</u>是個謎。

   (A) accept〔ək'sɛpt〕*v.* 接受   (B) decide〔dɪ'saɪd〕*v.* 決定
   (C) ***remain***〔rɪ'men〕*v.* 仍然   (D) excite〔ɪk'saɪt〕*v.* 使興奮
   * experiment〔ɪk'spɛrəmənt〕*n.* 實驗

5. (**C**) His <u>experiments</u> with herbal medicine earned him a Nobel prize. 他在草藥醫學上的<u>實驗</u>，使他贏得了諾貝爾獎。

   (A) sort〔sɔrt〕*n.* 種類
   (B) pilot〔'paɪlət〕*n.* 飛行員；領航員
   (C) ***experiment***〔ɪk'spɛrəmənt〕*n.* 實驗
   (D) society〔sə'saɪətɪ〕*n.* 社會
   * herbal〔'hɝbḷ, 'ɝbḷ〕*adj.* 草藥的

6. (**C**) His parents have long <u>anticipated</u> his returning home.
他的父母長久以來一直<u>期盼</u>他回家。

    (A) calculate (ˈkælkjəˌlet) *v.* 計算

    (B) reach (ritʃ) *v.* 達到

    (C) ***anticipate*** (ænˈtɪsəˌpet) *v.* 期盼

    (D) handle (ˈhændḷ) *v.* 處理

anti	+cipate
beforehand +	take (先拿)

7. (**B**) Ask the doctor about his <u>condition</u>.
問問醫生他的<u>情況</u>如何。

    (A) addition (əˈdɪʃən) *n.* 附加   (B) ***condition*** (kənˈdɪʃən) *n.* 情況

    (C) effect (ɪˈfɛkt) *n.* 效果   (D) attention (əˈtɛnʃən) *n.* 注意

8. (**B**) The <u>temperature</u> in the city can go down as low as 10 degrees below 0. 這城市的<u>溫度</u>可下降到零下十度。

    (A) technology (tɛkˈnɑlədʒɪ) *n.* 技術

    (B) ***temperature*** (ˈtɛmpərətʃɚ) *n.* 溫度

    (C) sincerity (sɪnˈsɛrətɪ) *n.* 誠懇

    (D) health (hɛlθ) *n.* 健康

9. (**B**) This bag is made of <u>genuine</u> leather.
這個手提包是由<u>真皮</u>製成的。

    (A) immediate (ɪˈmidɪɪt) *adj.* 立即的

    (B) ***genuine*** (ˈdʒɛnjuɪn) *adj.* 真正的

    (C) severe (səˈvɪr) *adj.* 嚴厲的；嚴重的

    (D) straight (stret) *adj.* 直的

10. (**C**) We'll be <u>exhibiting</u> our latest products at the show.
我們將在展覽會上<u>展示</u>最新的產品。

    (A) comfort (ˈkʌmfɚt) *v.* 安慰

    (B) follow (ˈfalo) *v.* 跟隨；遵守

    (C) ***exhibit*** (ɪgˈzɪbɪt) *v.* 展示

    (D) devote (dɪˈvot) *v.* 奉獻；致力於

ex	+hibit
out +	have (用手捧出來)

    * latest (ˈletɪst) *adj.* 最新的

      show (ʃo) *n.* 展覽會；表演

TEST 10

Directions: *Of the four words given after each sentence, choose the one most suitable for filling in the blank.*

1. The forces are now _____ the city.
   - (A) resulting
   - (B) attacking
   - (C) fascinating
   - (D) meaning   (   )

2. During his illness he found it difficult to _____ reality from dreams.
   - (A) attract
   - (B) fail
   - (C) distinguish
   - (D) organize   (   )

3. He is one of the country's ten most wanted _____.
   - (A) security
   - (B) criminals
   - (C) professions
   - (D) wisdom   (   )

4. A mission of the U.N. is to _____ peace and understanding.
   - (A) promote
   - (B) explore
   - (C) depend
   - (D) argue   (   )

5. The immigrants _____ a colony on the continent.
   - (A) founded
   - (B) wasted
   - (C) performed
   - (D) stressed   (   )

6. The _____ pounding of the sea has formed these caves.

   (A) tight
   (B) popular
   (C) responsible
   (D) constant   (   )

7. He will be _____ to bed for the next two weeks.

   (A) declined
   (B) disappointed
   (C) guaranteed
   (D) confined   (   )

8. There's a(n) _____ to every rule.

   (A) science
   (B) mystery
   (C) trade
   (D) exception   (   )

9. The police immediately _____ to the scene.

   (A) matched
   (B) rushed
   (C) wasted
   (D) reached   (   )

10. The witching hour starts when the clock _____ twelve.

   (A) strikes
   (B) raises
   (C) solves
   (D) restricts   (   )

TEST 10 詳解

1. (**B**) The forces are now <u>attacking</u> the city.
軍隊正在<u>攻擊</u>這座城市。

    (A) result〔rɪ'zʌlt〕*v.* 造成   (B) ***attack***〔ə'tæk〕*v.* 攻擊
    (C) fascinate〔'fæsn̩,et〕*v.* 使著迷   (D) mean〔min〕*v.* 意思是

    * forces〔'fɔrsɪz〕*n. pl.* 軍隊

2. (**C**) During his illness he found it difficult to <u>distinguish</u>
reality from dreams. 生病期間，他覺得很難<u>分辨</u>現實和幻夢。

    (A) attract〔ə'trækt〕*v.* 吸引   (B) fail〔fel〕*v.* 失敗
    (C) ***distinguish***〔dɪ'stɪŋgwɪʃ〕*v.* 分辨
    (D) organize〔'ɔrgən,aɪz〕*v.* 組織

3. (**B**) He is one of the country's ten most wanted <u>criminals</u>.
他是國內十大通緝要<u>犯</u>之一。

    (A) security〔sɪ'kjurətɪ〕*n.* 安全   (B) ***criminal***〔'krɪmənl̩〕*n.* 罪犯
    (C) profession〔prə'fɛʃən〕*n.* 職業   (D) wisdom〔'wɪzdəm〕*n.* 智慧

4. (**A**) A mission of the U.N. is to <u>promote</u> peace and understanding. 聯合國的任務之一就是要<u>促進</u>和平與了解。

    (A) ***promote***〔prə'mot〕*v.* 促進
    (B) explore〔ɪk'splor〕*v.* 探測
    (C) depend〔dɪ'pɛnd〕*v.* 依賴
    (D) argue〔'ɑrgju〕*v.* 爭論

pro	+mote
forward	+*move* (向前移動)

    * mission〔'mɪʃən〕*n.* 任務   U.N. 聯合國 (= *United Nations*)

5. (**A**) The immigrants <u>founded</u> a colony on the continent.
移民者在這一洲<u>建立</u>了殖民地。

    (A) ***found***〔faʊnd〕*v.* 建立   (B) waste〔west〕*v.* 浪費
    (C) perform〔pə'fɔrm〕*v.* 表演；執行
    (D) stress〔strɛs〕*v.* 強調

    * immigrant〔'ɪməgrənt〕*n.* 移民   colony〔'kɑlənɪ〕*n.* 殖民地
    continent〔'kɑntənənt〕*n.* 洲；大陸

6. (**D**) The <u>constant</u> pounding of the sea has formed these caves.
海水<u>不斷的</u>衝擊形成了這些洞穴。

(A) tight〔taɪt〕*adj.* 緊的
(B) popular〔'pɑpjələ〕*adj.* 流行的；受歡迎的
(C) responsible〔rɪ'spɑnsəbl〕*adj.* 負責任的
(D) *constant*〔'kɑnstənt〕*adj.* 不斷的

* pound〔'paʊnd〕*v.* 撞擊　　cave〔kev〕*n.* 洞穴

7. (**D**) He will be <u>confined</u> to bed for the next two weeks.
未來的兩個星期，他將會<u>臥病</u>在床。

(A) decline〔dɪ'klaɪn〕*v.* 衰退；拒絕
(B) disappoint〔,dɪsə'pɔɪnt〕*v.* 使失望
(C) guarantee〔,gærən'ti〕*v.* 保證
(D) *confine*〔kən'faɪn〕*v.* 限制

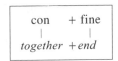

* *be confined to bed* 臥病在床

8. (**D**) There's an <u>exception</u> to every rule.
每項規則都有<u>例外</u>。

(A) science〔'saɪəns〕*n.* 科學
(B) mystery〔'mɪstrɪ〕*n.* 神秘
(C) trade〔tred〕*n.* 貿易
(D) *exception*〔ɪk'sɛpʃən〕*n.* 例外

9. (**B**) The police immediately <u>rushed</u> to the scene.
警方立刻<u>趕往</u>現場。

(A) match〔mætʃ〕*v.* 相配
(B) *rush*〔rʌʃ〕*v.* 趕往；衝去
(C) waste〔west〕*v.* 浪費
(D) reach〔ritʃ〕*v.* 到達（為及物動詞，不可與 to 連用）

* scene〔sin〕*n.* 現場

10. (**A**) The witching hour starts when the clock <u>strikes</u> twelve.
當鐘<u>敲</u>了十二下，午夜就來臨了。

(A) *strike*〔straɪk〕*v.*（鐘）敲響
(B) raise〔rez〕*v.* 提高
(C) solve〔sɑlv〕*v.* 解決
(D) restrict〔rɪ'strɪkt〕*v.* 限制

* *witching hour* (*of night*) 夜間巫師出沒的時刻；三更半夜

TEST 11

Directions: *Of the four words given after each sentence, choose the one most suitable for filling in the blank.*

1. The opera singer was greeted with a _____ round of applause.

 (A) solid
 (B) vivid
 (C) synthetic
 (D) tremendous   (   )

2. Margaret has been _____ to work in Germany.

 (A) assigned
 (B) embarrassed
 (C) recycled
 (D) annoyed   (   )

3. These _____ have been marked for slaughter.

 (A) paragraphs
 (B) cattle
 (C) origins
 (D) incidents   (   )

4. An _____ crowd waited outside the building for the results of the election.

 (A) incredible
 (B) ideal
 (C) anxious
 (D) illegal   (   )

5. The soldiers _____ the town bravely.

 (A) defended
 (B) consisted
 (C) instituted
 (D) reserved   (   )

6. The car suddenly _____ direction.
   - (A) predicted
   - (B) compiled
   - (C) reversed
   - (D) exaggerated   (   )

7. The accused _____ indifferently to the verdict.
   - (A) drowned
   - (B) reacted
   - (C) roared
   - (D) streamed   (   )

8. Elizabeth keeps a _____ of her daily work in the office.
   - (A) sake
   - (B) diligence
   - (C) psyche
   - (D) journal   (   )

9. A beggar _____ me for alms today.
   - (A) abused
   - (B) transmitted
   - (C) approached
   - (D) demonstrated   (   )

10. He _____ the photo with paste.
   - (A) attached
   - (B) ported
   - (C) removed
   - (D) rewarded   (   )

TEST 11 詳解

1. (**D**) The opera singer was greeted with a <u>tremendous</u> round of applause. 歌劇演唱家獲得一陣熱烈掌聲的歡迎。

    (A) solid〔ˋsɑlɪd〕*adj.* 固體的   (B) vivid〔ˋvɪvɪd〕*adj.* 生動的
    (C) synthetic〔sɪnˋθɛtɪk〕*adj.* 合成的
    (D) *tremendous*〔trɪˋmɛndəs〕*adj.* 熱烈的；極大的
    * applause〔əˋplɔz〕*n.* 鼓掌

2. (**A**) Margaret has been <u>assigned</u> to work in Germany.
瑪格麗特已被派到德國工作。

    (A) *assign*〔əˋsaɪn〕*v.* 指派
    (B) embarrass〔ɪmˋbærəs〕*v.* 使困窘
    (C) recycle〔riˋsaɪkḷ〕*v.* 回收；再利用
    (D) annoy〔əˋnɔɪ〕*v.* 使心煩

3. (**B**) These <u>cattle</u> have been marked for slaughter.
這些牛已被做記號，要用來屠宰。

    (A) paragraph〔ˋpærəˏgræf〕*n.* 段落
    (B) *cattle*〔ˋkætḷ〕*n.* 牛（集合名詞）
    (C) origin〔ˋɔrədʒɪn〕*n.* 起源   (D) incident〔ˋɪnsədənt〕*n.* 事件
    * slaughter〔ˋslɔtɚ〕*n.* 屠宰

4. (**C**) An <u>anxious</u> crowd waited outside the building for the results of the election. 焦急的群眾在大樓外等待選舉的結果。

    (A) incredible〔ɪnˋkrɛdəbḷ〕*adj.* 不可思議的
    (B) ideal〔aɪˋdiəl〕*adj.* 理想的   (C) *anxious*〔ˋæŋkʃəs〕*adj.* 焦慮的
    (D) illegal〔ɪˋligḷ〕*adj.* 非法的

5. (**A**) The soldiers <u>defended</u> the town bravely.
士兵們勇敢地保衛城鎮。

    (A) *defend*〔dɪˋfɛnd〕*v.* 保衛
    (B) consist〔kənˋsɪst〕*v.* 由～組成
    (C) institute〔ˋɪnstəˏtjut〕*v.* 設立
    (D) reserve〔rɪˋzɝv〕*v.* 預訂
    * bravely〔ˋbrevlɪ〕*adv.* 勇敢地

```
de  +  fend
 |        |
down + strike
```

6. (**C**) The car suddenly <u>reversed</u> direction. 汽車突然<u>轉了</u>方向。

    (A) predict〔prɪ'dɪkt〕*v.* 預測

    (B) compile〔kəm'paɪl〕*v.* 編輯

    (C) ***reverse***〔rɪ'vɜs〕*v.* 使逆轉

    (D) exaggerate〔ɪg'zædʒə‚ret〕*v.* 誇大

7. (**B**) The accused <u>reacted</u> indifferently to the verdict.
對於判決結果，被告<u>反應</u>冷淡。

    (A) drown〔draʊn〕*v.* 淹死

    (B) ***react***〔rɪ'ækt〕*v.* 反應

    (C) roar〔ror〕*v.* 吼叫

    (D) stream〔strim〕*v.* 流出

re	+	act
back	+	*act*

    * ***the accused*** 被告

    indifferently〔ɪn'dɪfərəntlɪ〕*adv.* 漠不關心地

    verdict〔'vɜdɪkt〕*n.* 判決

8. (**D**) Elizabeth keeps a <u>journal</u> of her daily work in the office.
伊莉莎白每天都會寫工作<u>日誌</u>。

    (A) sake〔sek〕*n.* 緣故   (B) diligence〔'dɪlədʒəns〕*n.* 勤勉

    (C) psyche〔'saɪkɪ〕*n.* 靈魂；精神   (D) ***journal***〔'dʒɜnḷ〕*n.* 日誌

9. (**C**) A beggar <u>approached</u> me for alms today.
今天有位乞丐<u>走向</u>我，乞求施捨。

    (A) abuse〔ə'bjuz〕*v.* 濫用；虐待

    (B) transmit〔træns'mɪt〕*v.* 傳送

    (C) ***approach***〔ə'protʃ〕*v.* 接近

    (D) demonstrate〔'dɛmən‚stret〕*v.* 示威；示範

ap	+	proach
to	+	*near*（向～靠近）

    * beggar〔'bɛgɚ〕*n.* 乞丐   alms〔ɑmz〕*n.* 施捨

10. (**A**) He <u>attached</u> the photo with paste. 他用漿糊把照片<u>貼上</u>。

    (A) ***attach***〔ə'tætʃ〕*v.* 貼

    (B) port〔port〕*v.* 端槍；使轉向左舷

    (C) remove〔rɪ'muv〕*v.* 除去

    (D) reward〔rɪ'wɔrd〕*v.* 獎賞；報酬

    * paste〔pest〕*n.* 漿糊

TEST 12

Directions: *Of the four words given after each sentence, choose the one most suitable for filling in the blank.*

1. Japanese ＿＿＿＿＿ on management are much admired in the West.
   - (A) concepts
   - (B) roots
   - (C) ambassadors
   - (D) negotiations   (   )

2. Walking in the park is part of his daily ＿＿＿＿＿.
   - (A) phenomenon
   - (B) evolution
   - (C) routine
   - (D) surgery   (   )

3. The Mennonite ＿＿＿＿＿ in the United States is noted for their simple way of living.
   - (A) flexibility
   - (B) community
   - (C) caution
   - (D) contempt   (   )

4. The ＿＿＿＿＿ of military training is meant to instill obedience in the soldier.
   - (A) rigidity
   - (B) wretch
   - (C) conscience
   - (D) irrigation   (   )

5. The detectives are now hot on his ＿＿＿＿＿.
   - (A) nerves
   - (B) cupboards
   - (C) tracks
   - (D) schedules   (   )

6. Everybody was _____ at the news that war might break out.

   (A) punished
   (B) alarmed
   (C) littered
   (D) approved   (   )

7. I'd like to _____ you that this food is safe for human consumption.

   (A) import
   (B) intensify
   (C) withdraw
   (D) assure   (   )

8. People often _____ snow with Santa Claus.

   (A) decrease
   (B) associate
   (C) select
   (D) authorize   (   )

9. President Mobuto of Zaire _____ his prime minister yesterday.

   (A) sacked
   (B) inherited
   (C) flourished
   (D) attempted   (   )

10. Thousands of people were _____ in the construction of the Hoover Dam.

    (A) conquered
    (B) observed
    (C) implied
    (D) employed   (   )

TEST 12 詳解

1. (**A**) Japanese <u>concepts</u> on management are much admired in the West. 日本的管理<u>概念</u>相當受到西方的推崇。

    (A) *concept* 〔'kɑnsɛpt 〕 *n.* 概念
    (B) root 〔 rut 〕 *n.* 根；根源
    (C) ambassador 〔 æm'bæsədɚ 〕 *n.* 大使
    (D) negotiation 〔 nɪ,goʃɪ'eʃən 〕 *n.* 談判；諮商
    * management 〔'mænɪdʒmənt 〕 *n.* 管理

2. (**C**) Walking in the park is part of his daily <u>routine</u>.
在公園散步是他每天<u>例行公事</u>的一部分。

    (A) phenomenon 〔 fə'nɑmə,nɑn 〕 *n.* 現象
    (B) evolution 〔,ɛvə'luʃən 〕 *n.* 進化
    (C) *routine* 〔 ru'tin 〕 *n.* 例行公事
    (D) surgery 〔'sɝdʒərɪ 〕 *n.* 外科手術

3. (**B**) The Mennonite <u>community</u> in the United States is noted for their simple way of living. 美國的孟諾教徒<u>社區</u>以生活簡樸聞名。

    (A) flexibility 〔,flɛksə'bɪlətɪ 〕 *n.* 彈性
    (B) *community* 〔 kə'mjunətɪ 〕 *n.* 社區
    (C) caution 〔'kɔʃən 〕 *n.* 小心
    (D) contempt 〔 kən'tɛmpt 〕 *n.* 輕視
    * Mennonite 〔'mɛnə,naɪt 〕 *n.* 孟諾派教徒   *be noted for* ~ 以~聞名

4. (**A**) The <u>rigidity</u> of military training is meant to instill obedience in the soldier. <u>嚴格</u>的軍事訓練是為了要灌輸士兵服從的觀念。

    (A) *rigidity* 〔 rɪ'dʒɪdətɪ 〕 *n.* 嚴格   (B) wretch 〔 rɛtʃ 〕 *n.* 可憐人
    (C) conscience 〔'kɑnʃəns 〕 *n.* 良心   (D) irrigation 〔,ɪrə'geʃən 〕 *n.* 灌溉
    * *be meant to* ~ 目的是為了~   instill 〔 ɪn'stɪl 〕 *v.* 灌輸

5. (**C**) The detectives are now hot on his <u>tracks</u>.
偵探現在正嚴密地跟<u>蹤</u>他。

    (A) nerve 〔 nɝv 〕 *n.* 神經   (B) cupboard 〔'kʌbɚd 〕 *n.* 碗櫥
    (C) *track* 〔 træk 〕 *n.* 行蹤；蹤跡   (D) schedule 〔'skɛdʒʊl 〕 *n.* 時間表
    * *be hot on* one's *track* 嚴密地跟蹤某人

6. (**B**) Everybody was <u>alarmed</u> at the news that war might break out. 一聽到可能會爆發戰爭的消息，每個人都很驚慌。

(A) punish〔ˈpʌnɪʃ〕*v.* 處罰

(B) ***alarm***〔əˈlɑrm〕*v.* 使驚慌

(C) litter〔ˈlɪtɚ〕*v.* 亂丟垃圾

(D) approve〔əˈpruv〕*v.* 贊成

```
al  +  arm
 |       |
to + weapon（去拿武器）
```

* ***break out***（火災、戰爭、疾病等）爆發

7. (**D**) I'd like to <u>assure</u> you that this food is safe for human consumption. 我願意向你保證，這食物絕對可以安心食用。

(A) import〔ɪmˈport〕*v.* 進口

(B) intensify〔ɪnˈtɛnsə͵faɪ〕*v.* 加強

(C) withdraw〔wɪðˈdrɔ〕*v.* 撤退

(D) ***assure***〔əˈʃur〕*v.* 保證

* consumption〔kənˈsʌmpʃən〕*n.* 吃喝；消耗

8. (**B**) People often <u>associate</u> snow with Santa Claus.
人們總是把雪和聖誕老人聯想在一起。

(A) decrease〔dɪˈkris〕*v.* 減少　　(B) ***associate***〔əˈsoʃɪ͵et〕*v.* 聯想

(C) select〔səˈlɛkt〕*v.* 挑選　　(D) authorize〔ˈɔθə͵raɪz〕*v.* 授權

9. (**A**) President Mobuto of Zaire <u>sacked</u> his prime minister yesterday. 薩伊總統莫布托昨天<u>開除</u>他的總理。

(A) ***sack***〔sæk〕*v.* 開除

(B) inherit〔ɪnˈhɛrɪt〕*v.* 繼承

(C) flourish〔ˈflɜɪʃ〕*v.* 興盛；繁榮

(D) attempt〔əˈtɛmpt〕*v.* 企圖；嘗試

* Zaire〔zɑˈir〕*n.* 薩伊　　***prime minister*** 首相；總理；行政院長

10. (**D**) Thousands of people were <u>employed</u> in the construction of the Hoover Dam. 為了建造胡佛水壩，<u>雇用</u>了上千名的人力。

(A) conquer〔ˈkɑŋkɚ〕*v.* 征服　　(B) observe〔əbˈzɝv〕*v.* 觀察；遵守

(C) imply〔ɪmˈplaɪ〕*v.* 暗示　　(D) ***employ***〔ɪmˈplɔɪ〕*v.* 雇用

* construction〔kənˈstrʌkʃən〕*n.* 建造　　dam〔dæm〕*n.* 水壩

TEST 13

Directions: *Of the four words given after each sentence, choose the one most suitable for filling in the blank.*

1. The _____ mounted when the police started to move in on the students.

   (A) tension
   (B) request
   (C) outcome
   (D) reception   (   )

2. Tracy is _____ to live her life as a housewife.

   (A) military
   (B) content
   (C) loose
   (D) invisible   (   )

3. We are here today on the _____ of Nigel and Audrey's 5th wedding anniversary.

   (A) religion
   (B) occasion
   (C) income
   (D) prescription   (   )

4. Trade is _____ to the economy of Taiwan.

   (A) nuclear
   (B) sharp
   (C) vital
   (D) facial   (   )

5. Golf is a very relaxing _____ .

   (A) perseverance
   (B) capacity
   (C) decency
   (D) recreation   (   )

6. Can we _____ like two normal human beings?

   (A) spring
   (B) establish
   (C) despair
   (D) behave   (   )

7. Adam _____ pedigree dogs.

   (A) breeds
   (B) reveals
   (C) delays
   (D) retires   (   )

8. Mr. Tanner, our neighborhood _____ , is looking for someone to help him mind the store.

   (A) trend
   (B) grocer
   (C) court
   (D) welfare   (   )

9. I had a _____ time at Disneyland.

   (A) capital
   (B) coherent
   (C) fantastic
   (D) chemical   (   )

10. A snake cannot _____ its food.

   (A) stretch
   (B) chew
   (C) contrast
   (D) represent   (   )

TEST 13 詳解

1. (**A**) The <u>tension</u> mounted when the police started to move in on the students. 當警方向學生逼近時，局勢更爲<u>緊張</u>。
 (A) ***tension***〔'tɛnʃən〕*n.* 緊張 (B) request〔rɪ'kwɛst〕*n.* 要求
 (C) outcome〔'aʊt,kʌm〕*n.* 結果 (D) reception〔rɪ'sɛpʃən〕*n.* 接待會
 * mount〔maʊnt〕*v.* 上升 ***move in on*** ~ 接近~

2. (**B**) Tracy is <u>content</u> to live her life as a housewife.
 崔西很<u>滿意</u>家庭主婦的生活。
 (A) military〔'mɪlə,tɛrɪ〕*adj.* 軍事的
 (B) ***content***〔kən'tɛnt〕*adj.* 滿意的
 (C) loose〔lus〕*adj.* 鬆的
 (D) invisible〔ɪn'vɪzəbl̩〕*adj.* 看不見的

3. (**B**) We are here today on the <u>occasion</u> of Nigel and Audrey's 5th wedding anniversary.
 我們今天在這裏，是爲了要<u>慶祝</u>奈吉爾和奧黛麗的五周年結婚紀念日。
 (A) religion〔rɪ'lɪdʒən〕*n.* 宗敎
 (B) ***occasion***〔ə'keʒən〕*n.* 慶祝；特殊的節日
 (C) income〔'ɪn,kʌm〕*n.* 收入
 (D) prescription〔prɪ'skrɪpʃən〕*n.* 藥方
 * wedding〔'wɛdɪŋ〕*n.* 婚禮 anniversary〔,ænə'vɜsərɪ〕*n.* 週年紀念日

4. (**C**) Trade is <u>vital</u> to the economy of Taiwan.
 貿易對台灣的經濟來說<u>很重要</u>。
 (A) nuclear〔'njuklɪɚ〕*adj.* 核子的 (B) sharp〔ʃɑrp〕*adj.* 尖銳的
 (C) ***vital***〔'vaɪtl̩〕*adj.* 非常重要的 (D) facial〔'feʃəl〕*adj.* 臉部的

5. (**D**) Golf is a very relaxing <u>recreation</u>.
 高爾夫是一項非常輕鬆的娛樂。
 (A) perseverance〔,pɜsə'vɪrəns〕*n.* 毅力
 (B) capacity〔kə'pæsətɪ〕*n.* 容量；能力
 (C) decency〔'disn̩sɪ〕*n.* 端莊；高雅
 (D) ***recreation***〔,rɛkrɪ'eʃən〕*n.* 娛樂

```
re  +creat(e)  +ion
 |       |        |
again +produce  +  n.
```

 * golf〔gɑlf〕*n.* 高爾夫球 relaxing〔rɪ'læksɪŋ〕*adj.* 輕鬆的

6. (**D**) Can we <u>behave</u> like two normal human beings?
我們兩個可不可以<u>表現</u>得像正常人一樣?

   (A) spring〔sprɪŋ〕*v.* 跳躍　　(B) establish〔ə'stæblɪʃ〕*v.* 建立
   (C) despair〔dɪ'spɛr〕*n.* 絕望　　(D) ***behave***〔bɪ'hev〕*v.* 行為;舉止

   ＊ normal〔'nɔrml̩〕*adj.* 正常的　　***human being*** 人類

7. (**A**) Adam <u>breeds</u> pedigree dogs.
亞當<u>飼養</u>純種狗。

   (A) ***breed***〔brid〕*v.* 飼養　　(B) reveal〔rɪ'vil〕*v.* 顯示
   (C) delay〔dɪ'le〕*v.* 延遲　　　(D) retire〔rɪ'taɪr〕*v.* 退休

   ＊ pedigree〔'pɛdə,gri〕*adj.* 純種的;有血統記錄的

8. (**B**) Mr. Tanner, our neighborhood <u>grocer</u>, is looking for
someone to help him mind the store.
我們附近的<u>雜貨店老闆</u>譚納先生,正在找人幫他看店。

   (A) trend〔trɛnd〕*n.* 趨勢　　(B) ***grocer***〔'grosɚ〕*n.* 雜貨店老闆
   (C) court〔kɔrt〕*n.* 法院　　　(D) welfare〔'wɛl,fɛr〕*n.* 福利

   ＊ neighborhood〔'nebɚ,hʊd〕*adj.* 鄰近地區的

9. (**C**) I had a <u>fantastic</u> time at Disneyland.
我在迪斯耐樂園玩得<u>很高興</u>。

   (A) capital〔'kæpətl̩〕*adj.* 首都的
   (B) coherent〔ko'hɪrənt〕*adj.* 有條理的
   (C) ***fantastic***〔fæn'tæstɪk〕*adj.* 極好的
   (D) chemical〔'kɛmɪkl̩〕*adj.* 化學的

   ＊ Disneyland〔'dɪznɪ,lænd〕*n.* 迪斯耐樂園

10. (**B**) A snake cannot <u>chew</u> its food.
蛇無法<u>咀嚼</u>食物。

   (A) stretch〔strɛtʃ〕*v.* 伸展
   (B) ***chew***〔tʃu〕*v.* 咀嚼
   (C) contrast〔kən'træst〕*v.* 與～成對比
   (D) represent〔,rɛprɪ'zɛnt〕*v.* 代表

   ＊ snake〔snek〕*n.* 蛇

TEST 14

Directions: *Of the four words given after each sentence, choose the one most suitable for filling in the blank.*

1. People _____ him like a plague.

   (A) avoided
   (B) reduced
   (C) entertained
   (D) preceded   (   )

2. His _____ is going to cost him his job.

   (A) diplomat
   (B) sense
   (C) attitude
   (D) chain   (   )

3. I've made a list of all the _____ in my luggage.

   (A) diseases
   (B) items
   (C) status
   (D) criticism   (   )

4. She _____ in wearing that old-fashioned hat.

   (A) persists
   (B) presses
   (C) provides
   (D) blames   (   )

5. He _____ in a solemn manner.

   (A) replied
   (B) majored
   (C) surprised
   (D) satisfied   (   )

6. He _____ to be a friend of yours.

   (A) imitates
   (B) claims
   (C) imposes
   (D) educates   (   )

7. This box _____ a first-aid kit among other things.

   (A) operates
   (B) deserts
   (C) contains
   (D) delights   (   )

8. This castle is _____ by this moat and these high walls.

   (A) reported
   (B) protected
   (C) mistaken
   (D) advertised   (   )

9. A crime of passion seems to be the _____ here.

   (A) grade
   (B) area
   (C) case
   (D) wealth   (   )

10. Aunt Rosie is _____ of keeping pets.

   (A) potential
   (B) objective
   (C) subject
   (D) fond   (   )

TEST 14 詳解

1. (**A**) People <u>avoided</u> him like a plague.
   人們<u>躲</u>他像是躲瘟疫。

   (A) ***avoid***〔ə'vɔɪd〕 v. 躲避　　(B) reduce〔rɪ'djus〕 v. 減少
   (C) entertain〔,ɛntə'ten〕 v. 娛樂　(D) precede〔prɪ'sid〕 v. 在～之前

   * plague〔pleg〕 n. 瘟疫；黑死病

2. (**C**) His <u>attitude</u> is going to cost him his job.
   他的<u>態度</u>會讓自己丟掉工作。

   (A) diplomat〔'dɪplə,mæt〕 n. 外交官
   (B) sense〔sɛns〕 n. 感覺
   (C) ***attitude***〔'ætə,tjud〕 n. 態度
   (D) chain〔tʃen〕 n. 鏈子

3. (**B**) I've made a list of all the <u>items</u> in my luggage.
   我把行李中的<u>物品</u>列出一張清單。

   (A) disease〔dɪ'ziz〕 n. 疾病　　(B) ***item***〔'aɪtəm〕 n. 物品；項目
   (C) status〔'stetəs〕 n. 地位　　(D) criticism〔'krɪtə,sɪzəm〕 n. 批評

   * luggage〔'lʌgɪdʒ〕 n. 行李

4. (**A**) She <u>persists</u> in wearing that old-fashioned hat.
   她<u>堅持</u>要戴那頂過時的帽子。

   (A) ***persist***〔pə'sɪst〕 v. 堅持
   (B) press〔prɛs〕 v. 壓
   (C) provide〔prə'vaɪd〕 v. 提供
   (D) blame〔blem〕 v. 責備

   ```
   per   + sist
    |        |
   through + stand（始終屹立）
   ```

   * old-fashioned〔'old'fæʃənd〕 adj. 過時的

5. (**A**) He <u>replied</u> in a solemn manner.
   他以嚴肅的態度<u>回答</u>。

   (A) ***reply***〔rɪ'plaɪ〕 v. 回答　　(B) major〔'medʒə〕 v. 主修
   (C) surprise〔sə'praɪz〕 v. 使驚訝　(D) satisfy〔'sætɪs,faɪ〕 v. 使滿意

   * solemn〔'saləm〕 adj. 嚴肅的　　manner〔'mænə〕 n. 態度

6. (**B**) He <u>claims</u> to be a friend of yours.
   他<u>聲稱</u>是你的朋友。

   (A) imitate〔'ɪmə,tet〕v. 模仿　　(B) **claim**〔klem〕v. 聲稱；宣稱

   (C) impose〔ɪm'poz〕v. 加於～之上　(D) educate〔'ɛdʒə,ket〕v. 教育

7. (**C**) This box <u>contains</u> a first-aid kit among other things.
   這箱子裡<u>包括</u>一個急救箱和其他的東西。

   (A) operate〔'ɑpə,ret〕v. 操作

   (B) desert〔dɪ'zɝt〕v. 拋棄

   (C) **contain**〔kən'ten〕v. 包含

   (D) delight〔dɪ'laɪt〕v. 使高興

   * **first-aid kit** 急救箱

8. (**B**) This castle is <u>protected</u> by this moat and these high walls.
   這座城堡有這些壕溝和圍牆<u>保護</u>。

   (A) report〔rɪ'port〕v. 報告

   (B) **protect**〔prə'tɛkt〕v. 保護

   (C) mistake〔mə'stek〕v. 誤解

   (D) advertise〔'ædvə,taɪz〕v. 刊登廣告

pro + tect
before + cover (遮蔽於前方)

   * castle〔'kæsḷ〕n. 城堡　　moat〔mot〕n. 壕溝

9. (**C**) A crime of passion seems to be the <u>case</u> here.
   這似乎是個情殺<u>案件</u>。

   (A) grade〔gred〕n. 等級；分數　(B) area〔'ɛrɪə〕n. 地區

   (C) **case**〔kes〕n. 案件；情況　(D) wealth〔wɛlθ〕n. 財富

   * passion〔'pæʃən〕n. 熱情

10. (**D**) Aunt Rosie is <u>fond</u> of keeping pets.
    蘿西阿姨<u>喜歡</u>養寵物。

    (A) potential〔pə'tɛnʃəl〕adj. 有潛力的

    (B) objective〔əb'dʒɛktɪv〕adj. 客觀的

    (C) subject〔'sʌbdʒɪkt〕adj. 服從的　n. 主題

    (D) **fond**〔fɑnd〕adj. 喜歡的　　**be fond of** 喜歡～

    * pet〔pɛt〕n. 寵物　　**keep a pet** 養寵物

TEST 15

Directions: *Of the four words given after each sentence, choose the one most suitable for filling in the blank.*

1. Dan _____ your friendship very much.
    (A) values
    (B) contributes
    (C) relaxes
    (D) invents   (   )

2. The trouble _____ in the engine.
    (A) accomplishes
    (B) lies
    (C) remembers
    (D) admires   (   )

3. Working late every night is not a small _____.
    (A) scholar
    (B) sacrifice
    (C) shortage
    (D) spirit   (   )

4. They _____ themselves to be very lucky.
    (A) strive
    (B) feed
    (C) consider
    (D) suffer   (   )

5. _____ killed the cat.
    (A) Ability
    (B) Quality
    (C) Security
    (D) Curiosity   (   )

6. Don't _____ to call me up.

(A) tend
(B) acquaint
(C) bother
(D) excel   (   )

7. He _____ his money in stocks and bonds.

(A) competed
(B) invested
(C) chose
(D) strove   (   )

8. The _____ time is two forty-eight.

(A) unwilling
(B) academic
(C) bare
(D) exact   (   )

9. The next _____ has been dubbed as the Pacific Century.

(A) favor
(B) fashion
(C) century
(D) career   (   )

10. The country is _____ between the haves and the have-nots.

(A) separated
(B) exchanged
(C) proposed
(D) supported   (   )

TEST 15 詳解

1.(**A**) Dan <u>values</u> your friendship very much.
丹很<u>重視</u>你的友誼。

    (A) **value**〔'vælju〕*v.* 重視
    (B) contribute〔kən'trıbjut〕*v.* 貢獻
    (C) relax〔rı'læks〕*v.* 放鬆   (D) invent〔ın'vɛnt〕*v.* 發明

2.(**B**) The trouble <u>lies</u> in the engine.
問題<u>在於</u>引擎。

    (A) accomplish〔ə'kɑmplıʃ〕*v.* 完成
    (B) **lie**〔laı〕*v.* 在 **lie in** 在於~
    (C) remember〔rı'mɛmbɚ〕*v.* 記得
    (D) admire〔əd'maır〕*v.* 欽佩

    * engine〔'ɛndʒın〕*n.* 引擎

3.(**B**) Working late every night is not a small <u>sacrifice</u>.
每天晚上工作到很晚，真是不小的<u>犧牲</u>。

    (A) scholar〔'skɑlɚ〕*n.* 學者
    (B) **sacrifice**〔'sækrə,faıs〕*n.* 犧牲
    (C) shortage〔'ʃɔrtıdʒ〕*n.* 缺乏
    (D) spirit〔'spırıt〕*n.* 精神

sacri	+	fice
sacred	+	*make*

4.(**C**) They <u>consider</u> themselves to be very lucky.
他們<u>認為</u>自己很幸運。

    (A) strive〔straıv〕*v.* 努力   (B) feed〔fid〕*v.* 餵食
    (C) **consider**〔kən'sıdɚ〕*v.* 認為   (D) suffer〔'sʌfɚ〕*v.* 受苦

5.(**D**) <u>Curiosity</u> killed the cat.
〔諺〕<u>好奇傷身</u>。

    (A) ability〔ə'bılətı〕*n.* 能力
    (B) quality〔'kwɑlətı〕*n.* 品質
    (C) security〔sı'kjurətı〕*n.* 安全
    (D) **curiosity**〔,kurı'ɑsətı〕*n.* 好奇心

6. (**C**) Don't <u>bother</u> to call me up.

不必費事打電話給我。

(A) tend〔tɛnd〕v. 傾向於

(B) acquaint〔ə'kwent〕v. 使認識

(C) ***bother***〔'bɑðɚ〕v. 費事；麻煩

(D) excel〔ɪk'sɛl〕v. 擅長；優越

＊ ***call sb. up*** 打電話給某人

7. (**B**) He <u>invested</u> his money in stocks and bonds.

他把錢投資在股票和債券上。

(A) compete〔kəm'pit〕v. 競爭 　(B) ***invest***〔ɪn'vɛst〕v. 投資

(C) choose〔tʃuz〕v. 選擇 　(D) strive〔straɪv〕v. 努力

＊ stock〔stɑk〕n. 股票 　bond〔bɑnd〕n. 債券

8. (**D**) The <u>exact</u> time is two forty-eight.

確切的時間是兩點四十八分。

(A) unwilling〔ʌn'wɪlɪŋ〕*adj.* 不願意的

(B) academic〔͵ækə'dɛmɪk〕*adj.* 學術的

(C) bare〔bɛr〕*adj.* 赤裸的；僅僅的

(D) ***exact***〔ɪg'zækt〕*adj.* 確切的；確實的

9. (**C**) The next <u>century</u> has been dubbed as the Pacific Century.

下一個世紀被稱爲太平洋世紀。

(A) favor〔'fevɚ〕n. 恩惠；偏愛 　(B) fashion〔'fæʃən〕n. 流行

(C) ***century***〔'sɛntʃərɪ〕n. 世紀 　(D) career〔kə'rɪr〕n. 職業

＊ dub〔dʌb〕v. 稱呼 　Pacific〔pə'sɪfɪk〕*adj.* 太平洋的

10. (**A**) The country is <u>separated</u> between the haves and the have-nots. 該國分爲富人與窮人兩種階級。

(A) ***separate***〔'sɛpə͵ret〕v. 區分

(B) exchange〔ɪks'tʃendʒ〕v. 交換

(C) propose〔prə'poz〕v. 提議

(D) support〔sə'port〕v. 支持

se	+	par	+ate
|		|	|
apart	+	*prepare*	+ *v.*

＊ ***the haves and the have-nots*** 富人與窮人

TEST 16

Directions: *Of the four words given after each sentence, choose the one most suitable for filling in the blank.*

1. His drinking _____ in an accident.
   (A) failed
   (B) attacked
   (C) apologized
   (D) resulted   (   )

2. This brochure gives a _____ description of the country.
   (A) tight
   (B) general
   (C) apparent
   (D) enthusiastic   (   )

3. The opposition is _____ a rally for tomorrow.
   (A) organizing
   (B) exploring
   (C) distinguishing
   (D) ruling   (   )

4. These people _____ on the sea for a living.
   (A) argue
   (B) depend
   (C) attract
   (D) fascinate   (   )

5. He was _____ at not being invited.
   (A) wasted
   (B) disappointed
   (C) promoted
   (D) confined   (   )

6. The children were _____ for cleaning their own rooms.

   (A) common
   (B) responsible
   (C) popular
   (D) individual   (   )

7. Doctor Greene will _____ the operation.

   (A) intend
   (B) mean
   (C) attract
   (D) perform   (   )

8. His strength slowly _____ .

   (A) declined
   (B) rushed
   (C) matched
   (D) concluded   (   )

9. An _____ thirteen-year-old child could understand it.

   (A) entire
   (B) average
   (C) honest
   (D) awful   (   )

10. I _____ an apartment with 4 people.

   (A) solve
   (B) raise
   (C) invent
   (D) share   (   )

TEST 16 詳解

1. (**D**) His drinking <u>resulted</u> in an accident. 他因喝酒<u>造成</u>了意外。
    (A) fail〔fel〕v. 失敗；不及格
    (B) attack〔əˋtæk〕v. 攻擊
    (C) apologize〔əˋpɑləˏdʒaɪz〕v. 道歉
    (D) **result**〔rɪˋzʌlt〕v. 造成　　**result in** 造成；導致
    * drinking〔ˋdrɪŋkɪŋ〕n. 喝酒　　accident〔ˋæksədənt〕n. 意外

2. (**B**) This brochure gives a <u>general</u> description of the country.
    這本小冊子<u>概略</u>地描述了這個國家。
    (A) tight〔taɪt〕adj. 緊的
    (B) **general**〔ˋdʒɛnərəl〕adj. 概略的；一般的
    (C) apparent〔əˋpɛrənt〕adj. 明顯的
    (D) enthusiastic〔ɪnˏθjuzɪˋæstɪk〕adj. 熱心的
    * brochure〔broˋʃʊr〕n. 小冊子　　description〔dɪˋskrɪpʃən〕n. 描述

3. (**A**) The opposition is <u>organizing</u> a rally for tomorrow.
    反對黨正在<u>組織</u>明天的示威運動。
    (A) **organize**〔ˋɔrgənˏaɪz〕v. 組織；發起
    (B) explore〔ɪkˋsplor〕v. 探索
    (C) distinguish〔dɪˋstɪŋgwɪʃ〕v. 分辨
    (D) rule〔rul〕v. 統治
    * opposition〔ˏɑpəˋzɪʃən〕n. 反對黨　　rally〔ˋrælɪ〕n. 示威運動

4. (**B**) These people <u>depend</u> on the sea for a living.
    這些人<u>靠</u>海洋爲生。
    (A) argue〔ˋɑrgju〕v. 爭論　　　　(B) **depend**〔dɪˋpɛnd〕v. 依靠
    (C) attract〔əˋtrækt〕v. 吸引　　(D) fascinate〔ˋfæsnˏet〕v. 使著迷

5. (**B**) He was <u>disappointed</u> at not being invited.
    他很<u>失望</u>自己沒被邀請。
    (A) waste〔west〕v. 浪費
    (B) **disappointed**〔ˏdɪsəˋpɔɪntɪd〕adj. 失望的
    (C) promote〔prəˋmot〕v. 升遷　　(D) confine〔kənˋfaɪn〕v. 限制

6. (**B**) The children were <u>responsible</u> for cleaning their own rooms. 小孩要<u>負責</u>打掃自己的房間。

    (A) common〔'kɑmən〕*adj.* 普通的;共有的

    (B) ***responsible***〔rɪ'spɑnsəbḷ〕*adj.* 有責任的

        be responsible for 對~負責

    (C) popular〔'pɑpjələ〕*adj.* 受歡迎的;流行的

    (D) individual〔ˌɪndə'vɪdʒuəl〕*adj.* 個別的

7. (**D**) Doctor Greene will <u>perform</u> the operation.
格林尼醫生要<u>執行</u>手術。

    (A) intend〔ɪn'tɛnd〕*v.* 打算

    (B) mean〔min〕*v.* 意思是

    (C) attract〔ə'trækt〕*v.* 吸引

    (D) ***perform***〔pɚ'fɔrm〕*v.* 執行

    * operation〔ˌɑpə'reʃən〕*n.* 手術 (= *surgery*)

8. (**A**) His strength slowly <u>declined</u>. 他的體力逐漸<u>衰退</u>。

    (A) ***decline***〔dɪ'klaɪn〕*v.* 衰退;減弱

    (B) rush〔rʌʃ〕*v.* 衝;催促

    (C) match〔mætʃ〕*v.* 相配

    (D) conclude〔kən'klud〕*v.* 下結論

```
de  + cline
 |      |
down +bend (向下彎曲)
```

9. (**B**) An <u>average</u> thirteen-year-old child could understand it.
<u>一般</u>十三歲的兒童都可以理解。

    (A) entire〔ɪn'taɪr〕*adj.* 全部的

    (B) ***average***〔'ævərɪdʒ〕*adj.* 平均的;一般的

    (C) honest〔'ɑnɪst〕*adj.* 誠實的

    (D) awful〔'ɔfḷ〕*adj.* 可怕的

10. (**D**) I <u>share</u> an apartment with 4 people.
我和四個人<u>共住</u>一間公寓。

    (A) solve〔sɑlv〕*v.* 解決   (B) raise〔rez〕*v.* 提高

    (C) invent〔ɪn'vɛnt〕*v.* 發明   (D) ***share***〔ʃɛr〕*v.* 共有;分享

    * apartment〔ə'pɑrtmənt〕*n.* 公寓

TEST 17

Directions: *Of the four words given after each sentence, choose the one most suitable for filling in the blank.*

1. A _____ set of encyclopedia now costs a fortune.
   - (A) immediate
   - (B) middle
   - (C) complete
   - (D) constant   (   )

2. Cigarette ads _____ the young to smoke.
   - (A) exhibit
   - (B) encourage
   - (C) advance
   - (D) pack   (   )

3. The former singer has _____ his candidacy.
   - (A) announced
   - (B) communicated
   - (C) stuck
   - (D) complained   (   )

4. To get a seat, I had to _____ my way in.
   - (A) discover
   - (B) afford
   - (C) deal
   - (D) force   (   )

5. One of the main goals of the colonists was to _____.
   the natives.
   - (A) civilize
   - (B) survive
   - (C) present
   - (D) pose   (   )

6. He deals in _____ currencies.

   (A) accurate
   (B) main
   (C) inevitable
   (D) foreign   (   )

7. These retards have the _____ of a five-year-old child.

   (A) effect
   (B) process
   (C) importance
   (D) intelligence   (   )

8. He has a very optimistic _____ of the future.

   (A) photography
   (B) discipline
   (C) vision
   (D) attention   (   )

9. Doris has her own _____ tutor.

   (A) scarce
   (B) essential
   (C) private
   (D) significant   (   )

10. Many sufferers have _____ from this drug.

   (A) persuaded
   (B) benefited
   (C) supplied
   (D) tasted   (   )

TEST 17 詳解

1. (**C**) A <u>complete</u> set of encyclopedia now costs a fortune.
現在一<u>整</u>套百科全書價格十分昂貴。

    (A) immediate〔ɪ'midɪɪt〕*adj.* 立即的
    (B) middle〔'mɪdḷ〕*adj.* 中間的
    (C) *complete*〔kəm'plit〕*adj.* 完整的
    (D) constant〔'kɑnstənt〕*adj.* 不斷的

    * encyclopedia〔ɪn,saɪklə'pidɪə〕*n.* 百科全書
       fortune〔'fɔrtʃən〕*n.* 財富

2. (**B**) Cigarette ads <u>encourage</u> the young to smoke.
香煙廣告會<u>鼓勵</u>年輕人吸煙。

    (A) exhibit〔ɪg'zɪbɪt〕*v.* 展示   (B) *encourage*〔ɪn'kɝɪdʒ〕*v.* 鼓勵
    (C) advance〔əd'væns〕*v.* 前進   (D) pack〔pæk〕*v.* 打包

    * ad〔æd〕*n.* 廣告 (= *advertisement*)   *the young* 年輕人

3. (**A**) The former singer has <u>announced</u> his candidacy.
昔日歌手<u>宣布</u>參選。

    (A) *announce*〔ə'naʊns〕*v.* 宣布
    (B) communicate〔kə'mjunə,ket〕*v.* 溝通
    (C) stick〔stɪk〕*v.* 黏住；堅持
    (D) complain〔kəm'plen〕*v.* 抱怨

    * former〔'fɔrmɚ〕*adj.* 早期的；昔日的
       candidacy〔'kændɪdəsɪ〕*n.* 候選資格

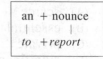

4. (**D**) To get a seat, I had to <u>force</u> my way in.
爲了要坐到位子，我必須<u>用力擠</u>進去。

    (A) discover〔dɪ'skʌvɚ〕*v.* 發現   (B) afford〔ə'fɔrd〕*v.* 負擔得起
    (C) deal〔dil〕*v.* 處理   (D) *force*〔fɔrs〕*v.* 用力推擠

5. (**A**) One of the main goals of the colonists was to <u>civilize</u> the natives. 殖民地居民的主要的目標之一，就是要<u>教化</u>當地的土著。

    (A) *civilize*〔'sɪvḷ,aɪz〕*v.* 教化   (B) survive〔sɚ'vaɪv〕*v.* 生還
    (C) present〔prɪ'zɛnt〕*v.* 呈現   (D) pose〔poz〕*v.* 擺姿勢

    * colonist〔'kɑlənɪst〕*n.* 殖民地居民   native〔'netɪv〕*n.* 土著

6. (**D**) He deals in <u>foreign</u> currencies. 他買賣<u>外</u>幣。

    (A) accurate〔'ækjərɪt〕*adj.* 準確的

    (B) main〔men〕*adj.* 主要的

    (C) inevitable〔ɪn'ɛvətəbl̩〕*adj.* 無法避免的

    (D) *foreign*〔'fɔrɪn〕*adj.* 國外的

    * *deal in* 買賣　currency〔'kɝənsɪ〕*n.* 貨幣

7. (**D**) These retards have the <u>intelligence</u> of a five-year-old child.
這些智障者只有五歲小孩的<u>智力</u>。

    (A) effect〔ɪ'fɛkt〕*n.* 效果

    (B) process〔'prɑsɛs〕*n.* 過程

    (C) importance〔ɪm'pɔrtn̩s〕*n.* 重要性

    (D) *intelligence*〔ɪn'tɛlədʒəns〕*n.* 智力

intel	+	lig	+ence
apart	+choose	+	n.

    * retard〔rɪ'tɑrd〕*n.* 智障者

8. (**C**) He has a very optimistic <u>vision</u> of the future.
他對未來抱持著非常樂觀的<u>憧憬</u>。

    (A) photography〔fə'tɑgrəfɪ〕*n.* 攝影

    (B) discipline〔'dɪsəplɪn〕*n.* 訓練；紀律

    (C) *vision*〔'vɪʒən〕*n.* 憧憬；想像

    (D) attention〔ə'tɛnʃən〕*n.* 注意

    * optimistic〔ˌɑptə'mɪstɪk〕*adj.* 樂觀的

9. (**C**) Doris has her own <u>private</u> tutor.
桃樂絲有自己的<u>私人</u>家教。

    (A) scarce〔skɛrs〕*adj.* 缺乏的；稀少的

    (B) essential〔ə'sɛnʃəl〕*adj.* 必要的

    (C) *private*〔'praɪvɪt〕*adj.* 私人的

    (D) significant〔sɪg'nɪfəkənt〕*adj.* 意義重大的

    * tutor〔'tutɚ〕*n.* 家庭教師

10. (**B**) Many sufferers have <u>benefited</u> from this drug.
許多患者因此藥而<u>受益</u>。

    (A) persuade〔pɚ'swed〕*v.* 說服　　(B) *benefit*〔'bɛnəfɪt〕*v.* 獲益

    (C) supply〔sə'plaɪ〕*v.* 供給　　(D) taste〔test〕*v.* 嚐起來

    * sufferer〔'sʌfərɚ〕*n.* 患者

TEST 18

Directions: *Of the four words given after each sentence, choose the one most suitable for filling in the blank.*

1. A _____ man by the name of Gerard was looking for you.

   (A) precious
   (B) certain
   (C) slight
   (D) straight   (   )

2. I've _____ only half of what I have hoped to do.

   (A) achieved
   (B) indicated
   (C) weighed
   (D) compared   (   )

3. These batteries have no more _____ .

   (A) profession
   (B) course
   (C) exception
   (D) energy   (   )

4. A sponge can _____ water.

   (A) consume
   (B) commit
   (C) absorb
   (D) challenge   (   )

5. This is the _____ speaking. We are now landing in Honolulu, Hawaii.

   (A) population
   (B) wisdom
   (C) order
   (D) pilot   (   )

6. The _____ capital of Xian is now a tourist attraction.

   (A) ancient
   (B) severe
   (C) rough
   (D) extreme   (   )

7. There were five different _____ of biscuits.

   (A) experiments
   (B) sorts
   (C) debts
   (D) factors   (   )

8. Engineers have _____ the cost to be $10 million.

   (A) calculated
   (B) transported
   (C) combined
   (D) followed   (   )

9. Diane _____ her life to the study of gorillas.

   (A) reached
   (B) judged
   (C) rejected
   (D) devoted   (   )

10. I hope these flowers can _____ you.

   (A) advise
   (B) hold
   (C) handle
   (D) comfort   (   )

TEST 18 詳解

1. (**B**) A <u>certain</u> man by the name of Gerard was looking for you.
　 某一位叫傑羅德的男士在找你。

　 (A) precious〔'prɛʃəs〕adj. 珍貴的　(B) ***certain***〔'sɝtn̩〕adj. 某一
　 (C) slight〔slaɪt〕adj. 輕微的　　(D) straight〔stret〕adj. 直的
　 * ***by the name of***~　名叫~

2. (**A**) I've <u>achieved</u> only half of what I have hoped to do.
　 我想做的事，目前只<u>完成</u>了一半。

　 (A) ***achieve***〔ə'tʃiv〕v. 完成　　(B) indicate〔'ɪndə͵ket〕v. 指出
　 (C) weigh〔we〕v. 重~；衡量　　(D) compare〔kəm'pɛr〕v. 比較

3. (**D**) These batteries have no more <u>energy</u>.
　 這些電池沒<u>電</u>了。

　 (A) profession〔prə'fɛʃən〕n. 職業
　 (B) course〔kors〕n. 課程
　 (C) exception〔ɪk'sɛpʃən〕n. 例外
　 (D) ***energy***〔'ɛnədʒɪ〕n. 能量
　 * battery〔'bætərɪ〕n. 電池

4. (**C**) A sponge can <u>absorb</u> water.
　 海綿會<u>吸</u>水。

　 (A) consume〔kən'sum〕v. 消耗；吃喝
　 (B) commit〔kə'mɪt〕v. 犯（罪）；委託
　 (C) ***absorb***〔əb'sɔrb〕v. 吸收
　 (D) challenge〔'tʃælɪndʒ〕v. 挑戰
　 * sponge〔spʌndʒ〕n. 海綿

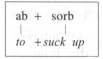

5. (**D**) This is the <u>pilot</u> speaking. We are now landing in Honolulu, Hawaii. 我是<u>駕駛員</u>。我們即將降落在夏威夷的檀香山。

　 (A) population〔͵papjə'leʃən〕n. 人口
　 (B) wisdom〔'wɪzdəm〕n. 智慧
　 (C) order〔'ɔrdə〕n. 順序
　 (D) ***pilot***〔'paɪlət〕n.（飛機）駕駛員；飛行員

6. (**A**) The <u>ancient</u> capital of Xian is now a tourist attraction.
　　　<u>古</u>都西安現在是個觀光勝地。

　　　(A) ***ancient*** ('enʃənt) *adj.* 古代的
　　　(B) severe (sə'vɪr) *adj.* 嚴厲的
　　　(C) rough (rʌf) *adj.* 粗糙的
　　　(D) extreme (ɪk'strim) *adj.* 極端的
　　　＊ capital ('kæpətl̩) *n.* 首都　　***tourist attraction*** 觀光勝地

7. (**B**) There were five different <u>sorts</u> of biscuits.
　　　有五<u>種</u>不同的餅乾。

　　　(A) experiment (ɪk'spɛrəmənt) *n.* 實驗
　　　(B) ***sort*** (sɔrt) *n.* 種類
　　　(C) debt (dɛt) *n.* 債務
　　　(D) factor ('fæktɚ) *n.* 因素
　　　＊ biscuit ('bɪskɪt) *n.* 餅乾

8. (**A**) Engineers have <u>calculated</u> the cost to be $10 million.
　　　工程師已經<u>計算</u>出費用為一千萬元。

　　　(A) ***calculate*** ('kælkjə,let) *v.* 計算
　　　(B) transport (træns'port) *v.* 運送
　　　(C) combine (kəm'baɪn) *v.* 結合
　　　(D) follow ('falo) *v.* 跟隨

calc +	ul	+ate
lime +	*small* +	*v.*

9. (**D**) Diane <u>devoted</u> her life to the study of gorillas.
　　　黛安一生都<u>致力</u>於研究大猩猩。

　　　(A) reach (ritʃ) *v.* 達到　　　(B) judge (dʒʌdʒ) *v.* 判斷
　　　(C) reject (rɪ'dʒɛkt) *v.* 拒絕　　(D) ***devote*** (dɪ'vot) *v.* 致力於
　　　＊ gorilla (gə'rɪlə) *n.* 大猩猩

10. (**D**) I hope these flowers can <u>comfort</u> you.
　　　我希望這些花能給你<u>安慰</u>。

　　　(A) advise (əd'vaɪz) *v.* 勸告
　　　(B) hold (hold) *v.* 握住；擁有
　　　(C) handle ('hændl̩) *v.* 處理
　　　(D) ***comfort*** ('kʌmfɚt) *v.* 安慰

com +	fort
together +	*strong*

TEST 19

Directions: *Of the four words given after each sentence, choose the one most suitable for filling in the blank.*

1. California _____ all kinds of fruits and vegetables.
   - (A) manages
   - (B) regards
   - (C) proves
   - (D) produces   (   )

2. I'm _____ with what you have achieved.
   - (A) limited
   - (B) impressed
   - (C) controlled
   - (D) characterized   (   )

3. He has had no _____ experience in this line of work.
   - (A) probable
   - (B) frank
   - (C) patient
   - (D) previous   (   )

4. Until being proven guilty, you are _____ innocent.
   - (A) presumed
   - (B) affected
   - (C) concentrated
   - (D) promised   (   )

5. The _____ has a long waiting list.
   - (A) sincerity
   - (B) dormitory
   - (C) temperature
   - (D) technology   (   )

6. This dog has been trained to ———— only one
master.

(A) horrify
(B) destroy
(C) apply
(D) obey   (   )

7. A computer is powerful in ———— of capacity and
speed.

(A) terms
(B) herds
(C) nations
(D) conditions   (   )

8. Mike has made a lot of ———— in recent months.

(A) economy
(B) progress
(C) evidence
(D) indifference   (   )

9. Harry has been ———— in several shady dealings in
the past.

(A) developed
(B) involved
(C) conducted
(D) injured   (   )

10. I'd like to ———— my deepest gratitude to you.

(A) excuse
(B) express
(C) exist
(D) excite   (   )

TEST 19 詳解

1. (**D**) California <u>produces</u> all kinds of fruits and vegetables.
加州<u>生產</u>各式各樣的水果和蔬菜。

    (A) manage〔'mænɪdʒ〕*v.* 設法   (B) regard〔rɪ'gɑrd〕*v.* 認為

    (C) prove〔pruv〕*v.* 證明   (D) ***produce***〔prə'djus〕*v.* 生產

2. (**B**) I'm <u>impressed</u> with what you have achieved.
你的成就讓我<u>印象深刻</u>。

    (A) limit〔'lɪmɪt〕*v.* 限制

    (B) ***impress***〔ɪm'prɛs〕*v.* 使印象深刻

    (C) control〔kən'trol〕*v.* 控制

    (D) characterize〔'kærɪktə,raɪz〕*v.* 以～為特色

    ＊ achieve〔ə'tʃiv〕*v.* 達到；完成

```
im +press
 |     |
on +press
```

3. (**D**) He has had no <u>previous</u> experience in this line of work.
他<u>先前</u>沒有這一行的工作經驗。

    (A) probable〔'prɑbəbḷ〕*adj.* 可能的

    (B) frank〔fræŋk〕*adj.* 坦白的

    (C) patient〔'peʃənt〕*adj.* 有耐心的

    (D) ***previous***〔'priviəs〕*adj.* 先前的

    ＊ line〔laɪn〕*n.* 行業

4. (**A**) Until being proven guilty, you are <u>presumed</u> innocent.
在證明有罪之前，你仍被<u>認為</u>是清白的。

    (A) ***presume***〔prɪ'zum〕*v.* 認為   (B) affect〔ə'fɛkt〕*v.* 影響

    (C) concentrate〔'kɑnsṇ,tret〕*v.* 專心於

    (D) promise〔'prɑmɪs〕*v.* 承諾；答應

    ＊ innocent〔'ɪnəsṇt〕*adj.* 清白的

5. (**B**) The <u>dormitory</u> has a long waiting list.
有一長串等候<u>宿舍</u>空位的名單。

    (A) sincerity〔sɪn'sɛrətɪ〕*n.* 誠懇

    (B) ***dormitory***〔'dɔrmə,torɪ〕*n.* 宿舍

    (C) temperature〔'tɛmpərətʃ⋰〕*n.* 溫度

    (D) technology〔tɛk'nɑlədʒɪ〕*n.* 科技

```
dormi + tory
  |        |
sleep  +place
```

6. (**D**) This dog has been trained to <u>obey</u> only one master.
這隻狗已被訓練成只<u>服從</u>一位主人。

(A) horrify〔ˈhɔrəˌfaɪ〕v. 使恐懼　　(B) destroy〔dɪˈstrɔɪ〕v. 破壞
(C) apply〔əˈplaɪ〕v. 申請；應徵　　(D) ***obey***〔oˈbe〕v. 服從；遵守

7. (**A**) A computer is powerful in <u>terms</u> of capacity and speed.
<u>以</u>容量和速度的<u>角度</u>來說，電腦非常有效力。

(A) ***term***〔tɝm〕n. 說法　***in terms of***~　以~的觀點；以~的角度
(B) herd〔hɝd〕n.(牛)群
(C) nation〔ˈneʃən〕n. 國家
(D) condition〔kənˈdɪʃən〕n. 情況；條件

* powerful〔ˈpaʊəfəl〕adj. 有效力的
　capacity〔kəˈpæsətɪ〕n. 容量

8. (**B**) Mike has made a lot of <u>progress</u> in recent months.
最近幾個月，麥可已有很大的<u>進步</u>。

(A) economy〔ɪˈkanəmɪ〕n. 經濟
(B) ***progress***〔ˈprogrɛs〕n. 進步
(C) evidence〔ˈɛvədəns〕n. 證據
(D) indifference〔ɪnˈdɪfərəns〕n. 漠不關心

* recent〔ˈrisn̩t〕adj. 最近的

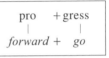

9. (**B**) Harry has been <u>involved</u> in several shady dealings in the past. 哈利過去曾<u>涉及</u>幾件可疑的交易。

(A) develop〔dɪˈvɛləp〕v. 發展
(B) ***involve***〔ɪnˈvalv〕v. 牽涉　***be involved in***~　牽涉到~之中
(C) conduct〔kənˈdʌkt〕v. 傳導；做(實驗)
(D) injure〔ˈɪndʒɚ〕v. 傷害

* shady〔ˈʃedɪ〕adj. 可疑的　　dealing〔ˈdilɪŋ〕n. 交易

10. (**B**) I'd like to <u>express</u> my deepest gratitude to you.
我要向你<u>表達</u>最深的謝意。

(A) excuse〔ɪkˈskjuz〕v. 原諒　　(B) ***express***〔ɪkˈsprɛs〕v. 表達
(C) exist〔ɪgˈzɪst〕v. 存在　　(D) excite〔ɪkˈsaɪt〕v. 使興奮

* gratitude〔ˈgrætəˌtjud〕n. 感激

TEST 20

Directions: *Of the four words given after each sentence, choose the one most suitable for filling in the blank.*

1. The police are here to _____ the crash.

   (A) interest
   (B) examine
   (C) ignore
   (D) create   (   )

2. The restaurant was _____ with people.

   (A) wondered
   (B) crowded
   (C) gained
   (D) delivered   (   )

3. I can't _____ you wearing that dress.

   (A) imagine
   (B) inform
   (C) appear
   (D) preserve   (   )

4. Can you _____ the table?

   (A) insist
   (B) instruct
   (C) measure
   (D) deem   (   )

5. Let me _____ the word for you.

   (A) pollute
   (B) define
   (C) figure
   (D) manage   (   )

6. The Asian and African elephants _____ in size.

- (A) differ
- (B) unite
- (C) refuse
- (D) tolerate   (   )

7. I _____ you will be selling the land.

- (A) memorize
- (B) object
- (C) suppose
- (D) substitute   (   )

8. Most men follow a double _____ when it comes to women.

- (A) independence
- (B) moment
- (C) weapon
- (D) standard   (   )

9. They have _____ a government in exile.

- (A) fitted
- (B) succeeded
- (C) suspected
- (D) formed   (   )

10. I made a mistake and I will _____ responsibility for it.

- (A) assume
- (B) participate
- (C) convince
- (D) relate   (   )

TEST 20 詳解

1. (**B**) The police are here to <u>examine</u> the crash.
   警方到這裡<u>檢查</u>失事原因。

   (A) interest〔'ɪntrɪst〕v. 使感興趣
   (B) *examine*〔ɪg'zæmɪn〕v. 檢查
   (C) ignore〔ɪg'nor〕v. 忽視
   (D) create〔krɪ'et〕v. 創造

   * crash〔kræʃ〕n.(飛機)失事;墜機

2. (**B**) The restaurant was <u>crowded</u> with people.
   餐廳裡<u>擠滿</u>了人。

   (A) wonder〔'wʌndɚ〕v. 想知道
   (B) *crowd*〔kraʊd〕v. 擁擠　　*be crowded with* 擠滿了~
   (C) gain〔gen〕v. 獲得
   (D) deliver〔dɪ'lɪvɚ〕v. 遞送

3. (**A**) I can't <u>imagine</u> you wearing that dress.
   我無法<u>想像</u>你穿上那件洋裝的樣子。

   (A) *imagine*〔ɪ'mædʒɪn〕v. 想像　　(B) inform〔ɪn'fɔrm〕v. 通知
   (C) appear〔ə'pɪr〕v. 出現;似乎　　(D) preserve〔prɪ'zɝv〕v. 保存

4. (**C**) Can you <u>measure</u> the table?
   你能<u>測量</u>一下桌子的大小嗎?

   (A) insist〔ɪn'sɪst〕v. 堅持　　(B) instruct〔ɪn'strʌkt〕v. 教導
   (C) *measure*〔'mɛʒɚ〕v. 測量　　(D) deem〔dim〕v. 認為

5. (**B**) Let me <u>define</u> the word for you.
   我來向你<u>解釋</u>這個字的意思。

   (A) pollute〔pə'lut〕v. 污染
   (B) *define*〔dɪ'faɪn〕v. 解釋;下定義
   (C) figure〔'fɪgjɚ〕v. 計算;想像
   (D) manage〔'mænɪdʒ〕v. 設法

de	+fine
down	+ end (定下界限)

6. (**A**) The Asian and African elephants <u>differ</u> in size.
亞洲象和非洲象的大小<u>不同</u>。

(A) ***differ*** ﹝'dɪfɚ﹞ *v.* 不同　　(B) unite ﹝ju'naɪt﹞ *v.* 聯合
(C) refuse ﹝rɪ'fjuz﹞ *v.* 拒絕　　(D) tolerate ﹝'talə,ret﹞ *v.* 容忍

* Asian ﹝'eʃən﹞ *adj.* 亞洲的　　African ﹝'æfrɪkən﹞ *adj.* 非洲的

7. (**C**) I <u>suppose</u> you will be selling the land.
我<u>想</u>你會出售這塊土地。

(A) memorize ﹝'mɛmə,raɪz﹞ *v.* 背誦
(B) object ﹝əb'dʒɛkt﹞ *v.* 反對
(C) ***suppose*** ﹝sə'poz﹞ *v.* 猜想；認為
(D) substitute ﹝'sʌbstə,tjut﹞ *v.* 代替

8. (**D**) Most men follow a double <u>standard</u> when it comes to women. 一提到女人，大部份的男人都有雙重<u>標準</u>。

(A) independence ﹝,ɪndɪ'pɛndəns﹞ *n.* 獨立
(B) moment ﹝'momənt﹞ *n.* 瞬間；片刻
(C) weapon ﹝'wɛpən﹞ *n.* 武器
(D) ***standard*** ﹝'stændɚd﹞ *n.* 標準

* follow ﹝'falo﹞ *v.* 遵循　　double ﹝'dʌbl̩﹞ *adj.* 雙重的
when it comes to~ 一提到~

9. (**D**) They have <u>formed</u> a government in exile.
他們已<u>成立</u>了流亡政府。

(A) fit ﹝fɪt﹞ *v.* 適合　　(B) succeed ﹝sək'sid﹞ *v.* 成功
(C) suspect ﹝sə'spɛkt﹞ *v.* 懷疑　　(D) ***form*** ﹝fɔrm﹞ *v.* 成立

* exile ﹝'ɛgzaɪl﹞ *n.* 流亡

10. (**A**) I made a mistake and I will <u>assume</u> responsibility for it.
我會為自己所犯的錯<u>承擔</u>責任。

(A) ***assume*** ﹝ə'sjum﹞ *v.* 承擔
(B) participate ﹝pɚ'tɪsə,pet﹞ *v.* 參加
(C) convince ﹝kən'vɪns﹞ *v.* 使相信
(D) relate ﹝rɪ'let﹞ *v.* 使有關聯

```
as + sume
 |      |
to  +  take
```

TEST 21

Directions: *Of the four words given after each sentence, choose the one most suitable for filling in the blank.*

1. I'd like to _____ a table for two.

    (A) reserve
    (B) observe
    (C) preserve
    (D) deserve   (   )

2. The statue of Lenin was _____ from the town square.

    (A) hesitated
    (B) astonished
    (C) assigned
    (D) removed   (   )

3. Maria _____ her maiden name after she was married.

    (A) annoyed
    (B) retained
    (C) postponed
    (D) divided   (   )

4. Let me _____ to you how this machine works.

    (A) demonstrate
    (B) recycle
    (C) expand
    (D) brighten   (   )

5. The Darwinian theory of _____ is really very ancient.

    (A) phenomenon
    (B) surgery
    (C) evolution
    (D) psyche   (   )

6. Malaria is _____ by mosquitoes.
   - (A) reacted
   - (B) transmitted
   - (C) abused
   - (D) compiled   (   )

7. The Gypsies have their _____ in India.
   - (A) origins
   - (B) sakes
   - (C) pessimism
   - (D) caves   (   )

8. If you always _____ , people will no longer believe you.
   - (A) institute
   - (B) approach
   - (C) exaggerate
   - (D) roar   (   )

9. It's hard to _____ the outcome of the elections.
   - (A) predict
   - (B) attach
   - (C) vanish
   - (D) surround   (   )

10. Five fishermen _____ in the sinking of the ship.
    - (A) witnessed
    - (B) drowned
    - (C) searched
    - (D) admitted   (   )

TEST 21 詳解

1. (**A**) I'd like to <u>reserve</u> a table for two.
我要<u>預訂</u>兩人坐的桌子。

(A) ***reserve*** (rɪ'zɝv) v. 預訂
(B) observe (əb'zɝv) v. 觀察；遵守
(C) preserve (prɪ'zɝv) v. 保存
(D) deserve (dɪ'zɝv) v. 應得

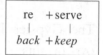

re ＋serve
back ＋keep

2. (**D**) The statue of Lenin was <u>removed</u> from the town square.
列寧雕像已被<u>搬離</u>廣場。

(A) hesitate ('hɛzə,tet) v. 猶豫
(B) astonish (ə'stɑnɪʃ) v. 使驚訝
(C) assign (ə'saɪn) v. 指派
(D) ***remove*** (rɪ'muv) v. 移開

＊ statue ('stætʃʊ) n. 雕像　　square (skwɛr) n. 廣場

3. (**B**) Maria <u>retained</u> her maiden name after she was married.
瑪麗亞婚後仍<u>保留</u>她的本姓。

(A) annoy (ə'nɔɪ) v. 使惱怒
(B) ***retain*** (rɪ'ten) v. 保留
(C) postpone (post'pon) v. 延期
(D) divide (də'vaɪd) v. 劃分

＊ ***maiden name*** 娘家姓氏；本姓

4. (**A**) Let me <u>demonstrate</u> to you how this machine works.
我向你<u>示範</u>如何操作這部機器。

(A) ***demonstrate*** ('dɛmən,stret) v. 示範
(B) recycle (ri'saɪkl̩) v. 回收；再利用
(C) expand (ɪk'spænd) v. 擴大
(D) brighten ('braɪtn̩) v. 使明亮

de ＋monstr ＋ate
｜　　｜　　｜
fully ＋ show ＋ v.

5. (**C**) The Darwinian theory of <u>evolution</u> is really very ancient.
達爾文的<u>進化</u>論，歷史非常悠久。

(A) phenomenon (fə'nɑmə,nɑn) n. 現象
(B) surgery ('sɝdʒərɪ) n. 外科手術
(C) ***evolution*** (,ɛvə'luʃən) n. 進化
(D) psyche ('saɪkɪ) n. 精神；靈魂

e ＋volut ＋ion
｜　　｜　　｜
out ＋ roll ＋ n.

＊ ancient ('enʃənt) adj. 古老的

6. (**B**) Malaria is <u>transmitted</u> by mosquitoes. 瘧疾是經由蚊子傳染。

    (A) react〔rɪ'ækt〕*v.* 反應

    (B) ***transmit***〔træns'mɪt〕*v.* 傳染；傳送

    (C) abuse〔ə'bjuz〕*v.* 濫用；虐待

    (D) compile〔kəm'paɪl〕*v.* 編輯

trans + mit
| |
across + send

    * malaria〔mə'lɛrɪə〕*n.* 瘧疾   mosquito〔mə'skito〕*n.* 蚊子

7. (**A**) The Gypsies have their <u>origins</u> in India.
　　吉普賽人起源於印度。

    (A) ***origin***〔'ɔrədʒɪn〕*n.* 起源   (B) sake〔sek〕*n.* 緣故

    (C) pessimism〔'pɛsə,mɪzəm〕*n.* 悲觀   (D) cave〔kev〕*n.* 洞穴

    * Gypsy〔'dʒɪpsɪ〕*n.* 吉普賽人   India〔'ɪndɪə〕*n.* 印度

8. (**C**) If you always <u>exaggerate</u>, people will no longer believe
　　you. 如果你一直誇大，就不會有人相信你。

    (A) institute〔'ɪnstə,tjut〕*v.* 設立

    (B) approach〔ə'protʃ〕*v.* 接近

    (C) ***exaggerate***〔ɪg'zædʒə,ret〕*v.* 誇大

    (D) roar〔ror〕*v.* 吼叫

ex + ag + ger + ate
| | | |
out + to + carry + v.

    * ***no longer*** 不再

9. (**A**) It's hard to <u>predict</u> the outcome of the elections.
　　很難預測選舉的結果。

    (A) ***predict***〔prɪ'dɪkt〕*v.* 預測

    (B) attach〔ə'tætʃ〕*v.* 貼上

    (C) vanish〔'vænɪʃ〕*v.* 消失

    (D) surround〔sə'raʊnd〕*v.* 圍繞

pre + dict
| |
before + say

    * outcome〔'aʊt,kʌm〕*n.* 結果   election〔ɪ'lɛkʃən〕*n.* 選舉

10. (**B**) Five fishermen <u>drowned</u> in the sinking of the ship.
　　這次沉船意外中，有五位漁民淹死。

    (A) witness〔'wɪtnɪs〕*v.* 目擊；作證   (B) ***drown***〔draʊn〕*v.* 淹死

    (C) search〔sɜtʃ〕*v.* 尋找   (D) admit〔əd'mɪt〕*v.* 承認

    * fisherman〔'fɪʃə·mən〕*n.* 漁夫   sinking〔'sɪŋkɪŋ〕*n.* 下沉

TEST 22

Directions: *Of the four words given after each sentence, choose the one most suitable for filling in the blank.*

1. This company was _____ in 1974.
   - (A) embraced
   - (B) deprived
   - (C) established
   - (D) corrected   (   )

2. Nuclear fusion is a(n) _____ source of energy for the next century.
   - (A) objective
   - (B) unwilling
   - (C) potential
   - (D) eager   (   )

3. Jack and I will _____ to climb Mount Everest next year.
   - (A) attempt
   - (B) crawl
   - (C) deceive
   - (D) represent   (   )

4. Don't put too much _____ in what the newspapers say.
   - (A) confidence
   - (B) prescription
   - (C) sorrow
   - (D) occasion   (   )

5. _____ shelters must be built for these refugees.
   - (A) Absolute
   - (B) False
   - (C) Content
   - (D) Temporary   (   )

6. The _____ towards international integration is becoming more pronounced every day.

   (A) status
   (B) recreation
   (C) trend
   (D) balance   (   )

7. His _____ from office has been widely speculated about.

   (A) dessert
   (B) departure
   (C) semester
   (D) climax   (   )

8. Most household detergents today are made from _____ materials.

   (A) chemical
   (B) dust
   (C) suspense
   (D) blank   (   )

9. An X-ray _____ a tumor in his brain.

   (A) revealed
   (B) recovered
   (C) extinguished
   (D) stretched   (   )

10. Farmers are predicting a record _____ this year.

   (A) harvest
   (B) version
   (C) permission
   (D) grocer   (   )

TEST 22 詳解

1. (**C**) This company was <u>established</u> in 1974.
這家公司<u>成立</u>於 1974 年。

    (A) embrace〔ɪm'bres〕*v.* 擁抱   (B) deprive〔dɪ'praɪv〕*v.* 剝奪
    (C) ***establish***〔ə'stæblɪʃ〕*v.* 建立   (D) correct〔kə'rɛkt〕*v.* 改正

2. (**C**) Nuclear fusion is a <u>potential</u> source of energy for the next century. 核融合是下一世紀非常<u>有潛力的</u>能源。

    (A) objective〔əb'dʒɛktɪv〕*adj.* 客觀的
    (B) unwilling〔ʌn'wɪlɪŋ〕*adj.* 不願意的
    (C) ***potential***〔pə'tɛnʃəl〕*adj.* 可能的；有潛力的
    (D) eager〔'igɚ〕*adj.* 渴望的；熱切的

    * nuclear〔'njuklɪɚ〕*adj.* 核子的   fusion〔'fjuʒən〕*n.* 融合

3. (**A**) Jack and I will <u>attempt</u> to climb Mount Everest next year.
我和傑克明年要<u>嘗試</u>攀登埃弗勒斯峰。

    (A) ***attempt***〔ə'tɛmpt〕*v.* 嘗試   (B) crawl〔krɔl〕*v.* 爬行
    (C) deceive〔dɪ'siv〕*v.* 欺騙
    (D) represent〔ˌrɛprɪ'zɛnt〕*v.* 代表

    * ***Mount Everest*** 埃佛勒斯峰；聖母峰

4. (**A**) Don't put too much <u>confidence</u> in what the newspapers say.
不要太<u>相信</u>報紙所說的。

    (A) ***confidence***〔'kɑnfədəns〕*n.* 信心
    (B) prescription〔prɪ'skrɪpʃən〕*n.* 藥方
    (C) sorrow〔'saro〕*n.* 悲傷
    (D) occasion〔ə'keʒən〕*n.* 場合

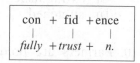

5. (**D**) <u>Temporary</u> shelters must be built for these refugees.
一定要爲這些難民搭建<u>臨時的</u>避難所。

    (A) absolute〔'æbsəˌlut〕*adj.* 絕對的
    (B) false〔fɔls〕*adj.* 錯誤的；假的
    (C) content〔kən'tɛnt〕*adj.* 滿足的
    (D) ***temporary***〔'tɛmpəˌrɛrɪ〕*adj.* 臨時的；暫時的

    * shelter〔'ʃɛltɚ〕*n.* 避難所   refugee〔ˌrɛfju'dʒi〕*n.* 難民

6. (**C**) The <u>trend</u> towards international integration is becoming more pronounced every day. 國際整合的<u>趨勢</u>日益明顯。

   (A) status〔'stetəs〕*n.* 地位

   (B) recreation〔ˌrɛkrɪ'eʃən〕*n.* 娛樂

   (C) ***trend***〔trɛnd〕*n.* 趨勢   (D) balance〔'bæləns〕*n.* 平衡

   * integration〔ˌɪntə'greʃən〕*n.* 整合

     pronounced〔prə'naʊnst〕*adj.* 顯著的

7. (**B**) His <u>departure</u> from office has been widely speculated about. 他已仔細考慮過<u>離職</u>的事。

   (A) dessert〔dɪ'zɝt〕*n.* 甜點   (B) ***departure***〔dɪ'partʃɚ〕*n.* 離開

   (C) semester〔sə'mɛstɚ〕*n.* 學期   (D) climax〔'klaɪmæks〕*n.* 高潮

   * office〔'ɔfɪs〕*n.* 職務   widely〔'waɪdlɪ〕*adv.* 廣大地；非常

     speculate〔'spɛkjəˌlet〕*v.* 思考

8. (**A**) Most household detergents today are made from <u>chemical</u> materials. 現今大部分的家用清潔劑都是由<u>化學</u>原料製成。

   (A) ***chemical***〔'kɛmɪkl̩〕*adj.* 化學的   (B) dust〔dʌst〕*n.* 灰塵

   (C) suspense〔sə'spɛns〕*n.* 懸疑   (D) blank〔blæŋk〕*n.* 空白

   * household〔'haʊsˌhold〕*adj.* 家庭的

     detergent〔dɪ'tɝdʒənt〕*n.* 清潔劑

9. (**A**) An X-ray <u>revealed</u> a tumor in his brain. X 光片<u>顯示</u>他腦部有腫瘤。

   (A) ***reveal***〔rɪ'vil〕*v.* 顯示

   (B) recover〔rɪ'kʌvɚ〕*v.* 恢復

   (C) extinguish〔ɪk'stɪŋgwɪʃ〕*v.* 熄滅

   (D) stretch〔strɛtʃ〕*v.* 伸展

   * tumor〔'tjumɚ〕*n.* 腫瘤

re	+ veal
back	+ veil (取下面紗)

10. (**A**) Farmers are predicting a record <u>harvest</u> this year. 農民預期今年會<u>豐收</u>。

   (A) ***harvest***〔'harvɪst〕*n.* 收穫   ***record harvest*** 豐收

   (B) version〔'vɝʒən〕*n.* 版本

   (C) permission〔pɚ'mɪʃən〕*n.* 允許

   (D) grocer〔'grosɚ〕*n.* 雜貨店老板

TEST 23

Directions: *Of the four words given after each sentence, choose the one most suitable for filling in the blank.*

1. I would consider it a _____ if you answer promptly.
   - (A) labor
   - (B) favor
   - (C) coward
   - (D) harmony   (   )

2. Teddy has to do some _____ in the library.
   - (A) effort
   - (B) factor
   - (C) century
   - (D) research   (   )

3. They _____ the show with a medley.
   - (A) concluded
   - (B) strove
   - (C) adapted
   - (D) pretended   (   )

4. Your prompt action _____ a serious accident.
   - (A) intended
   - (B) suffered
   - (C) prevented
   - (D) proposed   (   )

5. The course is a combination of _____ and practical work.
   - (A) academic
   - (B) optimistic
   - (C) frustrated
   - (D) aware   (   )

6. He is a _____ customer of ours.

    (A) tiny
    (B) unwilling
    (C) plastic
    (D) regular   (   )

7. The majority is for _____ the status quo.

    (A) contrasting
    (B) maintaining
    (C) acquainting
    (D) delaying   (   )

8. Mini-skirts are again in _____ .

    (A) recreation
    (B) event
    (C) fashion
    (D) diligence   (   )

9. A thousand people _____ the seminar.

    (A) separated
    (B) behaved
    (C) excelled
    (D) attended   (   )

10. Winners will be notified by _____ .

    (A) post
    (B) surgery
    (C) curiosity
    (D) factor   (   )

TEST 23 詳解

1. (**B**) I would consider it a <u>favor</u> if you answer promptly.
   如果你立刻回答，我會非常感激。

   (A) labor〔'lebɚ〕 *n.* 勞動　　　(B) ***favor***〔'fevɚ〕 *n.* 恩惠；偏愛
   (C) coward〔'kauɚd〕 *n.* 懦夫　　(D) harmony〔'harmənɪ〕 *n.* 和諧

   * promptly〔'pramptlɪ〕 *adv.* 迅速地

2. (**D**) Teddy has to do some <u>research</u> in the library.
   泰迪必須在圖書館做些研究。

   (A) effort〔'ɛfɚt〕 *n.* 努力　　　(B) factor〔'fæktɚ〕 *n.* 因素
   (C) century〔'sɛntʃərɪ〕 *n.* 世紀　(D) ***research***〔rɪ'sɝtʃ〕 *n.* 研究

3. (**A**) They <u>concluded</u> the show with a medley.
   他們以組曲結束這場表演。

   (A) ***conclude***〔kən'klud〕 *v.* 結束；下結論
   (B) strive〔straɪv〕 *v.* 努力
   (C) adapt〔ə'dæpt〕 *v.* 使適應；改編
   (D) pretend〔prɪ'tɛnd〕 *v.* 假裝

   * medley〔'mɛdlɪ〕 *n.* 混合曲；組曲

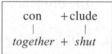

con　　+clude
│　　　　│
together　+　*shut*

4. (**C**) Your prompt action <u>prevented</u> a serious accident.
   你立即的行動阻止了一場嚴重意外的發生。

   (A) intend〔ɪn'tɛnd〕 *v.* 打算
   (B) suffer〔'sʌfɚ〕 *v.* 受苦
   (C) ***prevent***〔prɪ'vɛnt〕 *v.* 阻止；預防
   (D) propose〔prə'poz〕 *v.* 提議

   * prompt〔prampt〕 *adj.* 立即的

5. (**A**) The course is a combination of <u>academic</u> and practical work. 這項課程結合了理論與實務。

   (A) ***academic***〔,ækə'dɛmɪk〕 *adj.* 理論上的；學術上的
   (B) optimistic〔,aptə'mɪstɪk〕 *adj.* 樂觀的
   (C) frustrated〔'frʌstretɪd〕 *adj.* 沮喪的
   (D) aware〔ə'wɛr〕 *adj.* 知道的；察覺的

6. (**D**) He is a <u>regular</u> customer of ours. 他是我們的<u>老主顧</u>。

    (A) tiny〔'taɪnɪ〕*adj.* 極小的

    (B) unwilling〔ʌn'wɪlɪŋ〕*adj.* 不願意的

    (C) plastic〔'plæstɪk〕*adj.* 塑膠的

    (D) *regular*〔'rɛgjələ〕*adj.* 定期的；固定的

        a regular customer 老主顧

    ＊customer〔'kʌstəmə〕*n.* 顧客

7. (**B**) The majority is for <u>maintaining</u> the status quo.
大部分的人贊成<u>維持</u>現狀。

    (A) contrast〔kən'træst〕*v.* 與～成對比

    (B) *maintain*〔men'ten〕*v.* 維持

    (C) acquaint〔ə'kwent〕*v.* 使認識

    (D) delay〔dɪ'le〕*v.* 延遲

    ＊majority〔mə'dʒɔrətɪ〕*n.* 大多數

    介系詞 for 表「贊成」，而「反對」則用 against。

    status quo〔'stetəs'kwo〕*n.* 現狀

8. (**C**) Mini-skirts are again in <u>fashion</u>. 迷你裙又再度<u>流行</u>。

    (A) recreation〔ˌrɛkrɪ'eʃən〕*n.* 娛樂

    (B) event〔ɪ'vɛnt〕*n.* 事件

    (C) *fashion*〔'fæʃən〕*n.* 流行　　*in fashion* 流行

    (D) diligence〔'dɪlədʒəns〕*n.* 勤勉

    ＊mini-skirt〔'mɪnɪˌskɜt〕*n.* 迷你裙 (= *miniskirt*)

9. (**D**) A thousand people <u>attended</u> the seminar.
有一千人<u>參加</u>座談會。

    (A) separate〔'sɛpəˌret〕*v.* 分離　　(B) behave〔bɪ'hev〕*v.* 行為；舉止

    (C) excel〔ɪk'sɛl〕*v.* 擅長；優越　　(D) *attend*〔ə'tɛnd〕*v.* 參加

    ＊seminar〔'sɛməˌnɑr〕*n.* 座談會；研討會

10. (**A**) Winners will be notified by <u>post</u>. 得獎者將以<u>信件</u>通知。

    (A) *post*〔post〕*n.* 郵件

    (B) surgery〔'sɜdʒərɪ〕*n.* 外科手術 (= *operation*)

    (C) curiosity〔ˌkjʊrɪ'ɑsətɪ〕*n.* 好奇心

    (D) factor〔'fæktə〕*n.* 因素

    ＊winner〔'wɪnə〕*n.* 獲勝者；得獎者　　notify〔'notəˌfaɪ〕*v.* 通知

TEST 24

Directions: *Of the four words given after each sentence, choose the one most suitable for filling in the blank.*

1. _____ the solar system is the unknown.

   (A) Extreme
   (B) Beyond
   (C) Vital
   (D) Despite   (   )

2. The green light _____ go.

   (A) achieves
   (B) mentions
   (C) compares
   (D) indicates   (   )

3. This car _____ a lot of gas.

   (A) consumes
   (B) challenges
   (C) committed
   (D) shatters   (   )

4. The punishment is too _____.

   (A) single
   (B) mental
   (C) severe
   (D) certain   (   )

5. I knew that they would _____ my proposal.

   (A) combine
   (B) accept
   (C) classify
   (D) flutter   (   )

6. This movie is _____ to adults only.

   (A) reflected
   (B) frightened
   (C) resigned
   (D) restricted   (   )

7. People use the river to _____ goods.

   (A) neglect
   (B) dominate
   (C) subsist
   (D) transport   (   )

8. The ten _____ scholars were sent abroad to study.

   (A) primitive
   (B) immediate
   (C) outstanding
   (D) final   (   )

9. We _____ a deposit in advance.

   (A) require
   (B) remain
   (C) cease
   (D) murder   (   )

10. He likes a girl with long _____ hair.

   (A) mere
   (B) straight
   (C) extra
   (D) corrupt   (   )

TEST 24 詳解

1. (**B**) <u>Beyond</u> the solar system is the unknown.
太陽系<u>之外</u>，仍是未知的世界。

(A) extreme〔ɪk'strim〕*adj.* 極端的
(B) ***beyond***〔bɪ'jɑnd〕*prep.* 在～之外
(C) vital〔'vaɪtḷ〕*adj.* 極重要的
(D) despite〔dɪ'spaɪt〕*prep.* 儘管（= *in spite of*）

* ***solar system*** 太陽系　　unknown〔ʌn'non〕*adj.* 未知的

2. (**D**) The green light <u>indicates</u> go.
綠燈<u>表示</u>可以通行。

(A) achieve〔ə'tʃiv〕*v.* 達到　　(B) mention〔'mɛnʃən〕*v.* 提到
(C) compare〔kəm'pɛr〕*v.* 比較　　(D) ***indicate***〔'ɪndə͵ket〕*v.* 表示

3. (**A**) This car <u>consumes</u> a lot of gas. 這輛車很<u>耗油</u>。

(A) ***consume***〔kən'sum〕*v.* 消耗
(B) challenge〔'tʃælɪndʒ〕*v.* 挑戰
(C) commit〔kə'mɪt〕*v.* 犯（罪）；委託
(D) shatter〔'ʃætɚ〕*v.* 使粉碎

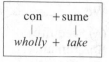

* gas〔gæs〕*n.* 汽油

4. (**C**) The punishment is too <u>severe</u>. 這處罰太<u>嚴厲</u>了。

(A) single〔'sɪŋgḷ〕*adj.* 單一的　　(B) mental〔'mɛntḷ〕*adj.* 心理的
(C) ***severe***〔sə'vɪr〕*adj.* 嚴厲的
(D) certain〔'sɝtṇ〕*adj.* 確定的；某一

* punishment〔'pʌnɪʃmənt〕*n.* 處罰

5. (**B**) I knew that they would <u>accept</u> my proposal.
我知道他們會<u>接受</u>我的提議。

(A) combine〔kəm'baɪn〕*v.* 結合
(B) ***accept***〔ək'sɛpt〕*v.* 接受
(C) classify〔'klæsə͵faɪ〕*v.* 分類
(D) flutter〔'flʌtɚ〕*v.* 拍動（翅膀）；飄動

6. (**D**) This movie is <u>restricted</u> to adults only.
　　　這部電影只<u>限</u>成人觀賞。

　　(A) reflect〔rɪˈflɛkt〕 v. 反映　　(B) frighten〔ˈfraɪtn̩〕 v. 驚嚇
　　(C) resign〔rɪˈzaɪn〕 v. 辭職　　　(D) **restrict**〔rɪˈstrɪkt〕 v. 限制
　　＊ adult〔əˈdʌlt〕 n. 成人

7. (**D**) People use the river to <u>transport</u> goods.
　　　人們利用河流來<u>運送</u>貨物。

　　(A) neglect〔nɪˈglɛkt〕 v. 忽略
　　(B) dominate〔ˈdɑməˌnet〕 v. 支配；控制
　　(C) subsist〔sʌbˈsɪst〕 v. 生存
　　(D) **transport**〔trænsˈport〕 v. 運送
　　＊ goods〔gʊdz〕 n. pl. 商品；貨物

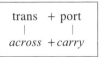

8. (**C**) The ten <u>outstanding</u> scholars were sent abroad to study.
　　　十位<u>傑出</u>的學者被送往國外深造。

　　(A) primitive〔ˈprɪmətɪv〕 adj. 原始的
　　(B) immediate〔ɪˈmidɪɪt〕 adj. 立即的
　　(C) **outstanding**〔aʊtˈstændɪŋ〕 adj. 傑出的
　　(D) final〔ˈfaɪn̩l〕 adj. 最後的
　　＊ scholar〔ˈskɑlɚ〕 n. 學者　　abroad〔əˈbrɔd〕 adv. 在國外

9. (**A**) We <u>require</u> a deposit in advance.　我們事先<u>需要</u>訂金。

　　(A) **require**〔rɪˈkwaɪr〕 v. 需要
　　(B) remain〔rɪˈmen〕 v. 仍然
　　(C) cease〔sis〕 v. 停止
　　(D) murder〔ˈmɝdɚ〕 v. 謀殺
　　＊ deposit〔dɪˈpɑzɪt〕 n. 訂金；押金　　**in advance** 事先

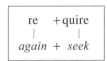

10. (**B**) He likes a girl with long <u>straight</u> hair.
　　　他喜歡留著<u>直</u>的長髮的女孩。

　　(A) mere〔mɪr〕 adj. 僅僅　　　(B) **straight**〔stret〕 adj. 直的
　　(C) extra〔ˈɛkstrə〕 adj. 額外的　(D) corrupt〔kəˈrʌpt〕 adj. 腐敗的

TEST 25

Directions: *Of the four words given after each sentence, choose the one most suitable for filling in the blank.*

1. How he _____ to find us is beyond me.

   (A) managed
   (B) produced
   (C) endured
   (D) published   (   )

2. The houses are _____ by red roofs.

   (A) impressed
   (B) characterized
   (C) produced
   (D) notified   (   )

3. The food in the refrigerator is _____ for the weekend.

   (A) previous
   (B) available
   (C) adequate
   (D) patient   (   )

4. The army has _____ the rebel base.

   (A) involved
   (B) demanded
   (C) disputed
   (D) destroyed   (   )

5. This award is being given in _____ of your contributions to the industry.

   (A) aspect
   (B) circumstance
   (C) recognition
   (D) diamond   (   )

6. The forest rangers _____ an unextinguished cigarette butt was the cause of the fire.

(A) starved
(B) suspected
(C) depressed
(D) canceled   (   )

7. His company has _____ a new kind of battery.

(A) developed
(B) weighed
(C) counted
(D) obeyed   (   )

8. Chimpanzees have the _____ of three men combined.

(A) evidence
(B) strength
(C) administration
(D) grass   (   )

9. Rubber cannot _____ electricity.

(A) convince
(B) contradict
(C) confuse
(D) conduct   (   )

10. I've _____ the staff to finish the work by tomorrow.

(A) injured
(B) disturbed
(C) encountered
(D) instructed   (   )

TEST 25 詳解

1.(**A**) How he <u>managed</u> to find us is beyond me.
我不知道他是如何設法找到我們的。

    (A) ***manage*** 〔'mænɪdʒ〕 *v.* 設法　　(B) produce 〔prə'djus〕 *v.* 生產

    (C) endure 〔ɪn'djʊr〕 *v.* 忍耐　　(D) publish 〔'pʌblɪʃ〕 *v.* 出版;刊登

    * ***beyond*** *sb*. 某人無法了解

2.(**B**) The houses are <u>characterized</u> by red roofs.
這些房子的<u>特色是紅色的屋頂</u>。

    (A) impress 〔ɪm'prɛs〕 *v.* 使印象深刻

    (B) ***characterize*** 〔'kærɪktə,raɪz〕 *v.* 以～為特色

        be characterized by～ 特色是～

    (C) produce 〔prə'djus〕 *v.* 生產

    (D) notify 〔'notə,faɪ〕 *v.* 通知

3.(**C**) The food in the refrigerator is <u>adequate</u> for the weekend.
冰箱裡的食物,<u>夠</u>週末時吃。

    (A) previous 〔'privɪəs〕 *adj.* 先前的

    (B) available 〔ə'veləbḷ〕 *adj.* 可獲得的

    (C) ***adequate*** 〔'ædəkwɪt〕 *adj.* 足夠的

    (D) patient 〔'peʃənt〕 *adj.* 有耐心的

4.(**D**) The army has <u>destroyed</u> the rebel base. 軍方已<u>摧毀叛軍的基地</u>。

    (A) involve 〔ɪn'vɑlv〕 *v.* 牽涉　　(B) demand 〔dɪ'mænd〕 *v.* 需要

    (C) dispute 〔dɪ'spjut〕 *v.* 爭論　　(D) ***destroy*** 〔dɪ'strɔɪ〕 *v.* 摧毀;破壞

    * army 〔'ɑrmɪ〕 *n.* 軍隊　　rebel 〔'rɛbḷ〕 *n.* 叛徒

      base 〔bes〕 *n.* 基地

5.(**C**) This award is being given in <u>recognition</u> of your contributions to the industry. 頒這座獎給你,是為了<u>表揚</u>你對工業的貢獻。

    (A) aspect 〔'æspɛkt〕 *n.* 方面

    (B) circumstance 〔'sɜkəm,stæns〕 *n.* 環境;情況

    (C) ***recognition*** 〔,rɛkəg'nɪʃən〕 *n.* 表揚;承認

    (D) diamond 〔'daɪəmənd〕 *n.* 鑽石

    * award 〔ə'wɔrd〕 *n.* 獎　　contribution 〔,kɑntrə'bjuʃən〕 *n.* 貢獻

6. (**B**) The forest rangers <u>suspected</u> an unextinguished cigarette butt was the cause of the fire.

森林看守員<u>懷疑</u>，未熄滅的煙蒂是造成森林大火的原因。

(A) starve〔stɑrv〕*v.* 餓
(B) ***suspect***〔sə'spɛkt〕*v.* 懷疑
(C) depress〔dɪ'prɛs〕*v.* 使沮喪
(D) cancel〔'kænsḷ〕*v.* 取消

* ranger〔'rendʒɚ〕*n.* 森林看守員；森林警備隊員
unextinguished〔ˌʌnɪk'stɪŋkwɪʃt〕*adj.* 未熄滅的
butt〔bʌt〕*n.* 煙蒂

7. (**A**) His company has <u>developed</u> a new kind of battery.

他的公司<u>發展</u>出新型的電池。

(A) ***develop***〔dɪ'vɛləp〕*v.* 發展　　(B) weigh〔we〕*v.* 衡量；重~
(C) count〔kaʊnt〕*v.* 數；重要　　(D) obey〔o'be〕*v.* 服從

8. (**B**) Chimpanzees have the <u>strength</u> of three men combined.

黑猩猩擁有三個人的<u>力氣</u>。

(A) evidence〔'ɛvədəns〕*n.* 證據
(B) ***strength***〔strɛŋθ〕*n.* 力氣
(C) administration〔ədˌmɪnə'streʃən〕*n.* 管理；行政
(D) grass〔græs〕*n.* 草

* chimpanzee〔ˌtʃɪmpæn'zi〕*n.* 黑猩猩
combine〔kəm'baɪn〕*v.* 結合

9. (**D**) Rubber cannot <u>conduct</u> electricity.　橡膠不能<u>導</u>電。

(A) convince〔kən'vɪns〕*v.* 使相信
(B) contradict〔ˌkɑntrə'dɪkt〕*v.* 反駁
(C) confuse〔kən'fjuz〕*v.* 使迷惑
(D) ***conduct***〔kən'dʌkt〕*v.* 傳導

* rubber〔'rʌbɚ〕*n.* 橡膠　　electricity〔ɪˌlɛk'trɪsətɪ〕*n.* 電

10. (**D**) I've <u>instructed</u> the staff to finish the work by tomorrow.

我已<u>命令</u>全體工作人員，明天以前將工作完成。

(A) injure〔'ɪndʒɚ〕*v.* 傷害
(B) disturb〔dɪ'stɝb〕*v.* 打擾
(C) encounter〔ɪn'kaʊntɚ〕*v.* 遭遇
(D) ***instruct***〔ɪn'strʌkt〕*v.* 指示；命令

in	+struct
into	+ build

TEST 26

Directions: *Of the four words given after each sentence, choose the one most suitable for filling in the blank.*

1. Rescue workers are _____ their search for the missing child.

   (A) intensifying
   (B) yielding
   (C) fluttering
   (D) preying   (   )

2. Mark is _____ me to take up his offer.

   (A) conflicting
   (B) urging
   (C) pretending
   (D) shifting   (   )

3. My monthly _____ was over twenty thousand NT dollars.

   (A) rigidity
   (B) caution
   (C) income
   (D) concept   (   )

4. The crowd _____ the streets with confetti.

   (A) punished
   (B) declared
   (C) assured
   (D) littered   (   )

5. The Mayas long ago used _____ to grow their crops.

   (A) pronunciation
   (B) conscience
   (C) irrigation
   (D) decency   (   )

6. Possession of firearms is ＿＿＿＿＿ in this country.

   (A) prosperous
   (B) nuclear
   (C) loose
   (D) illegal   (   )

7. Bernard has ＿＿＿＿＿ all his money from the bank.

   (A) associated
   (B) withdrawn
   (C) flourished
   (D) translated   (   )

8. The space shuttle is starting its ＿＿＿＿＿ towards earth.

   (A) descent
   (B) melody
   (C) flexibility
   (D) manufacturer   (   )

9. The government has ＿＿＿＿＿ all forms of dissent in the country.

   (A) robbed
   (B) baked
   (C) engaged
   (D) oppressed   (   )

10. Selective breeding ensures that only desirable ＿＿＿＿＿ are passed on to the next generation.

    (A) rhythms
    (B) traits
    (C) emergencies
    (D) obligations   (   )

TEST 26 詳解

1.(**A**) Rescue workers are <u>intensifying</u> their search for the missing child. 救援人員正<u>加緊</u>搜尋那名失蹤的小孩。

    (A) ***intensify*** ﹝ ɪn'tɛnsə͵faɪ ﹞ *v.* 加緊;加強
    (B) yield ﹝ jild ﹞ *v.* 屈服;生產
    (C) flutter ﹝'flʌtɚ﹞ *v.* 拍打(翅膀);飄動
    (D) prey ﹝ pre ﹞ *v.* 捕食
    ＊ rescue ﹝'rɛskju﹞ *n.* 拯救
       missing ﹝'mɪsɪŋ﹞ *adj.* 失蹤的

in	+	tens	+	ify
toward	+	stretch	+	make

2.(**B**) Mark is <u>urging</u> me to take up his offer.
馬克<u>勸</u>我接受他的提議。

    (A) conflict ﹝ kən'flɪkt ﹞ *v.* 衝突   (B) ***urge*** ﹝ ɝdʒ ﹞ *v.* 力勸;催促
    (C) pretend ﹝ prɪ'tɛnd ﹞ *v.* 假裝   (D) shift ﹝ ʃɪft ﹞ *v.* 改變
    ＊ ***take up*** 接受   offer ﹝'ɔfɚ﹞ *n.* 提議

3.(**C**) My monthly <u>income</u> was over twenty thousand NT dollars.
我每月的<u>收入</u>超過兩萬元新台幣。

    (A) rigidity ﹝ rɪ'dʒɪdətɪ ﹞ *n.* 堅硬;嚴格
    (B) caution ﹝'kɔʃən﹞ *n.* 小心;謹慎
    (C) ***income*** ﹝'ɪn͵kʌm﹞ *n.* 收入   (D) concept ﹝'kɑnsɛpt﹞ *n.* 概念
    ＊ monthly ﹝'mʌnθlɪ﹞ *adj.* 每月的

4.(**D**) The crowd <u>littered</u> the streets with confetti.
群眾把彩色紙片<u>隨意丟</u>在街道上。

    (A) punish ﹝'pʌnɪʃ﹞ *v.* 處罰   (B) declare ﹝ dɪ'klɛr ﹞ *v.* 宣布
    (C) assure ﹝ ə'ʃur ﹞ *v.* 確保   (D) ***litter*** ﹝'lɪtɚ﹞ *v.* 亂丟
    ＊ confetti ﹝ kən'fɛtɪ ﹞ *n.* 五彩碎紙

5.(**C**) The Mayas long ago used <u>irrigation</u> to grow their crops.
很久以前,馬雅人利用<u>灌溉</u>來種植農作物。

    (A) pronunciation ﹝ prə͵nʌnsɪ'eʃən ﹞ *n.* 發音
    (B) conscience ﹝'kɑnʃəns﹞ *n.* 良心
    (C) ***irrigation*** ﹝͵ɪrə'geʃən﹞ *n.* 灌溉
    (D) decency ﹝'disn̩sɪ﹞ *n.* 端莊;高尚
    ＊ Maya ﹝'majə﹞ *n.* 馬雅人   crop ﹝ krɑp ﹞ *n.* 農作物

ir	+	rigat	+	ion
upon	+	wet	+	n.

6. (**D**) Possession of firearms is <u>illegal</u> in this country.
在這個國家，持有槍械是<u>違法的</u>。

(A) prosperous〔'prɑspərəs〕*adj.* 繁榮的

(B) nuclear〔'njuklɪə〕*adj.* 核子的

(C) loose〔lus〕*adj.* 鬆的

(D) ***illegal***〔ɪ'ligl̩〕*adj.* 違法的

* possession〔pə'zɛʃən〕*n.* 擁有　　firearm〔'faɪrˌɑrm〕*n.* 槍枝

7. (**B**) Bernard has <u>withdrawn</u> all his money from the bank.
伯納德已把他所有的錢從銀行裡<u>提</u>出來。

(A) associate〔ə'soʃɪˌet〕*v.* 使有關聯　　(B) ***withdraw***〔wɪð'drɔ〕*v.* 提款

(C) flourish〔'flɝɪʃ〕*v.* 興盛；繁榮

(D) translate〔træns'let〕*v.* 翻譯

8. (**A**) The space shuttle is starting its <u>descent</u> towards earth.
太空梭正開始<u>降落</u>地球。

(A) ***descent***〔dɪ'sɛnt〕*n.* 下降　　(B) melody〔'mɛlədɪ〕*n.* 旋律

(C) flexibility〔ˌflɛksə'bɪlətɪ〕*n.* 彈性

(D) manufacturer〔ˌmænjə'fæktʃərə〕*n.* 製造商；廠商

* ***space shuttle*** 太空梭

9. (**D**) The government has <u>oppressed</u> all forms of dissent in the country. 這國家的政府<u>打壓</u>國內一切的反對聲浪。

(A) rob〔rɑb〕*v.* 搶劫

(B) bake〔bek〕*v.* 烘烤

(C) engage〔ɪn'gedʒ〕*v.* 從事

(D) ***oppress***〔ə'prɛs〕*v.* 打壓；壓迫

* dissent〔dɪ'sɛnt〕*n.* 異議；反對意見

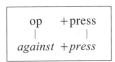

10. (**B**) Selective breeding ensures that only desirable <u>traits</u> are passed on to the next generation.
優生學（選擇性）生育能確保只將良好的<u>特徵</u>傳給下一代。

(A) rhythm〔'rɪðəm〕*n.* 節奏　　(B) ***trait***〔tret〕*n.* 特徵；特點

(C) emergency〔ɪ'mɝdʒənsɪ〕*n.* 緊急情況

(D) obligation〔ˌɑblə'geʃən〕*n.* 義務

* breeding〔'bridɪŋ〕*n.* 生育　　desirable〔dɪ'zaɪrəbl̩〕*adj.* 令人滿意的

TEST 27

Directions: *Of the four words given after each sentence, choose the one most suitable for filling in the blank.*

1. A small _____ of alcohol has been found in his blood.

    (A) amount
    (B) area
    (C) item
    (D) chain   (   )

2. Don't _____ to this matter again, please.

    (A) bend
    (B) refer
    (C) tie
    (D) avoid   (   )

3. It's hard to _____ his charms.

    (A) insist
    (B) resist
    (C) persist
    (D) consist   (   )

4. The _____ has been overthrown by a coup.

    (A) disease
    (B) pressure
    (C) barbarian
    (D) government   (   )

5. He _____ his teacher for his failure.

    (A) blamed
    (B) introduced
    (C) mistook
    (D) provided   (   )

6. This room has an excellent _____ of the mountains.

   (A) welfare
   (B) gesture
   (C) dignity
   (D) view   (   )

7. We could see the top of the high mountain _____ well.

   (A) fairly
   (B) gradually
   (C) further
   (D) actually   (   )

8. 3.0 is the passing _____ for this course.

   (A) fault
   (B) theory
   (C) obstacle
   (D) grade   (   )

9. Circuses never fail to _____ children.

   (A) minimize
   (B) envy
   (C) wrinkle
   (D) delight   (   )

10. The trains are _____ to delays when there is fog.

    (A) naughty
    (B) subject
    (C) insufficient
    (D) pure   (   )

TEST 27 詳解

1. (**A**) A small <u>amount</u> of alcohol has been found in his blood.
   在他的血液中，發現有少量的酒精。

   (A) **amount** 〔 ə'maʊnt 〕 n. 數量　　(B) area 〔'ɛrɪə〕 n. 地區
   (C) item 〔'aɪtəm 〕 n. 項目　　(D) chain 〔 tʃen 〕 n. 鏈子

   * alcohol 〔'ælkə,hɔl 〕 n. 酒精　　blood 〔 blʌd 〕 n. 血液

2. (**B**) Don't <u>refer</u> to this matter again, please.
   拜託別再<u>提</u>這件事了。

   (A) bend 〔 bɛnd 〕 v. 彎曲
   (B) **refer** 〔 rɪ'fɝ 〕 v. 提到　　**refer to** 提到
   (C) tie 〔 taɪ 〕 v. 綁
   (D) avoid 〔 ə'vɔɪd 〕 v. 避免

3. (**B**) It's hard to <u>resist</u> his charms. 他的魅力令人難以<u>抗拒</u>。

   (A) insist 〔 ɪn'sɪst 〕 v. 堅持
   (B) **resist** 〔 rɪ'zɪst 〕 v. 抵抗
   (C) persist 〔 pə'sɪst 〕 v. 堅持；持續
   (D) consist 〔 kən'sɪst 〕 v. 由～組成

   * charm 〔 tʃɑrm 〕 n. 魅力

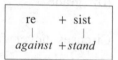

4. (**D**) The <u>government</u> has been overthrown by a coup.
   一場政變推翻了<u>政府</u>。

   (A) disease 〔 dɪ'ziz 〕 n. 疾病
   (B) pressure 〔'prɛʃə 〕 n. 壓力
   (C) barbarian 〔 bɑr'bɛrɪən 〕 n. 野蠻人
   (D) **government** 〔'gʌvənmənt 〕 n. 政府

   * overthrow 〔,ovə'θro 〕 v. 推翻　　coup 〔 ku 〕 n. 政變

5. (**A**) He <u>blamed</u> his teacher for his failure.
   他把失敗<u>歸咎</u>於他的老師。

   (A) **blame** 〔 blem 〕 v. 歸咎於；責備
   (B) introduce 〔,ɪntrə'djus 〕 v. 介紹
   (C) mistake 〔 mə'stek 〕 v. 誤解　　(D) provide 〔 prə'vaɪd 〕 v. 提供

6. (**D**) This room has an excellent <u>view</u> of the mountains.
從這個房間可看到優美的山景。

(A) welfare 〔'wɛl,fɛr 〕 *n.* 福利　　(B) gesture 〔'dʒɛstʃə 〕 *n.* 手勢
(C) dignity 〔'dɪgnətɪ 〕 *n.* 尊嚴　　(D) *view* 〔 vju 〕 *n.* 景色

＊ excellent 〔'ɛksl̩ənt 〕 *adj.* 非常好的

7. (**A**) We could see the top of the high mountain <u>fairly</u> well.
我們可以<u>很清楚地</u>看見高山的山頂。

(A) *fairly* 〔'fɛrlɪ 〕 *adv.* 非常地 (= *very*)
(B) gradually 〔'grædʒuəlɪ 〕 *adv.* 逐漸地
(C) further 〔'fɜðə 〕 *adv.* 更進一步地
(D) actually 〔'æktʃuəlɪ 〕 *adv.* 實際上

8. (**D**) 3.0 is the passing <u>grade</u> for this course.
這門課的及格分數是 3.0。

(A) fault 〔 fɔlt 〕 *n.* 錯誤　　(B) theory 〔'θiərɪ 〕 *n.* 理論
(C) obstacle 〔'ɑbstəkl̩ 〕 *n.* 障礙　　(D) *grade* 〔 gred 〕 *n.* 分數；成績

＊ passing 〔'pæsɪŋ 〕 *adj.* 及格的
passing grade 及格分數 (= *passing mark*)

9. (**D**) Circuses never fail to <u>delight</u> children.
馬戲團總是能<u>使孩子高興</u>。

(A) minimize 〔'mɪnə,maɪz 〕 *v.* 使減到最小
(B) envy 〔'ɛnvɪ 〕 *v.* 嫉妒
(C) wrinkle 〔'rɪŋkl̩ 〕 *v.* 起皺紋
(D) *delight* 〔 dɪ'laɪt 〕 *v.* 使高興

＊ circus 〔'sɜkəs 〕 *n.* 馬戲團　　*fail to* 無法

10. (**B**) The trains are <u>subject</u> to delays when there is fog.
有霧時，火車<u>容易</u>誤點。

(A) naughty 〔'nɔtɪ 〕 *adj.* 頑皮的
(B) *subject* 〔'sʌbdʒɪkt 〕 *adj.* 易於　　*be subject to* 容易～
(C) insufficient 〔,ɪnsə'fɪʃənt 〕 *adj.* 不足的
(D) pure 〔 pjʊr 〕 *adj.* 純粹的

＊ delay 〔 dɪ'le 〕 *n.* 延誤　　fog 〔 fɔg 〕 *n.* 霧

TEST 28

Directions: *Of the four words given after each sentence, choose the one most suitable for filling in the blank.*

1. The children were _____ by all the toys in the shop windows.

   (A) fascinated
   (B) resulted
   (C) declined
   (D) distinguished   (   )

2. Columbus never got to _____ the New World.

   (A) attract
   (B) found
   (C) explore
   (D) confine   (   )

3. The new product has generated a(n) _____ response from the public.

   (A) general
   (B) average
   (C) tight
   (D) enthusiastic   (   )

4. He _____ the importance of better public relations.

   (A) ruled
   (B) stressed
   (C) wasted
   (D) disappointed   (   )

5. I _____ to make you as good as new.

   (A) guarantee
   (B) perform
   (C) depend
   (D) organize   (   )

6. It was one of those ideas that changed the ＿＿＿＿＿＿ of history.

(A) criminal
(B) course
(C) exception
(D) trade   (   )

7. ＿＿＿＿＿＿ in a country town, he went to New York at the age of eighteen.

(A) Rushed
(B) Raised
(C) Wasted
(D) Sympathized   (   )

8. This clock keeps ＿＿＿＿＿＿ time.

(A) accurate
(B) entire
(C) terrible
(D) responsible   (   )

9. This dress ＿＿＿＿＿＿ your eyes.

(A) matches
(B) strikes
(C) shares
(D) solves   (   )

10. Water is a(n) ＿＿＿＿＿＿ resource we can't waste.

(A) entire
(B) constant
(C) honest
(D) precious   (   )

TEST 28 詳解

1. (**A**) The children were <u>fascinated</u> by all the toys in the shop windows. 孩子們對商店櫥窗裡的各種玩具非常著迷。

   (A) *fascinate*〔'fæsṇ,et〕v. 使著迷
   (B) result〔rɪ'zʌlt〕v. 導致
   (C) decline〔dɪ'klaɪn〕v. 衰退；拒絕
   (D) distinguish〔dɪ'stɪŋgwɪʃ〕v. 分辨

2. (**C**) Columbus never got to <u>explore</u> the New World.
   哥倫布從未探索新世界。

   (A) attract〔ə'trækt〕v. 吸引　　(B) found〔faʊnd〕v. 建立
   (C) *explore*〔ɪk'splor〕v. 探索　(D) confine〔kən'faɪn〕v. 限制

3. (**D**) The new product has generated an <u>enthusiastic</u> response from the public. 新產品引起了大眾熱烈的迴響。

   (A) general〔'dʒɛnərəl〕*adj.* 一般的；概略的
   (B) average〔'ævərɪdʒ〕*adj.* 平均的；一般的
   (C) tight〔taɪt〕*adj.* 緊的
   (D) *enthusiastic*〔ɪn,θjuzɪ'æstɪk〕*adj.* 熱烈的；熱心的

   ＊generate〔'dʒɛnə,ret〕v. 產生；引起　response〔rɪ'spɑns〕n. 反應

4. (**B**) He <u>stressed</u> the importance of better public relations.
   他強調改善公共關係的重要性。

   (A) rule〔rul〕v. 統治　　　　(B) *stress*〔strɛs〕v. 強調
   (C) waste〔west〕v. 浪費
   (D) disappoint〔,dɪsə'pɔɪnt〕v. 使失望

5. (**A**) I <u>guarantee</u> to make you as good as new.
   我保證讓你從此煥然一新。

   (A) *guarantee*〔,gærən'ti〕v. 保證
   (B) perform〔pɚ'fɔrm〕v. 表演；執行
   (C) depend〔dɪ'pɛnd〕v. 依賴；視～而定
   (D) organize〔'ɔrgən,aɪz〕v. 組織

   ＊*as good as* 幾乎

6. (**B**) It was one of those ideas that changed the <u>course</u> of history. 這是改變歷史演進的想法之一。

    (A) criminal〔'krɪmənḷ〕*n.* 罪犯
    (B) *course*〔kors〕*n.* 演變　　*the course of history* 歷史的演進
    (C) exception〔ɪk'sɛpʃən〕*n.* 例外
    (D) trade〔tred〕*n.* 貿易

7. (**B**) <u>Raised</u> in a country town, he went to New York at the age of eighteen. 他<u>生長</u>於鄉下的小鎮，十八歲時前往紐約。

    (A) rush〔rʌʃ〕*v.* 衝；催促
    (B) *raise*〔rez〕*v.* 養育
    (C) waste〔west〕*v.* 浪費
    (D) sympathize〔'sɪmpə,θaɪz〕*v.* 同情

8. (**A**) This clock keeps <u>accurate</u> time.
這個鐘很<u>準</u>。

    (A) *accurate*〔'ækjərɪt〕*adj.* 準確的
    (B) entire〔ɪn'taɪr〕*adj.* 全部的
    (C) terrible〔'tɛrəbḷ〕*adj.* 可怕的
    (D) responsible〔rɪ'spɑnsəbḷ〕*adj.* 有責任的

ac +	cur	+ ate
to +take	care	+ adj.

9. (**A**) This dress <u>matches</u> your eyes.
這件洋裝很<u>配</u>你的眼睛。

    (A) *match*〔mætʃ〕*v.* 相配
    (B) strike〔straɪk〕*v.* 敲打
    (C) share〔ʃɛr〕*v.* 分享
    (D) solve〔sɑlv〕*v.* 解決

10. (**D**) Water is a <u>precious</u> resource we can't waste.
水是<u>珍貴的</u>資源，我們不可以浪費。

    (A) entire〔ɪn'taɪr〕*adj.* 全部的
    (B) constant〔'kɑnstənt〕*adj.* 不斷的
    (C) honest〔'ɑnɪst〕*adj.* 誠實的
    (D) *precious*〔'prɛʃəs〕*adj.* 珍貴的

    ＊resource〔rɪ'sors〕*n.* 資源

TEST 29

Directions: *Of the four words given after each sentence, choose the one most suitable for filling in the blank.*

1. _____ is the mother of invention.

   (A) Corner
   (B) Contact
   (C) Powder
   (D) Necessity   (   )

2. The United States is the _____ export market of Taiwan.

   (A) sharp
   (B) whole
   (C) scarce
   (D) main   (   )

3. Julia made a(n) _____ in the lottery.

   (A) conference
   (B) atmosphere
   (C) fortune
   (D) alcohol   (   )

4. I'm glad you _____ to your principles.

   (A) begged
   (B) complained
   (C) stuck
   (D) announced   (   )

5. He pulled hard, but without any noticeable _____.

   (A) shell
   (B) attention
   (C) effect
   (D) threat   (   )

6. The fall of Communism is —————— .

   (A) inevitable
   (B) double
   (C) aggressive
   (D) mute   (   )

7. The whole world is now in the —————— of Westernization.

   (A) importance
   (B) mayor
   (C) feast
   (D) process   (   )

8. Don't —————— me of my blunders.

   (A) force
   (B) afford
   (C) discover
   (D) remind   (   )

9. The teacher —————— his class when the bell rang.

   (A) dismissed
   (B) communicated
   (C) lacked
   (D) advanced   (   )

10. She —————— her degree from Stanford.

    (A) encouraged
    (B) obtained
    (C) displeased
    (D) supplied   (   )

TEST 29 詳解

1. (**D**) <u>Necessity</u> is the mother of invention.
〔諺〕<u>需要</u>是發明之母。

(A) corner〔'kɔrnɚ〕*n.* 角落　　(B) contact〔'kɑntækt〕*n.* 接觸
(C) powder〔'paʊdɚ〕*n.* 粉末　　(D) *necessity*〔nə'sɛsətɪ〕*n.* 需要

＊ invention〔ɪn'vɛnʃən〕*n.* 發明

2. (**D**) The United States is the <u>main</u> export market of Taiwan.
美國是台灣<u>主要的</u>外銷市場。

(A) sharp〔ʃɑrp〕*adj.* 尖銳的　　(B) whole〔hol〕*adj.* 全部的
(C) scarce〔skɛrs〕*adj.* 稀少的　　(D) *main*〔men〕*adj.* 主要的

＊ export〔ɪks'port〕*n.* 外銷；出口

3. (**C**) Julia made a <u>fortune</u> in the lottery.
茱莉亞中了彩券發了<u>大財</u>。

(A) conference〔'kɑnfərəns〕*n.* 會議
(B) atmosphere〔'ætməs,fɪr〕*n.* 氣氛；大氣層
(C) *fortune*〔'fɔrtʃən〕*n.* 大筆的錢；財富　　*make a fortune* 發大財
(D) alcohol〔'ælkə,hol〕*n.* 酒精

＊ lottery〔'lɑtərɪ〕*n.* 彩券

4. (**C**) I'm glad you <u>stuck</u> to your principles.
我很高興你能<u>堅持</u>自己的原則。

(A) beg〔bɛg〕*v.* 乞求　　(B) complain〔kəm'plen〕*v.* 抱怨
(C) *stick*〔stɪk〕*v.* 堅持　　(D) announce〔ə'naʊns〕*v.* 宣布

＊ principle〔'prɪnsəpl̩〕*n.* 原則

5. (**C**) He pulled hard, but without any noticeable <u>effect</u>.
他很用力地拉，卻沒有明顯的<u>效果</u>。

(A) shell〔ʃɛl〕*n.* 貝殼　　(B) attention〔ə'tɛnʃən〕*n.* 注意
(C) *effect*〔ɪ'fɛkt〕*n.* 效果　　(D) threat〔θrɛt〕*n.* 威脅

＊ pull〔pʊl〕*v.* 拉　　hard〔hɑrd〕*adv.* 用力地
noticeable〔'notɪsəbl̩〕*adj.* 顯著的

6. (**A**) The fall of Communism is <u>inevitable</u>.
    共產主義的衰落是<u>不可避免的</u>。

    (A) ***inevitable*** 〔 ɪnˈɛvətəbḷ 〕 *adj.* 不可避免的
    (B) double 〔ˈdʌbḷ 〕 *adj.* 雙重的
    (C) aggressive 〔 əˈgrɛsɪv 〕 *adj.* 具攻擊性的；積極進取的
    (D) mute 〔 mjut 〕 *adj.* 啞的
    ＊ fall 〔 fɔl 〕 *n.* 衰落；滅亡
       Communism 〔ˈkɑmjʊˌnɪzəm 〕 *n.* 共產主義

7. (**D**) The whole world is now in the <u>process</u> of Westernization.
    全世界現在正處於西化的<u>過程</u>中。

    (A) importance 〔 ɪmˈpɔrtṇs 〕 *n.* 重要性
    (B) mayor 〔ˈmeɚ 〕 *n.* 市長
    (C) feast 〔 fist 〕 *n.* 盛宴
    (D) ***process*** 〔ˈprɑsɛs 〕 *n.* 過程

8. (**D**) Don't <u>remind</u> me of my blunders. 別<u>使我想起</u>我所犯的錯誤。

    (A) force 〔 fors 〕 *v.* 強迫   (B) afford 〔 əˈford 〕 *v.* 負擔得起
    (C) discover 〔 dɪsˈkʌvɚ 〕 *v.* 發現   (D) ***remind*** 〔 rɪˈmaɪnd 〕 *v.* 使想起
    ＊ blunder 〔ˈblʌndɚ 〕 *n.* (愚蠢或粗心的) 錯誤

9. (**A**) The teacher <u>dismissed</u> his class when the bell rang.
    鈴聲一響，老師就<u>下</u>課了。

    (A) ***dismiss*** 〔 dɪsˈmɪs 〕 *v.* 解散；下 (課)
    (B) communicate 〔 kəˈmjunəˌket 〕 *v.* 溝通
    (C) lack 〔 læk 〕 *v.* 缺乏
    (D) advance 〔 ədˈvæns 〕 *v.* 前進
    ＊ bell 〔 bɛl 〕 *n.* 鐘；鈴   ring 〔 rɪŋ 〕 *v.* (鈴) 響

10. (**B**) She <u>obtained</u> her degree from Stanford.
    她在史丹福大學<u>得到</u>學位。

    (A) encourage 〔 ɪnˈkɝɪdʒ 〕 *v.* 鼓勵
    (B) ***obtain*** 〔 əbˈten 〕 *v.* 獲得
    (C) displease 〔 dɪsˈpliz 〕 *v.* 使生氣
    (D) supply 〔 səˈplaɪ 〕 *v.* 供給
    ＊ degree 〔 dɪˈgri 〕 *n.* 學位

```
ob   +  tain
 |       |
near  + hold
```

TEST 30

Directions: *Of the four words given after each sentence, choose the one most suitable for filling in the blank.*

1. My lawyers are _____ me to sell the land.

    (A) preparing
    (B) persuading
    (C) presenting
    (D) qualifying   (   )

2. Child rearing practices have a(n) _____ role in a country's development.

    (A) foreign
    (B) international
    (C) pleasant
    (D) significant   (   )

3. If you _____ him, he'll stop crying.

    (A) wonder
    (B) ignore
    (C) crowd
    (D) create   (   )

4. He suffered no _____ injury.

    (A) steady
    (B) fresh
    (C) physical
    (D) recent   (   )

5. We were _____ that two prisoners had escaped.

    (A) imagined
    (B) informed
    (C) appeared
    (D) created   (   )

6. The children are playing in the _____ .

   (A) field
   (B) insect
   (C) journey
   (D) victory   (   )

7. Can you _____ out how this thing works?

   (A) define
   (B) figure
   (C) object
   (D) pollute   (   )

8. I have _____ the apples for peaches.

   (A) substituted
   (B) delivered
   (C) interested
   (D) concerned   (   )

9. The dry desert air has _____ the mummy.

   (A) refused
   (B) determined
   (C) preserved
   (D) memorized   (   )

10. It's hard to find shoes that will _____ me.

   (A) fit
   (B) tolerate
   (C) oppose
   (D) treat   (   )

TEST 30 詳解

1. (**B**) My lawyers are <u>persuading</u> me to sell the land.
   我的律師正在<u>說服</u>我賣掉土地。

   (A) prepare〔prɪ'pɛr〕*v.* 準備
   (B) ***persuade***〔pɚ'swed〕*v.* 說服
   (C) present〔prɪ'zɛnt〕*v.* 呈現
   (D) qualify〔'kwɑlə,faɪ〕*v.* 使有資格

   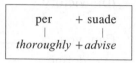

2. (**D**) Child rearing practices have a <u>significant</u> role in a country's development.
   教養兒童的工作在國家發展中扮演<u>重要的</u>角色。

   (A) foreign〔'fɔrɪn〕*adj.* 外國的
   (B) international〔,ɪntɚ'næʃənl̩〕*adj.* 國際的
   (C) pleasant〔'plɛznt〕*adj.* 愉快的
   (D) ***significant***〔sɪg'nɪfəkənt〕*adj.* 重要的；意義重大的

   * rear〔rɪr〕*v.* 教養　practice〔'præktɪs〕*n.* 工作

3. (**B**) If you <u>ignore</u> him, he'll stop crying.
   只要你<u>不理</u>他，他就不會哭了。

   (A) wonder〔'wʌndɚ〕*v.* 想知道　(B) ***ignore***〔ɪg'nor〕*v.* 忽視；不理
   (C) crowd〔kraʊd〕*v.* 擠滿　　　(D) create〔krɪ'et〕*v.* 創造

4. (**C**) He suffered no <u>physical</u> injury. 他並沒有遭受<u>肉體上的</u>傷害。

   (A) steady〔'stɛdɪ〕*adj.* 穩定的
   (B) fresh〔frɛʃ〕*adj.* 新鮮的
   (C) ***physical***〔'fɪzɪkl̩〕*adj.* 肉體的；身體的
   (D) recent〔'risnt〕*adj.* 最近的

   * suffer〔'sʌfɚ〕*v.* 遭受　injury〔'ɪndʒərɪ〕*n.* 傷害

5. (**B**) We were <u>informed</u> that two prisoners had escaped.
   我們<u>得知</u>兩名囚犯逃走了。

   (A) imagine〔ɪ'mædʒɪn〕*v.* 想像　(B) ***inform***〔ɪn'fɔrm〕*v.* 通知
   (C) appear〔ə'pɪr〕*v.* 出現；似乎　(D) create〔krɪ'et〕*v.* 創造

   * prisoner〔'prɪznɚ〕*n.* 囚犯

6. (**A**) The children are playing in the <u>field</u>.
孩子們在<u>田野</u>上玩耍。

(A) ***field*** 〔 fild 〕 *n.* 田野
(B) insect 〔'ɪnsɛkt 〕 *n.* 昆蟲
(C) journey 〔'dʒɜnɪ 〕 *n.* 旅程
(D) victory 〔'vɪktərɪ 〕 *n.* 勝利

7. (**B**) Can you <u>figure</u> out how this thing works?
你<u>知道</u>這個東西是如何運作嗎?

(A) define 〔 dɪ'faɪn 〕 *v.* 下定義
(B) ***figure*** 〔'fɪgjɚ 〕 *v.* 想;認為　***figure out*** 理解
(C) object 〔 əb'dʒɛkt 〕 *v.* 反對
(D) pollute 〔 pə'lut 〕 *v.* 污染
＊ work 〔 wɜk 〕 *v.* 運作

8. (**A**) I have <u>substituted</u> the apples for peaches.
我用蘋果<u>代替</u>桃子。

(A) ***substitute*** 〔'sʌbstə,tjut 〕 *v.* 代替
substitute A ***for*** B　以 A 代替 B

sub	+stitute
under	+ stand

(B) deliver 〔 dɪ'lɪvɚ 〕 *v.* 遞送
(C) interest 〔'ɪntrɪst 〕 *v.* 使感興趣
(D) concern 〔 kən'sɜn 〕 *v.* 關心
＊ peach 〔 pitʃ 〕 *n.* 桃子

9. (**C**) The dry desert air has <u>preserved</u> the mummy.
沙漠乾燥的空氣使木乃伊得以<u>保存</u>。

(A) refuse 〔 rɪ'fjuz 〕 *v.* 拒絕
(B) determine 〔 dɪ'tɜmɪn 〕 *v.* 決定
(C) ***preserve*** 〔 prɪ'zɜv 〕 *v.* 保存

pre	+serve
before	+ keep

(D) memorize 〔'mɛmə,raɪz 〕 *v.* 背誦
＊ desert 〔'dɛzɚt 〕 *n.* 沙漠　　mummy 〔'mʌmɪ 〕 *n.* 木乃伊

10. (**A**) It's hard to find shoes that will <u>fit</u> me.
很難找到<u>適合</u>我穿的鞋子。

(A) ***fit*** 〔 fɪt 〕 *v.* 適合
(B) tolerate 〔'tɑlə,ret 〕 *v.* 容忍
(C) oppose 〔 ə'poz 〕 *v.* 反對
(D) treat 〔 trit 〕 *v.* 對待

TEST 31

Directions: *Of the four words given after each sentence, choose the one most suitable for filling in the blank.*

1. Two important secrets of long life are regular exercise and _____ from worry.
   - (A) process
   - (B) freedom
   - (C) motion
   - (D) favor   (   )

2. The policemen have _____ the whole area but haven't found the criminal yet.
   - (A) looked
   - (B) improved
   - (C) searched
   - (D) discovered   (   )

3. If you want to become a good tennis player, you have to _____ your skill.
   - (A) sharpen
   - (B) increase
   - (C) progress
   - (D) realize   (   )

4. Newspapers are _____ with advertisements for all kinds of consumer goods.
   - (A) full
   - (B) filled
   - (C) fitted
   - (D) fixed   (   )

5. After spending one hour on this math problem, John still could not _____ it.
   - (A) count
   - (B) figure
   - (C) add
   - (D) solve   (   )

6. The _____ of the story was when the dog saved the little girl from the bad man.
   - (A) version
   - (B) climax
   - (C) attempt
   - (D) system   (   )

7. Tell me what happened at the end of the game. Don't keep me in _____ .
   - (A) suspense
   - (B) record
   - (C) memory
   - (D) permission   (   )

8. My poor test score does not _____ how much I know about this subject.
   - (A) reflect
   - (B) vanish
   - (C) adapt
   - (D) contain   (   )

9. The _____ I have of the principal is that of a very kind and gentle person.
   - (A) aspect
   - (B) effect
   - (C) image
   - (D) message   (   )

10. My apartment has one _____ I like. It has a fireplace in the living room.
    - (A) mystery
    - (B) triumph
    - (C) product
    - (D) feature   (   )

TEST 31 詳解

1. (**B**) Two important secrets of long life are regular exercise and <u>freedom</u> from worry.

長壽的兩大重要秘訣是規律的運動以及<u>免除</u>煩憂。

(A) process ('prasɛs) *n.* 過程   (B) **freedom** ('fridəm) *n.* 免除
(C) motion ('moʃən) *n.* 動作   (D) favor ('fevə) *n.* 恩惠；偏愛

2. (**C**) The policemen have <u>searched</u> the whole area but haven't found the criminal yet. 警察<u>搜尋</u>了整個地區，仍未找到罪犯。

(A) look (lʊk) *v.* 看   (B) improve (ɪm'pruv) *v.* 改善
(C) **search** (sɝtʃ) *v.* 搜尋   (D) discover (dɪs'kʌvə) *v.* 發現

    * criminal ('krɪmənḷ) *n.* 罪犯

3. (**A**) If you want to become a good tennis player, you have to <u>sharpen</u> your skill.

如果你想成爲網球好手，必須<u>磨練</u>球技。

(A) **sharpen** ('ʃɑrpṇ) *v.* 加強；使敏銳
(B) increase (ɪn'kris) *v.* 增加
(C) progress (prə'grɛs) *v.* 進步
(D) realize ('rɪə,laɪz) *v.* 了解；實現

sharp + en
| |
sharp + *v.*

4. (**B**) Newspapers are <u>filled</u> with advertisements for all kinds of consumer goods. 報紙上<u>充滿</u>了各種商品的廣告。

(A) full (fʊl) *adj.* 充滿的   (B) **fill** (fɪl) *v.* 使充滿
(C) fit (fɪt) *v.* 適合   (D) fix (fɪks) *v.* 修理

    * **be filled with** 充滿了~ (= *be full of*)
    consumer goods 消費商品

5. (**D**) After spending one hour on this math problem, John still could not <u>solve</u> it.

約翰花了一個鐘頭做這題數學，還是<u>解</u>不出來。

(A) count (kaʊnt) *v.* 數   (B) figure ('fɪgjə) *v.* 計算；想
(C) add (æd) *v.* 加   (D) **solve** (salv) *v.* 解答；解決

6. (**B**) The <u>climax</u> of the story was when the dog saved the little girl from the bad man.

這故事的<u>高潮</u>是當小狗從壞人手中救出小女孩的時候。

(A) version〔'vɝʒən〕*n.* 版本
(B) *climax*〔'klaɪmæks〕*n.* 高潮
(C) attempt〔ə'tɛmpt〕*n.* 嘗試；企圖
(D) system〔'sɪstəm〕*n.* 系統

7. (**A**) Tell me what happened at the end of the game. Don't keep me in <u>suspense</u>. 快告訴我比賽的結果，別讓我窮<u>緊張</u>。

(A) *suspense*〔sə'spɛns〕*n.* 緊張；懸疑
　　keep sb. in suspense 使某人緊張
(B) record〔'rɛkəd〕*n.* 記錄
(C) memory〔'mɛmərɪ〕*n.* 記憶
(D) permission〔pə'mɪʃən〕*n.* 許可

8. (**A**) My poor test score does not <u>reflect</u> how much I know about this subject.

考試成績不好，並不能<u>反映</u>我對這個科目的理解程度。

(A) *reflect*〔rɪ'flɛkt〕*v.* 反映　　(B) vanish〔'vænɪʃ〕*v.* 消失
(C) adapt〔ə'dæpt〕*v.* 使適應　　(D) contain〔kən'ten〕*v.* 包含

* score〔skor〕*n.* 分數；成績　　subject〔'sʌbdʒɪkt〕*n.* 科目

9. (**C**) The <u>image</u> I have of the principal is that of a very kind and gentle person. 校長給我的<u>印象</u>是一個非常親切和藹的人。

(A) aspect〔'æspɛkt〕*n.* 方面　　(B) effect〔ɪ'fɛkt〕*n.* 效果
(C) *image*〔'ɪmɪdʒ〕*n.* 印象；形象　(D) message〔'mɛsɪdʒ〕*n.* 訊息

* principal〔'prɪnsəpḷ〕*n.* 中小學校長　　gentle〔'dʒɛntḷ〕*adj.* 溫和的

10. (**D**) My apartment has one <u>feature</u> I like. It has a fireplace in the living room.

我的公寓有個我喜歡的<u>特點</u>，那就是客廳有個壁爐。

(A) mystery〔'mɪstrɪ〕*n.* 奧秘　　(B) triumph〔'traɪəmf〕*n.* 勝利
(C) product〔'prɑdəkt〕*n.* 產品　(D) *feature*〔'fitʃə〕*n.* 特色

* apartment〔ə'pɑrtmənt〕*n.* 公寓　　fireplace〔'faɪr‚ples〕*n.* 壁爐

TEST 32

Directions: *Of the four words given after each sentence, choose the one most suitable for filling in the blank.*

1. Knowledge is important, and imagination is _____ important.

   (A) equally
   (B) apparently
   (C) hardly
   (D) roughly   (   )

2. Being _____ industrialized, this country has become very prosperous.

   (A) highly
   (B) likely
   (C) briefly
   (D) merely   (   )

3. Our _____ have passed down to us a rich cultural tradition.

   (A) grandparents
   (B) citizens
   (C) officials
   (D) ancestors   (   )

4. Several politicians have been _____ of corruption.

   (A) accused
   (B) removed
   (C) protested
   (D) obtained   (   )

5. Complicated work requires a _____ person to carry it out.

   (A) careless
   (B) hostile
   (C) patient
   (D) naive   (   )

6. Nowadays many people drive _____ cars to show off their wealth.
   - (A) casual
   - (B) luxurious
   - (C) economical
   - (D) modest   (   )

7. Some people find it difficult to _____ ideas with others.
   - (A) suggest
   - (B) propose
   - (C) exchange
   - (D) expose   (   )

8. A successful artist knows how to _____ on his work.
   - (A) establish
   - (B) maintain
   - (C) approach
   - (D) concentrate   (   )

9. The English language has _____ many words from other languages.
   - (A) dismissed
   - (B) absorbed
   - (C) arranged
   - (D) invested   (   )

10. In a library, you will find a great many _____ of knowledge and literature.
    - (A) treasures
    - (B) devices
    - (C) shadows
    - (D) margins   (   )

TEST 32 詳解

1. (**A**) Knowledge is important, and imagination is <u>equally</u> important.
知識很重要，而想像力也<u>同樣地</u>重要。

    (A) ***equally*** (ˈikwəlɪ) *adv.* 同樣地

    (B) apparently (əˈpɛrəntlɪ) *adv.* 顯然地

    (C) hardly (ˈhɑrdlɪ) *adv.* 幾乎不

    (D) roughly (ˈrʌflɪ) *adv.* 大約

2. (**A**) Being <u>highly</u> industrialized, this country has become very prosperous. 這個國家因<u>高度</u>工業化，十分繁榮。

    (A) ***highly*** (ˈhaɪlɪ) *adv.* 高度地   (B) likely (ˈlaɪklɪ) *adj.* 可能的

    (C) briefly (ˈbriflɪ) *adv.* 簡短地   (D) merely (ˈmɪrlɪ) *adv.* 僅僅

    * industrialize (ɪnˈdʌstrɪəl‚aɪz) *v.* 使工業化

    prosperous (ˈprɑspərəs) *adj.* 繁榮的

3. (**D**) Our <u>ancestors</u> have passed down to us a rich cultural tradition. 我們的<u>祖先</u>留給我們豐富的文化傳統。

    (A) grandparents (ˈgrænd‚pɛrənts) *n. pl.* 祖父母

    (B) citizen (ˈsɪtɪzn̩) *n.* 公民

    (C) official (əˈfɪʃəl) *n.* 官員

    (D) ***ancestor*** (ˈænsɛstə) *n.* 祖先

    * ***pass down*** 留傳

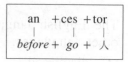

4. (**A**) Several politicians have been <u>accused</u> of corruption.
有幾位政客被<u>控</u>貪污。

    (A) ***accuse*** (əˈkjuz) *v.* 指控   (B) remove (rɪˈmuv) *v.* 除去

    (C) protest (prəˈtɛst) *v.* 抗議   (D) obtain (əbˈten) *v.* 獲得

    * politician (‚pɑləˈtɪʃən) *n.* 政客

    corruption (kəˈrʌpʃən) *n.* 貪污；腐敗

5. (**C**) Complicated work requires a <u>patient</u> person to carry it out.
複雜的工作需要<u>有耐心的</u>人來完成。

    (A) careless (ˈkɛrlɪs) *adj.* 不在乎的   (B) hostile (ˈhɑstɪl) *adj.* 有敵意的

    (C) ***patient*** (ˈpeʃənt) *adj.* 有耐心的   (D) naive (nɑˈiv) *adj.* 天眞的

    * complicated (ˈkɑmplə‚ketɪd) *adj.* 複雜的   ***carry out*** 實行

6. (**B**) Nowadays many people drive <u>luxurious</u> cars to show off their wealth. 現在有很多人開豪華轎車來炫耀他們的財富。

(A) casual〔'kæʒʊəl〕*adj.* 休閒的
(B) *luxurious*〔lʌk'ʃʊrɪəs〕*adj.* 豪華的；奢侈的
(C) economical〔‚ikə'nɑmɪkḷ〕*adj.* 節儉的
(D) modest〔'mɑdɪst〕*adj.* 謙虛的
 * *show off* 炫耀 wealth〔wɛlθ〕*n.* 財富

7. (**C**) Some people find it difficult to <u>exchange</u> ideas with others. 有些人覺得很難和別人交換意見。

(A) suggest〔sə'dʒɛst〕*v.* 建議 (B) propose〔prə'poz〕*v.* 提議
(C) *exchange*〔ɪks'tʃendʒ〕*v.* 交換 (D) expose〔ɪk'spoz〕*v.* 暴露

8. (**D**) A successful artist knows how to <u>concentrate</u> on his work. 成功的藝術家知道如何專心於他的作品。

(A) establish〔ə'stæblɪʃ〕*v.* 建立
(B) maintain〔men'ten〕*v.* 保持
(C) approach〔ə'protʃ〕*v.* 接近
(D) *concentrate*〔'kɑnsn̩‚tret〕*v.* 專心

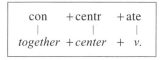

  concentrate on 專心於~ work〔wɝk〕*n.* 作品

9. (**B**) The English language has <u>absorbed</u> many words from other languages. 英語從其他語言吸收了許多的字彙。

(A) dismiss〔dɪs'mɪs〕*v.* 解散；下 (課)
(B) *absorb*〔əb'sɔrb〕*v.* 吸收
(C) arrange〔ə'rendʒ〕*v.* 安排
(D) invest〔ɪn'vɛst〕*v.* 投資

10. (**A**) In a library, you will find a great many <u>treasures</u> of knowledge and literature.
你可以在圖書館裡找到許多知識和文學的寶藏。

(A) *treasure*〔'trɛʒɚ〕*n.* 寶藏
(B) device〔dɪ'vaɪs〕*n.* 裝置
(C) shadow〔'ʃædo〕*n.* 影子
(D) margin〔'mɑrdʒɪn〕*n.* 邊緣；頁邊的空白
 * literature〔'lɪtərətʃɚ〕*n.* 文學

TEST 33

Directions: *Of the four words given after each sentence, choose the one most suitable for filling in the blank.*

1. When a public official is found involved in a ＿＿＿＿＿＿ , he usually has to resign.
   - (A) request
   - (B) tension
   - (C) scandal
   - (D) hardship   (   )

2. The transportation in this city is terrible and people have many ＿＿＿＿＿＿ about it.
   - (A) transcripts
   - (B) complaints
   - (C) accounts
   - (D) results   (   )

3. Movies, sports and reading are forms of ＿＿＿＿＿＿ . They help us relax.
   - (A) entertainment
   - (B) advertisement
   - (C) tournament
   - (D) commitment   (   )

4. After reading for nearly two hours, Carol felt ＿＿＿＿＿＿ to go out for some fresh air.
   - (A) dismissed
   - (B) tired
   - (C) tempted
   - (D) attached   (   )

5. A polite person never ＿＿＿＿＿＿ others while they are discussing important matters.
   - (A) initiates
   - (B) instills
   - (C) inhabits
   - (D) interrupts   (   )

6. Some students get _____ aid from the government to support their education.

(A) financial
(B) vocational
(C) professional
(D) intellectual   (   )

7. Henry, my old classmate, has _____ a true friend of mine all over the years.

(A) retained
(B) remained
(C) regained
(D) respected   (   )

8. He was very shy, so his smile was barely _____ when he met his teacher.

(A) deliberate
(B) extensive
(C) noticeable
(D) residential   (   )

9. They had not seen each other for years until they met _____ in Taipei last week.

(A) distinctly
(B) enormously
(C) precisely
(D) accidentally   (   )

10. The king was _____ for all his cruelties to the people.

(A) feverish
(B) notorious
(C) spiritual
(D) generous   (   )

TEST 33 詳解

1. (**C**) When a public official is found involved in a <u>scandal</u>, he usually has to resign. 當公務員被發現有醜聞時，通常必須辭職。

    (A) request〔rɪ'kwɛst〕*n.* 要求　　(B) tension〔'tɛnʃən〕*n.* 緊張
    (C) *scandal*〔'skændl̩〕*n.* 醜聞　　(D) hardship〔'hardʃɪp〕*n.* 辛苦

2. (**B**) The transportation in this city is terrible and people have many <u>complaints</u> about it.
這城市的交通很糟糕，居民有不少的怨言。

    (A) transcript〔'træn,skrɪpt〕*n.* 成績單
    (B) *complaint*〔kəm'plent〕*n.* 抱怨
    (C) account〔ə'kaʊnt〕*n.* 帳戶
    (D) result〔rɪ'zʌlt〕*n.* 結果

    ＊ transportation〔,trænspə'teʃən〕*n.* 交通；運輸

3. (**A**) Movies, sports and reading are forms of <u>entertainment</u>. They help us relax.
電影、運動和閱讀都是<u>休閒活動</u>，能幫助我們放鬆心情。

    (A) *entertainment*〔,ɛntə'tenmənt〕*n.* 休閒活動；娛樂
    (B) advertisement〔,ædvə'taɪzmənt〕*n.* 廣告
    (C) tournament〔'tɜnəmənt,tʊr-〕*n.* 錦標賽
    (D) commitment〔kə'mɪtmənt〕*n.* 承諾

4. (**C**) After reading for nearly two hours, Carol felt <u>tempted</u> to go out for some fresh air.
讀了將近兩小時的書後，卡蘿<u>想</u>出去走走，呼吸新鮮空氣。

    (A) dismiss〔dɪs'mɪs〕*v.* 解散　　(B) tired〔taɪrd〕*adj.* 疲倦的
    (C) *tempt*〔tɛmpt〕*v.* 引誘；想要　(D) attach〔ə'tætʃ〕*v.* 貼上

5. (**D**) A polite person never <u>interrupts</u> others while they are discussing important matters.
有禮貌的人，絕不會在別人討論重要事情時插嘴。

    (A) initiate〔ɪ'nɪʃɪ,et〕*v.* 創始　　(B) instill〔ɪn'stɪl〕*v.* 灌輸
    (C) inhabit〔ɪn'hæbɪt〕*v.* 居住於　(D) *interrupt*〔,ɪntə'rʌpt〕*v.* 插嘴

6. (**A**) Some students get <u>financial</u> aid from the government to support their education.

有些學生的教育費用來自於政府的<u>財務</u>補助。

(A) ***financial***〔faɪ'nænʃəl〕 *adj.* 財務上的

(B) vocational〔vo'keʃənl̩〕 *adj.* 職業的

(C) professional〔prə'fɛʃənl̩〕 *adj.* 專業的

(D) intellectual〔ˌɪntl̩'ɛktʃʊəl〕 *adj.* 聰明的；智力的

7. (**B**) Henry, my old classmate, has <u>remained</u> a true friend of mine all over the years. 我的老同學亨利，多年來<u>仍然</u>是我很真心的朋友。

(A) retain〔rɪ'ten〕 *v.* 保留　　(B) ***remain***〔rɪ'men〕 *v.* 仍然

(C) regain〔rɪ'gen〕 *v.* 恢復　　(D) respect〔rɪ'spɛkt〕 *v.* 尊敬

8. (**C**) He was very shy, so his smile was barely <u>noticeable</u> when he met his teacher.

他很害羞，所以碰到老師時，臉上的微笑並不<u>明顯</u>。

(A) deliberate〔dɪ'lɪbərɪt〕 *adj.* 故意的

(B) extensive〔ɪk'stɛnsɪv〕 *adj.* 廣泛的

(C) ***noticeable***〔'notɪsəbl̩〕 *adj.* 明顯的

(D) residential〔ˌrɛzə'dɛnʃəl〕 *adj.* 住宅的

* shy〔ʃaɪ〕 *adj.* 害羞的　　barely〔'bɛrlɪ〕 *adv.* 幾乎不（= *hardly*）

9. (**D**) They had not seen each other for years until they met <u>accidentally</u> in Taipei last week.

他們好幾年沒見面了，直到上星期才<u>意外地</u>在台北碰面。

(A) distinctly〔dɪ'stɪŋktlɪ〕 *adv.* 清楚地

(B) enormously〔ɪ'nɔrməslɪ〕 *adv.* 巨大地

(C) precisely〔prɪ'saɪslɪ〕 *adv.* 精確地

(D) ***accidentally***〔ˌæksə'dɛntl̩ɪ〕 *adv.* 意外地

10. (**B**) The king was <u>notorious</u> for all his cruelties to the people.

那位國王因虐待人民而<u>惡名昭彰</u>。

(A) feverish〔'fivərɪʃ〕 *adj.* 發燒的；狂熱的

(B) ***notorious***〔no'torɪəs〕 *adj.* 惡名昭彰的（= *infamous*）

(C) spiritual〔'spɪrɪtʃʊəl〕 *adj.* 精神上的

(D) generous〔'dʒɛnərəs〕 *adj.* 慷慨的

TEST 34

Directions: *Of the four words given after each sentence, choose the one most suitable for filling in the blank.*

1. He will forgive you because he is a very _____ man.
   - (A) persuasive
   - (B) realistic
   - (C) reasonable
   - (D) sensitive   (   )

2. So far no _____ has been found to the problem.
   - (A) award
   - (B) formula
   - (C) instruction
   - (D) solution   (   )

3. Few people truly _____ how seriously we have polluted the environment.
   - (A) concern
   - (B) identify
   - (C) initiate
   - (D) realize   (   )

4. All students without _____ should take the math exam.
   - (A) avocation
   - (B) exception
   - (C) connection
   - (D) resolution   (   )

5. Susan's smile _____ that she would like to come with us.
   - (A) admits
   - (B) displays
   - (C) implies
   - (D) recalls   (   )

6. The foreigner was found _____ in a bank robbery.
   - (A) devoted
   - (B) complicated
   - (C) involved
   - (D) implied   (   )

7. The new policy _____ greatly to the economic growth of the country.
   - (A) attributes
   - (B) contributes
   - (C) contemplates
   - (D) stimulates   (   )

8. The athlete _____ a hope of winning an Olympic gold medal.
   - (A) cherishes
   - (B) enchants
   - (C) insists
   - (D) reserves   (   )

9. The boy was _____ in reading a detective story.
   - (A) absorbed
   - (B) curious
   - (C) diligent
   - (D) enthusiastic   (   )

10. The manager resigned in _____ against the company's new regulation.
   - (A) complaint
   - (B) concession
   - (C) protest
   - (D) request   (   )

TEST 34 詳解

1. (**C**) He will forgive you because he is a very <u>reasonable</u> man.
   他會原諒你的,因為他是個非常<u>明理的</u>人。
   - (A) persuasive〔pɚ'swesɪv〕*adj.* 有說服力的
   - (B) realistic〔‚riə'lɪstɪk〕*adj.* 寫實的
   - (C) **reasonable**〔'riznəbḷ〕*adj.* 明理的;合理的
   - (D) sensitive〔'sɛnsətɪv〕*adj.* 敏感的
   - * forgive〔fɚ'gɪv〕*v.* 原諒

2. (**D**) So far no <u>solution</u> has been found to the problem.
   目前這個問題仍無<u>解決之道</u>。
   - (A) award〔ə'wɔrd〕*n.* 獎;獎賞　　(B) formula〔'fɔrmjələ〕*n.* 公式
   - (C) instruction〔ɪn'strʌkʃən〕*n.* 指導
   - (D) **solution**〔sə'luʃən〕*n.* 解決之道
   - * **so far** 到目前為止

3. (**D**) Few people truly <u>realize</u> how seriously we have polluted the environment. 很少人真正<u>了解</u>環境污染有多嚴重。
   - (A) concern〔kən'sɝn〕*v.* 關心(須與 about 連用)
   - (B) identify〔aɪ'dɛntə‚faɪ〕*v.* 辨認
   - (C) initiate〔ɪ'nɪʃɪ‚et〕*v.* 創始
   - (D) **realize**〔'riə‚laɪz〕*v.* 了解;實現
   - * environment〔ɪn'vaɪrənmənt〕*n.*(自然)環境

4. (**B**) All students without <u>exception</u> should take the math exam.
   所有學生都得參加數學考試,沒有人能<u>例外</u>。
   - (A) avocation〔‚ævə'keʃən〕*n.* 副業　　(B) **exception**〔ɪk'sɛpʃən〕*n.* 例外
   - (C) connection〔kə'nɛkʃən〕*n.* 連接
   - (D) resolution〔‚rɛzə'luʃən〕*n.* 決心

5. (**C**) Susan's smile <u>implies</u> that she would like to come with us.
   蘇珊的微笑<u>暗示</u>著她想和我們一起來。
   - (A) admit〔əd'mɪt〕*v.* 承認
   - (B) display〔dɪ'sple〕*v.* 展示
   - (C) **imply**〔ɪm'plaɪ〕*v.* 暗示
   - (D) recall〔rɪ'kɔl〕*v.* 回想起

   ```
   im + ply
    |     |
   in + fold (摺疊其中)
   ```

6. (**C**) The foreigner was found <u>involved</u> in a bank robbery.
那名外國人被發現<u>涉及</u>一件銀行搶案。

    (A) devoted〔dɪˈvotɪd〕*adj.* 專心的；熱衷的

    (B) complicated〔ˈkɑmpləˌketɪd〕*adj.* 複雜的

    (C) ***involved***〔ɪnˈvɑlvd〕*adj.* 牽涉在內的

    (D) implied〔ɪmˈplaɪd〕*adj.* 含蓄的

    * foreigner〔ˈfɔrɪnɚ〕*n.* 外國人　　***bank robbery*** 銀行搶案

7. (**B**) The new policy <u>contributes</u> greatly to the economic growth of the country. 新政策非常<u>有助於</u>國家的經濟成長。

    (A) attribute〔əˈtrɪbjut〕*v.* 歸因於

    (B) ***contribute***〔kənˈtrɪbjut〕*v.* 貢獻；有助於　***contribute to*** 有助於

    (C) contemplate〔ˈkɑntəmˌplet〕*v.* 沈思

    (D) stimulate〔ˈstɪmjəˌlet〕*v.* 刺激

8. (**A**) The athlete <u>cherishes</u> a hope of winning an Olympic gold medal. 運動員<u>懷抱著</u>贏得奧運金牌的希望。

    (A) ***cherish***〔ˈtʃɛrɪʃ〕*v.* 懷抱著（希望）

    (B) enchant〔ɪnˈtʃænt〕*v.* 使著迷

    (C) insist〔ɪnˈsɪst〕*v.* 堅持　　(D) reserve〔rɪˈzɝv〕*v.* 預訂

    * athlete〔ˈæθlit〕*n.* 運動員　　Olympic〔oˈlɪmpɪk〕*adj.* 奧林匹克的

    medal〔ˈmɛdl̩〕*n.* 獎牌　　***gold medal*** 金牌

9. (**A**) The boy was <u>absorbed</u> in reading a detective story.
那男孩正<u>全神貫注</u>地看偵探小說。

    (A) ***absorbed***〔əbˈsɔrbd〕*adj.* 全神貫注的；專心的

    be absorbed in 專心於～

    (B) curious〔ˈkjʊrɪəs〕*adj.* 好奇的

    (C) diligent〔ˈdɪlədʒənt〕*adj.* 勤勉的

    (D) enthusiastic〔ɪnˌθjuzɪˈæstɪk〕*adj.* 熱心的

    * detective〔dɪˈtɛktɪv〕*adj.* 偵探的　　story〔ˈstorɪ〕*n.* 故事；小說

10. (**C**) The manager resigned in <u>protest</u> against the company's new regulation. 經理辭職以<u>抗議</u>公司的新規定。

    (A) complaint〔kəmˈplent〕*n.* 抱怨

    (B) concession〔kənˈsɛʃən〕*n.* 讓步

    (C) ***protest***〔ˈprotɛst〕*n.* 抗議

    (D) request〔rɪˈkwɛst〕*n.* 要求

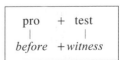

TEST 35

Directions: Of the four words given after each sentence, choose the one most suitable for filling in the blank.

1. The _____ of 18, 13, and 14 is 15.
   (A) division
   (B) balance
   (C) average
   (D) total
   (　　)

2. There are many _____ that the economy will recover from a recession.
   (A) indications
   (B) organizations
   (C) contributions
   (D) traditions
   (　　)

3. Intelligence does not _____ mean success. You need diligence as well.
   (A) honestly
   (B) formally
   (C) merely
   (D) necessarily
   (　　)

4. The report says that _____ driving has killed more than 20 persons since June.
   (A) patient
   (B) serious
   (C) thorough
   (D) reckless
   (　　)

5. How can you expect me to _____ exactly what happened twelve years ago?
   (A) remind
   (B) recall
   (C) refill
   (D) reserve
   (　　)

6. The man made a _____ effort to look happy, though deep in his heart he was very sad.

(A) cheerful
(B) friendly
(C) conscious
(D) laughing   (   )

7. Most children find it difficult to _____ the temptation of ice cream, especially on a hot summer day.

(A) purchase
(B) resist
(C) stare at
(D) accustom to   (   )

8. We cannot give you a _____ answer now; there are still many uncertainties on this issue.

(A) definite
(B) familiar
(C) courteous
(D) hollow   (   )

9. The report is much too long — you must _____ it, using as few words as possible.

(A) strengthen
(B) destroy
(C) eliminate
(D) condense   (   )

10. Mary is having a tough time deciding whether to dress _____ or formally for the party tonight.

(A) individually
(B) casually
(C) respectively
(D) deliberately   (   )

TEST 35 詳解

1. (**C**) The <u>average</u> of 18, 13, and 14 is 15.
   18、13 和 14 的<u>平均值</u>是 15。

   (A) division〔dəˈvɪʒən〕*n.* 劃分　　(B) balance〔ˈbæləns〕*n.* 平衡
   (C) *average*〔ˈævərɪdʒ〕*n.* 平均值　(D) total〔ˈtotl〕*n.* 總數

2. (**A**) There are many <u>indications</u> that the economy will recover from a recession. 許多<u>跡象</u>顯示經濟不景氣即將好轉。

   (A) *indication*〔ˌɪndəˈkeʃən〕*n.* 跡象；指標
   (B) organization〔ˌɔrgənaɪˈzeʃən〕*n.* 組織
   (C) contribution〔ˌkɑntrəˈbjuʃən〕*n.* 貢獻
   (D) tradition〔trəˈdɪʃən〕*n.* 傳統

   * recover〔rɪˈkʌvɚ〕*v.* 恢復　　recession〔rɪˈsɛʃən〕*n.* 不景氣

3. (**D**) Intelligence does not <u>necessarily</u> mean success. You need diligence as well. 聰明才智並不<u>一定</u>等於成功，你還需要努力。

   (A) honestly〔ˈɑnɪstlɪ〕*adv.* 誠實地
   (B) formally〔ˈfɔrməlɪ〕*adv.* 正式地
   (C) merely〔ˈmɪrlɪ〕*adv.* 僅僅
   (D) *necessarily*〔ˈnɛsəˌsɛrəlɪ〕*adv.* 必定

   * intelligence〔ɪnˈtɛlədʒəns〕*n.* 聰明；才智
   diligence〔ˈdɪlədʒəns〕*n.* 勤勉　　*as well* 也（= *too*）

4. (**D**) The report says that <u>reckless</u> driving has killed more than 20 persons since June.
   報導指出，從六月至今已有二十多人死於<u>魯莽</u>駕駛。

   (A) patient〔ˈpeʃənt〕*adj.* 有耐心的　(B) serious〔ˈsɪrɪəs〕*adj.* 嚴重的
   (C) thorough〔ˈθɝo〕*adj.* 徹底的　　(D) *reckless*〔ˈrɛklɪs〕*adj.* 魯莽的

5. (**B**) How can you expect me to <u>recall</u> exactly what happened twelve years ago?
   你怎能期望我還能清楚<u>記得</u>十二年前發生過的事？

   (A) remind〔rɪˈmaɪnd〕*v.* 提醒　　(B) *recall*〔rɪˈkɔl〕*v.* 回想起
   (C) refill〔riˈfɪl〕*v.* 再填滿　　(D) reserve〔rɪˈzɝv〕*v.* 預訂

6. (**C**) The man made a <u>conscious</u> effort to look happy, though deep in his heart he was very sad.

他心裡雖然很難過，但卻<u>刻意</u>表現出很快樂的樣子。

(A) cheerful〔'tʃɪrfəl〕*adj.* 高興的
(B) friendly〔'frɛndlɪ〕*adj.* 友善的
(C) *conscious*〔'kɑnʃəs〕*adj.* 有意的
(D) laughing〔'læfɪŋ〕*adj.* 愉快的

7. (**B**) Most children find it difficult to <u>resist</u> the temptation of ice cream, especially on a hot summer day.

大部份的孩子很難<u>抗拒</u>冰淇淋的誘惑，尤其是在炎熱的夏天。

(A) purchase〔'pɝtʃəs〕*v.* 購買   (B) *resist*〔rɪ'zɪst〕*v.* 抵抗
(C) stare at 瞪著~   (D) accustom〔ə'kʌstəm〕*v.* 使習慣

8. (**A**) We cannot give you a <u>definite</u> answer now; there are still many uncertainties on this issue.

我們現在無法給你一個<u>明確的</u>答案；關於這項問題，仍有許多變數。

(A) *definite*〔'dɛfənɪt〕*adj.* 明確的
(B) familiar〔fə'mɪljɚ〕*adj.* 熟悉的
(C) courteous〔'kɝtɪəs〕*adj.* 有禮貌的
(D) hollow〔'hɑlo〕*adj.* 中空的

9. (**D**) The report is much too long—you must <u>condense</u> it, using as few words as possible.

這份報告太長了——你必須把它<u>濃縮</u>，用字儘量精簡。

(A) strengthen〔'strɛŋθən〕*v.* 強化
(B) destroy〔dɪ'strɔɪ〕*v.* 破壞
(C) eliminate〔ɪ'lɪmə,net〕*v.* 除去
(D) *condense*〔kən'dɛns〕*v.* 濃縮

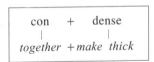

con   +   dense
| |
together +*make thick*

10. (**B**) Mary is having a tough time deciding whether to dress <u>casually</u> or formally for the party tonight.

瑪麗很難做決定，不知道要穿得很<u>休閒</u>，還是要盛裝出席晚上的宴會。

(A) individually〔,ɪndə'vɪdʒuəlɪ〕*adv.* 個別地
(B) *casually*〔'kæʒuəlɪ〕*adv.* 休閒地；非正式地
(C) respectively〔rɪ'spɛktɪvlɪ〕*adv.* 個別地
(D) deliberately〔dɪ'lɪbərɪtlɪ〕*adv.* 故意地

TEST 36

Directions: *Of the four words given after each sentence, choose the one most suitable for filling in the blank.*

1. It was quite _____ that she was a good student; she always got high scores.
   - (A) apparent
   - (B) elegant
   - (C) urgent
   - (D) efficient   (   )

2. That could not be a mere accident. He did it _____ to hurt him.
   - (A) necessarily
   - (B) dogmatically
   - (C) deliberately
   - (D) inevitably   (   )

3. The _____ for robbery is death. There can be no exception to the law.
   - (A) hostility
   - (B) penalty
   - (C) mystery
   - (D) safety   (   )

4. The prosperity that we enjoy now is _____ to the efforts of our forefathers.
   - (A) accustomed
   - (B) sympathetic
   - (C) urgent
   - (D) due   (   )

5. The taste of the cake suddenly _____ her of her happy childhood.
   - (A) reminded
   - (B) adopted
   - (C) rewarded
   - (D) approved   (   )

6. We have made every effort to _____ her. However, her loss was so great that she simply cannot overcome her grief.

   (A) consist
   (B) contribute
   (C) criticize
   (D) console ( )

7. Doesn't he have any _____ for the poor? He is too selfish indeed.

   (A) compassion
   (B) preparation
   (C) conflict
   (D) oppression ( )

8. After the quarrel they came to a _____ understanding and became friends eventually.

   (A) curious
   (B) mutual
   (C) stubborn
   (D) vulgar ( )

9. His is a personality _____ by good humor; no one seems able to irritate him.

   (A) shattered
   (B) astonished
   (C) characterized
   (D) compared ( )

10. It was a _____ that he should survive the accident; the other passengers were all killed.

   (A) revenge
   (B) miracle
   (C) protest
   (D) preference ( )

TEST 36 詳解

1. (**A**) It was quite <u>apparent</u> that she was a good student; she always got high scores. 很明顯地，她是個好學生；她總是得高分。

    (A) ***apparent*** ﹝ə'pɛrənt﹞ *adj.* 明顯的

    (B) elegant ﹝'ɛləgənt﹞ *adj.* 高雅的

    (C) urgent ﹝'ɝdʒənt﹞ *adj.* 迫切的

    (D) efficient ﹝ə'fɪʃənt﹞ *adj.* 有效率的

    * score ﹝skor﹞ *n.* 分數

2. (**C**) That could not be a mere accident. He did it <u>deliberately</u> to hurt him. 這絕不只是一件意外，他是故意要傷害他。

    (A) necessarily ﹝'nɛsə,sɛrəlɪ﹞ *adv.* 必定

    (B) dogmatically ﹝dɔg'mætɪk̩lɪ﹞ *adv.* 武斷地

    (C) ***deliberately*** ﹝dɪ'lɪbərɪtlɪ﹞ *adv.* 故意地

    (D) inevitably ﹝ɪn'ɛvətəb̩lɪ﹞ *adv.* 不可避免地

3. (**B**) The <u>penalty</u> for robbery is death. There can be no exception to the law. 搶劫的刑罰是死刑，沒有例外。

    (A) hostility ﹝has'tɪlətɪ﹞ *n.* 敵意　　(B) ***penalty*** ﹝'pɛn̩ltɪ﹞ *n.* 刑罰

    (C) mystery ﹝'mɪstrɪ﹞ *n.* 奧秘　　(D) safety ﹝'seftɪ﹞ *n.* 安全

    * robbery ﹝'rabərɪ﹞ *n.* 搶劫　　exception ﹝ɪk'sɛpʃən﹞ *n.* 例外

4. (**D**) The prosperity that we enjoy now is <u>due</u> to the efforts of our forefathers. 我們現在所享受的繁榮，是由於祖先努力的結果。

    (A) accustomed ﹝ə'kʌstəmd﹞ *adj.* 習慣的

    (B) sympathetic ﹝,sɪmpə'θɛtɪk﹞ *adj.* 同情的

    (C) urgent ﹝'ɝdʒənt﹞ *adj.* 迫切的

    (D) ***due*** ﹝dju﹞ *adj.* 由於　***due to*** 由於

    * prosperity ﹝pras'pɛrətɪ﹞ *n.* 繁榮　　forefather ﹝'for,faðɚ﹞ *n.* 祖先

5. (**A**) The taste of the cake suddenly <u>reminded</u> her of her happy childhood. 蛋糕的味道使她突然想起快樂的童年。

    (A) ***remind*** ﹝rɪ'maɪnd﹞ *v.* 使想起　　(B) adopt ﹝ə'dapt﹞ *v.* 採用

    (C) reward ﹝rɪ'word﹞ *v.* 獎賞；報酬　(D) approve ﹝ə'pruv﹞ *v.* 同意

    * childhood ﹝'tʃaɪld,hʊd﹞ *n.* 童年

6. (**D**) We have made every effort to <u>console</u> her. However, her loss was so great that she simply cannot overcome her grief.
我們已盡力<u>安慰</u>她。但損失實在太大，她無法平撫傷痛。

    (A) consist〔kən'sɪst〕*v.* 由～組成
    (B) contribute〔kən'trɪbjut〕*v.* 貢獻
    (C) criticize〔'krɪtə,saɪz〕*v.* 批評   (D) ***console*** 〔kən'sol〕*v.* 安慰
    * ***make every effort*** 盡力   overcome〔,ovə'kʌm〕*v.* 克服
    grief〔grif〕*n.* 悲傷

7. (**A**) Doesn't he have any <u>compassion</u> for the poor ? He is too selfish indeed. 難道他對窮人沒有絲毫的<u>同情心</u>嗎？他真是太自私了。

    (A) ***compassion***〔kəm'pæʃən〕*n.* 同情
    (B) preparation〔,prɛpə'reʃən〕*n.* 準備
    (C) conflict〔'kɑnflɪkt〕*n.* 衝突
    (D) oppression〔ə'prɛʃən〕*n.* 壓迫

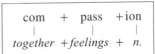

com	+	pass	+ion
together	+	*feelings*	+ *n.*

8. (**B**) After the quarrel they came to a <u>mutual</u> understanding and became friends eventually.
爭吵之後，他們終於能<u>互相</u>了解，最後成為朋友。

    (A) curious〔'kjurɪəs〕*adj.* 好奇的
    (B) ***mutual***〔'mjutʃuəl〕*adj.* 互相的
    (C) stubborn〔'stʌbən〕*adj.* 頑固的   (D) vulgar〔'vʌlgə〕*adj.* 粗俗的

9. (**C**) His is a personality <u>characterized</u> by good humor; no one seems able to irritate him.
他性格上的<u>特點</u>是脾氣好。似乎沒有人能激怒他。

    (A) shatter〔'ʃætə〕*v.* 使粉碎   (B) astonish〔ə'stɑnɪʃ〕*v.* 使吃驚
    (C) ***characterize***〔'kærɪktə,raɪz〕*v.* 以～為特色
    (D) compare〔kəm'pɛr〕*v.* 比較
    * humor〔'hjumə〕*n.* 性情   irritate〔'ɪrə,tet〕*v.* 激怒

10. (**B**) It was a <u>miracle</u> that he should survive the accident; the other passengers were all killed.
他能從這次意外中生還，真是<u>奇蹟</u>。其他乘客都已罹難。

    (A) revenge〔rɪ'vɛndʒ〕*n.* 報復   (B) ***miracle***〔'mɪrəkl̩〕*n.* 奇蹟
    (C) protest〔'protɛst〕*n.* 抗議
    (D) preference〔'prɛfərəns〕*n.* 偏愛
    * survive〔sə'vaɪv〕*v.* 自～中生還   ***be killed*** （因意外）死亡

TEST 37

Directions: *Of the four words given after each sentence, choose the one most suitable for filling in the blank.*

1. My recent trip to Europe has left a _____ impression on me.
   - (A) final
   - (B) lasting
   - (C) forever
   - (D) long   (   )

2. A _____ of migrant birds flew to our island yesterday.
   - (A) flock
   - (B) host
   - (C) crew
   - (D) set   (   )

3. Jack fell down while playing tennis and _____ his ankle very badly.
   - (A) bent
   - (B) crippled
   - (C) turned
   - (D) twisted   (   )

4. These two photographs are too small. Let's have them _____ .
   - (A) increased
   - (B) formalized
   - (C) enlarged
   - (D) expanded   (   )

5. This museum is famous for its _____ of modern paintings.
   - (A) construction
   - (B) reduction
   - (C) affection
   - (D) collection   (   )

6. The professor did his best to _____ the students with new ideas.

   (A) witness
   (B) review
   (C) acquaint
   (D) display   (   )

7. Their determination to fight to the last man was really _____ .

   (A) admirable
   (B) disposable
   (C) replaceable
   (D) portable   (   )

8. All of us must have the _____ that there is no free lunch.

   (A) know-how
   (B) wonder
   (C) dispute
   (D) awareness   (   )

9. A large poster in beautiful colors _____ the attention of many people.

   (A) called
   (B) caught
   (C) charted
   (D) caused   (   )

10. It rains _____ this summer. The water we've got is not enough for this area.

   (A) frequently
   (B) occasionally
   (C) precisely
   (D) previously   (   )

TEST 37 詳解

1. (**B**) My recent trip to Europe has left a <u>lasting</u> impression on me. 最近的歐洲之旅，留給我<u>永遠</u>難忘的印象。

    (A) final〔'faɪnḷ〕*adj.* 最後的   (B) ***lasting***〔'læstɪŋ〕*adj.* 永遠的
    (C) forever〔fɚ'ɛvɚ〕*adv.* 永遠地   (D) long〔lɔŋ〕*adj.* 長的
    * recent〔'risṇt〕*adj.* 最近的   impression〔ɪm'prɛʃən〕*n.* 印象

2. (**A**) A <u>flock</u> of migrant birds flew to our island yesterday. 有一<u>群</u>候鳥昨天飛到我們島上。

    (A) ***flock***〔flɑk〕*n.* (鳥) 群   (B) host〔host〕*n.* 主人；多數
    (C) crew〔kru〕*n.* 全體工作人員   (D) set〔sɛt〕*n.* 套；組
    * migrant〔'maɪgrənt〕*adj.* 遷移的

3. (**D**) Jack fell down while playing tennis and <u>twisted</u> his ankle very badly. 傑克在打網球時跌倒，腳踝嚴重地<u>扭傷</u>。

    (A) bend〔bɛnd〕*v.* 使彎曲   (B) cripple〔'krɪpḷ〕*v.* 使殘廢
    (C) turn〔tɝn〕*v.* 轉動   (D) ***twist***〔twɪst〕*v.* 扭傷
    * ankle〔'æŋkḷ〕*n.* 腳踝

4. (**C**) These two photographs are too small. Let's have them <u>enlarged</u>. 這兩張相片太小了。我們把它們<u>放大</u>吧。

    (A) increase〔ɪn'kris〕*v.* 增加
    (B) formalize〔'fɔrmḷ,aɪz〕*v.* 使正式
    (C) ***enlarge***〔ɪn'lardʒ〕*v.* 放大
    (D) expand〔ɪk'spænd〕*v.* 擴大

en ＋ large
　｜　　｜
make ＋ *large*

5. (**D**) This museum is famous for its <u>collection</u> of modern paintings. 這座美術館以現代畫的<u>收藏</u>而聞名。

    (A) construction〔kən'strʌkʃən〕*n.* 建造
    (B) reduction〔rɪ'dʌkʃən〕*n.* 減少
    (C) affection〔ə'fɛkʃən〕*n.* 情感
    (D) ***collection***〔kə'lɛkʃən〕*n.* 收藏
    * museum〔mju'ziəm〕*n.* 美術館；博物館

6. (**C**) The professor did his best to <u>acquaint</u> the students with new ideas. 教授努力讓學生認識新觀念。

(A) witness〔'wɪtnɪs〕 *v.* 目擊；作證   (B) review〔rɪ'vju〕 *v.* 複習

(C) ***acquaint***〔ə'kwent〕 *v.* 使認識   (D) display〔dɪ'sple〕 *v.* 展示

＊professor〔prə'fɛsə〕 *n.* 教授   ***do one's best*** 盡力

7. (**A**) Their determination to fight to the last man was really <u>admirable</u>. 他們要奮戰到底的決心真是<u>令人欽佩</u>。

(A) ***admirable***〔'ædmərəbḷ〕 *adj.* 令人欽佩的

(B) disposable〔dɪ'spozəbḷ〕 *adj.* 用完即丟的

(C) replaceable〔rɪ'plesəbḷ〕 *adj.* 可取代的

(D) portable〔'portəbḷ〕 *adj.* 手提的

＊determination〔dɪ,tɜmə'neʃən〕 *n.* 決心

8. (**D**) All of us must have the <u>awareness</u> that there is no free lunch. 我們必須<u>知道</u>天下沒有白吃的午餐。

(A) know-how〔'no,haʊ〕 *n.* 實用知識

(B) wonder〔'wʌndə〕 *n.* 驚奇

(C) dispute〔dɪ'spjut〕 *n.* 爭論

(D) ***awareness***〔ə'wɛrnɪs〕 *n.* 知道

9. (**B**) A large poster in beautiful colors <u>caught</u> the attention of many people. 一張色彩亮麗的大型海報<u>吸引</u>了許多人的注意。

(A) call〔kɔl〕 *v.* 喊叫；打電話

(B) ***catch***〔kætʃ〕 *v.* 引起（注意）；吸引（視線）

(C) chart〔tʃɑrt〕 *v.* 以圖表表示

(D) cause〔kɔz〕 *v.* 造成

＊poster〔'postə〕 *n.* 海報   attention〔ə'tɛnʃən〕 *n.* 注意力

10. (**B**) It rains <u>occasionally</u> this summer. The water we've got is not enough for this area.

今年夏天<u>偶爾</u>才下雨。我們的蓄水量不足以供應本地區使用。

(A) frequently〔'frikwəntlɪ〕 *adv.* 經常

(B) ***occasionally***〔ə'keʒənḷɪ〕 *adv.* 偶爾

(C) precisely〔prɪ'saɪslɪ〕 *adv.* 精確地

(D) previously〔'privɪəslɪ〕 *adv.* 先前

TEST 38

Directions: *Of the four words given after each sentence, choose the one most suitable for filling in the blank.*

1. Mark walked away _____ when he failed to find his name on the list.
   - (A) fleetingly
   - (B) heartily
   - (C) devotedly
   - (D) dejectedly   (   )

2. One thing people seem to like about deep-fried food is its _____ .
   - (A) crunch
   - (B) carbonation
   - (C) softness
   - (D) toughness   (   )

3. I don't want you to read from a prepared script; I'd like a _____ speech.
   - (A) sarcastic
   - (B) conceited
   - (C) spontaneous
   - (D) pompous   (   )

4. Are you _____ of how many unnecessary plastic bags you collect over a week?
   - (A) aware
   - (B) alienated
   - (C) disposable
   - (D) unreasonable   (   )

5. Here — put this _____ on first or you'll get grease all over your clothes.
   - (A) dress
   - (B) apron
   - (C) stocking
   - (D) belt   (   )

6. The rest of you can wait in the _____ before it's your turn to be interviewed.

(A) lounge
(B) rest room
(C) elevator
(D) closet   (   )

7. Only people who have never been _____ of a crime are allowed to be independent taxi drivers; others must work under a company.

(A) alleviated
(B) repented
(C) convicted
(D) tangled   (   )

8. That's a very _____ idea, but it doesn't sound too practical to me.

(A) fierce
(B) radiant
(C) admirable
(D) harsh   (   )

9. You'd better hang up that suit so it doesn't _____ .

(A) succumb
(B) wrinkle
(C) resign
(D) clash   (   )

10. I got a rather _____ response when I asked for volunteers to do clean-up; so in the end I had to do most of it myself.

(A) enthused
(B) reckless
(C) extravagant
(D) lukewarm   (   )

TEST 38 詳解

1. (**D**) Mark walked away <u>dejectedly</u> when he failed to find his name on the list. 當馬克發現他的名字不在名單上時，就<u>沮喪地</u>離開了。
   (A) fleetingly (ˈflitɪŋlɪ) *adv.* 短暫地　(B) heartily (ˈhɑrtɪlɪ) *adv.* 衷心地
   (C) devotedly (dɪˈvotɪdlɪ) *adv.* 專心地；熱衷地
   (D) *dejectedly* (dɪˈdʒɛktɪdlɪ) *adv.* 沮喪地
   * *fail to* 未能

2. (**A**) One thing people seem to like about deep-fried food is its <u>crunch</u>. 人們喜歡油炸食物的原因，在於它<u>酥脆的</u>口感。
   (A) *crunch* (krʌntʃ) *n.* 咬碎聲
   (B) carbonation (ˌkɑrbəˈneʃən) *n.* 碳化作用
   (C) softness (ˈsɔftnɪs) *n.* 柔軟　(D) toughness (ˈtʌfnɪs) *n.* 堅強
   * deep-fried (ˈdipˈfraɪd) *adj.* 油炸的

3. (**C**) I don't want you to read from a prepared script; I'd like a <u>spontaneous</u> speech.
   我不希望你唸準備好的稿子；我要的是<u>自然脫口而出</u>的演講。
   (A) sarcastic (sɑrˈkæstɪk) *adj.* 諷刺的
   (B) conceited (kənˈsitɪd) *adj.* 自負的
   (C) *spontaneous* (spɑnˈtenɪəs) *adj.* 自然的
   (D) pompous (ˈpɑmpəs) *adj.* 自大的
   * script (skrɪpt) *n.* 手稿；腳本

4. (**A**) Are you <u>aware</u> of how many unnecessary plastic bags you collect over a week? 你<u>知道</u>你一星期用了多少不必要的塑膠袋嗎？
   (A) *aware* (əˈwɛr) *adj.* 知道的
   (B) alienated (ˈeljənˌetɪd) *adj.* 疏遠的
   (C) disposable (dɪˈspozəbḷ) *adj.* 用完即丟的
   (D) unreasonable (ʌnˈriznəbḷ) *adj.* 不合理的

5. (**B**) Here — put this <u>apron</u> on first or you'll get grease all over your clothes. 來，先把這件<u>圍裙</u>穿上，要不然衣服會沾滿油。
   (A) dress (drɛs) *n.* 洋裝　　(B) *apron* (ˈeprən) *n.* 圍裙
   (C) stocking (ˈstɑkɪŋ) *n.* 長襪　(D) belt (bɛlt) *n.* 皮帶
   * *put on* 穿上　　grease (griz) *n.* 油脂

6. (**A**) The rest of you can wait in the <u>lounge</u> before it's your turn to be interviewed. 其餘還未輪到面試的人，可在<u>休息室</u>稍候。

(A) *lounge*〔laundʒ〕*n.* 休息室　　(B) rest room 廁所
(C) elevator〔'ɛlə,vetɚ〕*n.* 電梯　　(D) closet〔'klɑzɪt〕*n.* 櫥櫃

* turn〔tʒn〕*n.* 輪流　　interview〔'ɪntɚ,vju〕*v.* 面試

7. (**C**) Only people who have never been <u>convicted</u> of a crime are allowed to be independent taxi drivers; others must work under a company. 只有從未被<u>判定有罪</u>的人可以成為獨立的計程車司機，否則都得加入車行。

(A) alleviate〔ə'livɪ,et〕*v.* 減輕
(B) repent〔rɪ'pɛnt〕*v.* 懊悔
(C) *convict*〔kən'vɪkt〕*v.* 定罪　　*be convicted of* 被判有～罪
(D) tangle〔'tæŋgl̩〕*v.* 使糾纏

8. (**C**) That's a very <u>admirable</u> idea, but it doesn't sound too practical to me. 那個想法<u>非常好</u>，但我覺得不太實際。

(A) fierce〔fɪrs〕*adj.* 猛烈的
(B) radiant〔'redɪənt〕*adj.* 光輝燦爛的；容光煥發的
(C) *admirable*〔'ædmərəbl̩〕*adj.* 值得讚賞的
(D) harsh〔hɑrʃ〕*adj.* 嚴厲的

9. (**B**) You'd better hang up that suit so it doesn't <u>wrinkle</u>.
你最好把那套西裝掛起來，免得弄<u>皺</u>了。

(A) succumb〔sə'kʌm〕*v.* 屈服　　(B) *wrinkle*〔'rɪŋkl̩〕*v.* 起皺紋
(C) resign〔rɪ'zaɪn〕*v.* 辭職　　(D) clash〔klæʃ〕*v.* 衝突；相撞

10. (**D**) I got a rather <u>lukewarm</u> response when I asked for volunteers to do clean-up; so in the end I had to do most of it myself.
當我徵求自願打掃的人時，得到非常<u>冷淡的</u>反應，最後我只好自己負責大部分的工作。

(A) enthused〔ɪn'θjuzd〕*adj.* 熱心的
(B) reckless〔'rɛklɪs〕*adj.* 魯莽的
(C) extravagant〔ɪk'strævəgənt〕*adj.* 奢侈的
(D) *lukewarm*〔'luk'wɔrm〕*adj.* 冷淡的

* clean-up〔'klin,ʌp〕*n.* 清掃　　volunteer〔,vɑlən'tɪr〕*n.* 自願者

TEST 39

Directions: *Of the four words given after each sentence, choose the one most suitable for filling in the blank.*

1. The functions of this machine are described _____ in the handbook.

    (A) steadily
    (B) precisely
    (C) extremely
    (D) forcibly   (   )

2. His _____ for power led him into a tragedy.

    (A) cause
    (B) fame
    (C) issue
    (D) greed   (   )

3. The candidate found every way to _____ her election materials to the voters.

    (A) operate
    (B) recognize
    (C) distribute
    (D) cultivate   (   )

4. John is so _____ that he does not accept others' opinions.

    (A) delicate
    (B) intimate
    (C) obstinate
    (D) considerate   (   )

5. Every country needs strong national _____ against enemy invasions.

    (A) defense
    (B) balance
    (C) analysis
    (D) response   (   )

6. At the finish, the winner of the race raised her arms
   _____ .

   (A) enormously
   (B) frequently
   (C) generously
   (D) triumphantly   (   )

7. He can _____ a motorcycle if he is given all the
   parts.

   (A) transmit
   (B) assemble
   (C) reform
   (D) proceed   (   )

8. He told me in _____ that he would do everything
   to help me.

   (A) action
   (B) manner
   (C) earnest
   (D) progress   (   )

9. This exhibition of Chinese paintings is _____ .
   Indeed, it's the best in ten years.

   (A) marvelous
   (B) potential
   (C) artificial
   (D) populous   (   )

10. Each of these bottles _____ 1,000 cc of mineral
    water, and it sells for NT$50.

    (A) attains
    (B) remains
    (C) sustains
    (D) contains   (   )

TEST 39 詳解

1. (**B**) The functions of this machine are described <u>precisely</u> in the handbook. 這台機器的功能在手冊中有<u>精確的</u>描述。

(A) steadily〔'stɛdəlɪ〕 *adv.* 穩定地

(B) ***precisely***〔prɪ'saɪslɪ〕 *adv.* 精確地

(C) extremely〔ɪk'strimlɪ〕 *adv.* 極端地

(D) forcibly〔'forsəblɪ〕 *adv.* 強制地

* handbook〔'hænd,bʊk〕 *n.* 手冊

2. (**D**) His <u>greed</u> for power led him into a tragedy.
他對權利的<u>貪婪</u>導致了他的悲劇。

(A) cause〔kɔz〕 *n.* 原因   (B) fame〔fem〕 *n.* 名聲

(C) issue〔'ɪʃʊ〕 *n.* 問題   (D) ***greed***〔grid〕 *n.* 貪婪

* tragedy〔'trædʒədɪ〕 *n.* 悲劇

3. (**C**) The candidate found every way to <u>distribute</u> her election materials to the voters.
這名候選人想盡辦法要把她的競選資料<u>分發</u>給投票人。

(A) operate〔'ɑpə,ret〕 *v.* 操作

(B) recognize〔'rɛkəg,naɪz〕 *v.* 認得

(C) ***distribute***〔dɪ'strɪbjut〕 *v.* 分發

(D) cultivate〔'kʌltə,vet〕 *v.* 培養

```
dis  +  tribute
 |         |
apart + bestow
```

* candidate〔'kændə,det〕 *n.* 候選人   voter〔'votɚ〕 *n.* 投票者

4. (**C**) John is so <u>obstinate</u> that he does not accept others' opinions.
約翰很<u>固執</u>，不肯接受別人的意見。

(A) delicate〔'dɛləkət〕 *adj.* 細緻的

(B) intimate〔'ɪntəmɪt〕 *adj.* 親密的

(C) ***obstinate***〔'ɑbstənɪt〕 *adj.* 固執的

(D) considerate〔kən'sɪdərɪt〕 *adj.* 體貼的

5. (**A**) Every country needs strong national <u>defense</u> against enemy invasions. 每個國家都需要強大的<u>國防</u>，以抵抗外敵的入侵。

(A) ***defense***〔dɪ'fɛns〕 *n.* 防衛   ***national defense*** 國防

(B) balance〔'bæləns〕 *n.* 平衡   (C) analysis〔ə'næləsɪs〕 *n.* 分析

(D) response〔rɪ'spɑns〕 *n.* 反應；回答

* invasion〔ɪn'veʒən〕 *n.* 侵略

6. (**D**) At the finish, the winner of the race raised her arms
triumphantly. 快抵達終點時，獲勝的跑者<u>得意地</u>高舉雙臂。

(A) enormously〔ɪ'nɔrməslɪ〕*adv.* 巨大地

(B) frequently〔'frikwəntlɪ〕*adv.* 經常地

(C) generously〔'dʒɛnərəslɪ〕*adv.* 慷慨地

(D) ***triumphantly***〔traɪ'ʌmfəntlɪ〕*adv.* 得意地

* finish〔'fɪnɪʃ〕*n.* 最後的階段　　race〔res〕*n.* 賽跑

7. (**B**) He can <u>assemble</u> a motorcycle if he is given all the
parts. 如果他有全部的零件，就能<u>裝配</u>一輛摩托車。

(A) transmit〔træns'mɪt〕*v.* 傳送　　(B) ***assemble***〔ə'sɛmbl̩〕*v.* 裝配

(C) reform〔rɪ'fɔrm〕*v.* 改革　　(D) proceed〔prə'sid〕*v.* 前進

8. (**C**) He told me in <u>earnest</u> that he would do everything to help
me. 他<u>認真</u>地告訴我，他會盡一切力量來幫助我。

(A) action〔'ækʃən〕*n.* 行動

(B) manner〔'mænɚ〕*n.* 態度；方式

(C) ***earnest***〔'ɝnɪst〕*n.* 認真　　***in earnest*** 認真地；鄭重地

(D) progress〔'progrɛs〕*n.* 進步

9. (**A**) This exhibition of Chinese paintings is <u>marvelous</u>. Indeed,
it's the best in ten years.
這場國畫展實在<u>太棒了</u>。的確是十年來最好的一場。

(A) ***marvelous***〔'marvələs〕*adj.* 太棒了

(B) potential〔pə'tɛnʃəl〕*adj.* 有潛力的；可能的

(C) artificial〔ˌartə'fɪʃəl〕*adj.* 人造的

(D) populous〔'papjələs〕*adj.* 人口稠密的

* exhibition〔ˌɛksə'bɪʃən〕*n.* 展覽　　indeed〔ɪn'did〕*adv.* 的確

10. (**D**) Each of these bottles <u>contains</u> 1,000 cc of mineral water,
and it sells for NT$50.
這些瓶子各<u>裝有</u>一千西西的礦泉水，每瓶售價五十元。

(A) attain〔ə'ten〕*v.* 達到　　(B) remain〔rɪ'men〕*v.* 仍然

(C) sustain〔sə'sten〕*v.* 維持　　(D) ***contain***〔kən'ten〕*v.* 包含

* mineral〔'mɪnərəl〕*n.* 礦物　　***mineral water*** 礦泉水

TEST 40

Directions: *Of the four words given after each sentence, choose the one most suitable for filling in the blank.*

1. I always _____ my notes before taking a test.
   - (A) review
   - (B) repeat
   - (C) refuse
   - (D) reply
   (　　)

2. Don't just _____ what someone else does — try to come up with your own original idea.
   - (A) suppose
   - (B) remove
   - (C) reflect
   - (D) imitate
   (　　)

3. Water is _____ in deserts.
   - (A) cheap
   - (B) bleak
   - (C) rare
   - (D) dry
   (　　)

4. Ms. Wang is well-informed; she reads _____ .
   - (A) extensively
   - (B) formally
   - (C) basically
   - (D) irregularly
   (　　)

5. We'd all like to express our deepest _____ at the death of your grandfather.
   - (A) stress
   - (B) sympathy
   - (C) congratulations
   - (D) conflict
   (　　)

6. I can't be around when someone's sweeping; I have allergies and the dust makes me _____ .

   (A) relax
   (B) slip
   (C) hiccup
   (D) sneeze   (   )

7. The course on the history of UFOs sounded interesting, but it turned out to be very _____ .

   (A) useful
   (B) funny
   (C) stimulating
   (D) dull   (   )

8. _____ we had to do all the housework ourselves, but now we have a maid.

   (A) Deliberately
   (B) Previously
   (C) Quietly
   (D) Accidentally   (   )

9. Please knock before you come in. I'd like a little _____ , if you don't mind.

   (A) interaction
   (B) privacy
   (C) openness
   (D) discussion   (   )

10. Helen blew up the balloon until it _____ in her face.

   (A) escaped
   (B) engaged
   (C) exploded
   (D) excluded   (   )

TEST 40 詳解

1. (**A**) I always <u>review</u> my notes before taking a test.
考試前，我都會<u>複習</u>筆記。

(A) ***review*** ﹝rɪ'vju﹞ *v.* 複習
(B) repeat ﹝rɪ'pit﹞ *v.* 重覆
(C) refuse ﹝rɪ'fjuz﹞ *v.* 拒絕
(D) reply ﹝rɪ'plaɪ﹞ *v.* 回答
* note ﹝not﹞ *n.* 筆記

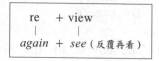

2. (**D**) Don't just <u>imitate</u> what someone else does — try to come up with your own original idea.
別只是<u>模仿</u>別人──試著找出自己獨特的想法。

(A) suppose ﹝sə'poz﹞ *v.* 以為 (B) remove ﹝rɪ'muv﹞ *v.* 除去
(C) reflect ﹝rɪ'flɛkt﹞ *v.* 反映 (D) ***imitate*** ﹝'ɪmə,tet﹞ *v.* 模仿
* ***come up with*** 想出 original ﹝ə'rɪdʒənḷ﹞ *adj.* 獨創的

3. (**C**) Water is <u>rare</u> in deserts. 沙漠中水很<u>稀少</u>。

(A) cheap ﹝tʃip﹞ *adj.* 便宜的 (B) bleak ﹝blik﹞ *adj.* 荒涼的
(C) ***rare*** ﹝rɛr﹞ *adj.* 稀少的 (D) dry ﹝draɪ﹞ *adj.* 乾的
* desert ﹝'dɛzət﹞ *n.* 沙漠

4. (**A**) Ms. Wang is well-informed; she reads <u>extensively</u>.
王小姐見聞廣博；她<u>廣泛地</u>閱讀各種書籍。

(A) ***extensively*** ﹝ɪk'stɛnsɪvlɪ﹞ *adv.* 廣泛地
(B) formally ﹝'fɔrməlɪ﹞ *adv.* 正式地
(C) basically ﹝'besɪkəlɪ﹞ *adv.* 基本地
(D) irregularly ﹝ɪ'rɛgjələlɪ﹞ *adv.* 不規則地
* well-informed ﹝'wɛlɪn'fɔrmd﹞ *adj.* 見聞廣博的

5. (**B**) We'd all like to express our deepest <u>sympathy</u> at the death of your grandfather.
對於你祖父的去世，我們要表達最深的<u>同情</u>。

(A) stress ﹝strɛs﹞ *n.* 壓力 (B) ***sympathy*** ﹝'sɪmpəθɪ﹞ *n.* 同情
(C) congratulations ﹝kən,grætʃə'leʃənz﹞ *n. pl.* 恭喜
(D) conflict ﹝'kɑnflɪkt﹞ *n.* 衝突

6. (**D**) I can't be around when someone's sweeping; I have allergies and the dust makes me <u>sneeze</u>.

我周圍不能有人掃地；我會過敏，灰塵會使我<u>打噴嚏</u>。

(A) relax〔rɪˋlæks〕v. 放鬆　　　(B) slip〔slɪp〕v. 滑倒
(C) hiccup〔ˋhɪkəp〕v. 打嗝　　　(D) **sneeze**〔sniz〕v. 打噴嚏
＊ sweep〔swip〕v. 掃地　　allergy〔ˋælɚdʒɪ〕n. 過敏症

7. (**D**) The course on the history of UFOs sounded interesting, but it turned out to be very <u>dull</u>.

這門探討幽浮歷史的課程聽起來很有趣，結果卻很<u>無聊</u>。

(A) useful〔ˋjusfəl〕adj. 有用的　　(B) funny〔ˋfʌnɪ〕adj. 可笑的
(C) stimulating〔ˋstɪmjəˏletɪŋ〕adj. 刺激的
(D) **dull**〔dʌl〕adj. 無聊的
＊ UFO（unidentified flying object）幽浮（不明飛行物體）

8. (**B**) <u>Previously</u> we had to do all the housework ourselves, but now we have a maid.

<u>以前</u>我們得自己做全部的家事，但現在我們有了女傭。

(A) deliberately〔dɪˋlɪbərɪtlɪ〕adv. 故意地
(B) **previously**〔ˋpriviəslɪ〕adv. 以前
(C) quietly〔ˋkwaɪətlɪ〕adv. 安靜地
(D) accidentally〔ˏæksəˋdɛntḷɪ〕adv. 意外地
＊ housework〔ˋhausˏwɝk〕n. 家事　　maid〔med〕n. 女傭

9. (**B**) Please knock before you come in. I'd like a little <u>privacy</u>, if you don't mind

進來前請你先敲門，我想保有一點<u>隱私</u>，希望你不要介意。

(A) interaction〔ˏɪntɚˋækʃən〕n. 互動
(B) **privacy**〔ˋpraɪvəsɪ〕n. 隱私　　(C) openness〔ˋopənnɪs〕n. 公開
(D) discussion〔dɪˋskʌʃən〕n. 討論

10. (**C**) Helen blew up the balloon until it <u>exploded</u> in her face.

海倫對氣球吹氣，直到氣球在她面前<u>爆開</u>為止。

(A) escape〔əˋskep〕v. 逃走　　(B) engage〔ɪnˋgedʒ〕v. 從事
(C) **explode**〔ɪkˋsplod〕v. 爆炸　　(D) exclude〔ɪkˋsklud〕v. 除外
＊ **blow up** 吹氣　　balloon〔bəˋlun〕n. 氣球

TEST 41

Directions: Of the four words given after each sentence, choose the one most suitable for filling in the blank.

1. I sometimes take John's coat for my own, because the two of them look so _____ .
   - (A) original
   - (B) cheerful
   - (C) curious
   - (D) similar   (   )

2. George at first had difficulty swimming across the pool, but he finally succeeded on his fourth _____ .
   - (A) attempt
   - (B) process
   - (C) instance
   - (D) display   (   )

3. Several motorists were _____ waiting for the light to change.
   - (A) impossibly
   - (B) impracticably
   - (C) importantly
   - (D) impatiently   (   )

4. Mary wrote a letter of _____ to the manufacturer after her new car broke down three times in the same week.
   - (A) complaint
   - (B) repair
   - (C) depression
   - (D) madness   (   )

5. John's poor math score must have _____ him a lot, because he is not attending the class any more.
   - (A) expelled
   - (B) discouraged
   - (C) impressed
   - (D) finished   (   )

6. The issue of environmental protection has not received much attention until very _____ .

   (A) seriously
   (B) recently
   (C) amazingly
   (D) dangerously   (   )

7. The old man could _____ swallow because his throat was too dry.

   (A) actually
   (B) strictly
   (C) exactly
   (D) hardly   (   )

8. We are more than willing to _____ our ties with those countries that are friendly to us.

   (A) appeal
   (B) strengthen
   (C) expect
   (D) connect   (   )

9. The artist is famous for his genius and great _____ .

   (A) fragrance
   (B) originality
   (C) sculptor
   (D) therapy   (   )

10. Although some things are _____ , they nevertheless exist.

   (A) important
   (B) intelligible
   (C) invisible
   (D) interesting   (   )

TEST 41 詳解

1. (**D**) I sometimes take John's coat for my own, because the two of them look so <u>similar</u>.
我有時會把約翰的外套誤認為是我的,因為這兩件外套很<u>相似</u>。
(A) original〔ə'rɪdʒənḷ〕*adj.* 原本的
(B) cheerful〔'tʃɪrfəl〕*adj.* 高興的
(C) curious〔'kjurɪəs〕*adj.* 好奇的 (D) *similar*〔'sɪmələ〕*adj.* 相似的
* *take* **A** *for* **B** 把 A 誤認為 B

2. (**A**) George at first had difficulty swimming across the pool, but he finally succeeded on his fourth <u>attempt</u>.
起初喬治無法游過游泳池,最後<u>嘗試</u>第四次時終於成功了。
(A) *attempt*〔ə'tɛmpt〕*n.* 嘗試   (B) process〔'prɑsɛs〕*n.* 過程
(C) instance〔'ɪnstəns〕*n.* 例證   (D) display〔dɪ'sple〕*n.* 展示

3. (**D**) Several motorists were <u>impatiently</u> waiting for the light to change. 有好幾個汽車駕駛人<u>正不耐煩地</u>等著燈號轉變。
(A) impossibly〔ɪm'pɑsəblɪ〕*adv.* 不可能地
(B) impracticably〔ɪm'præktɪkəblɪ〕*adv.* 不能實行地
(C) importantly〔ɪm'pɔrtṇtlɪ〕*adv.* 重要地
(D) *impatiently*〔ɪm'peʃəntlɪ〕*adv.* 不耐煩地
* motorist〔'motərɪst〕*n.* 汽車駕駛人

4. (**A**) Mary wrote a letter of <u>complaint</u> to the manufacturer after her new car broke down three times in the same week.
瑪麗的新車一週內壞了三次,於是她就寫了一封<u>抱怨</u>信給廠商。
(A) *complaint*〔kəm'plent〕*n.* 抱怨 (B) repair〔rɪ'pɛr〕*n.* 修理
(C) depression〔dɪ'prɛʃən〕*n.* 沮喪 (D) madness〔'mædnɪs〕*n.* 瘋狂
* manufacturer〔ˌmænjə'fæktʃərə〕*n.* 廠商   *break down* 故障

5. (**B**) John's poor math score must have <u>discouraged</u> him a lot, because he is not attending the class any more.
約翰再也不來上課了,一定是數學成績不好讓他覺得很<u>氣餒</u>。
(A) expel〔ɪk'spɛl〕*v.* 驅逐
(B) *discourage*〔dɪs'kɝɪdʒ〕*v.* 使氣餒
(C) impress〔ɪm'prɛs〕*v.* 使印象深刻
(D) finish〔'fɪnɪʃ〕*v.* 結束

dis	+	courage
away	+	*courage*

6. (**B**) The issue of environmental protection has not received much attention until very <u>recently</u>.
直到<u>最近</u>，環保問題才受到大家的注意。
(A) seriously (ˈsɪrɪəslɪ) *adv.* 嚴重地
(B) ***recently*** (ˈrisn̩tlɪ) *adv.* 最近
(C) amazingly (əˈmezɪŋlɪ) *adv.* 令人驚訝地
(D) dangerously (ˈdendʒərəslɪ) *adv.* 危險地
* issue (ˈɪʃu) *n.* 問題　***environmental protection*** 環保

7. (**D**) The old man could <u>hardly</u> swallow because his throat was too dry. 這老人<u>幾乎不</u>能吞嚥，因爲他的喉嚨太乾了。
(A) actually (ˈæktʃʊəlɪ) *adv.* 實際上
(B) strictly (ˈstrɪktlɪ) *adv.* 嚴格地
(C) exactly (ɪgˈzæktlɪ) *adv.* 確實地
(D) ***hardly*** (ˈhɑrdlɪ) *adv.* 幾乎不
* swallow (ˈswɑlo) *v.* 吞

8. (**B**) We are more than willing to <u>strengthen</u> our ties with those countries that are friendly to us.
我們非常願意<u>加強</u>和那些友好國家的關係。
(A) appeal (əˈpil) *v.* 吸引；懇求
(B) ***strengthen*** (ˈstrɛŋθən) *v.* 加強
(C) expect (ɪkˈspɛkt) *v.* 期待
(D) connect (kəˈnɛkt) *v.* 連接

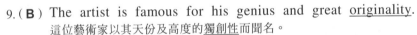

strength ＋en
　|　　　 |
strength ＋ v.

* ***more than*** 非常　　willing (ˈwɪlɪŋ) *adj.* 願意的　tie (taɪ) *n.* 關係

9. (**B**) The artist is famous for his genius and great <u>originality</u>.
這位藝術家以其天份及高度的<u>獨創性</u>而聞名。
(A) fragrance (ˈfregrəns) *n.* 香味
(B) ***originality*** (ə,rɪdʒəˈnælətɪ) *n.* 獨創性；創意
(C) sculptor (ˈskʌlptɚ) *n.* 雕刻家　(D) therapy (ˈθɛrəpɪ) *n.* 治療法
* genius (ˈdʒinjəs) *n.* 天才；天賦

10. (**C**) Although some things are <u>invisible</u>, they nevertheless exist.
有些東西是<u>看不見的</u>，但它們仍然存在。
(A) important (ɪmˈpɔrtn̩t) *adj.* 重要的
(B) intelligible (ɪnˈtɛlədʒəbl̩) *adj.* 可理解的
(C) ***invisible*** (ɪnˈvɪzəbl̩) *adj.* 看不見的
(D) interesting (ˈɪntrɪstɪŋ) *adj.* 有趣的

in ＋vis ＋ible
 |　　|　　 |
not ＋see ＋adj.

* nevertheless (,nɛvɚðəˈlɛs) *adv.* 然而　　exist (ɪgˈzɪst) *v.* 存在

TEST 42

Directions: *Of the four words given after each sentence, choose the one most suitable for filling in the blank.*

1. Because Mr. Chang has been busy these days, it's
_____ whether he will come to the party.
   (A) unlikely
   (B) impossible
   (C) doubtful
   (D) inevitable   (   )

2. I'm quite _____ to the weather in Taiwan, so I think
I'll stay here for another year.
   (A) devoted
   (B) satisfied
   (C) pleased
   (D) accustomed   (   )

3. Mr. Smith won't tolerate talking during class; he says it
_____ others.
   (A) disturbs
   (B) deserves
   (C) destroys
   (D) dismisses   (   )

4. On the basis of the clues, can you predict the _____
of the story?
   (A) outcome
   (B) headline
   (C) cause
   (D) performance   (   )

5. A good reader can often figure out what new words mean
by using _____ .
   (A) contact
   (B) context
   (C) content
   (D) contest   (   )

6. I wonder why she _____ turned up the radio when I was studying.

   (A) sympathetically
   (B) primarily
   (C) deliberately
   (D) thoroughly   (   )

7. It suddenly _____ me that I had to get to the airport to meet a friend.

   (A) took
   (B) struck
   (C) occurred
   (D) surprised   (   )

8. Being a very careful person, he is quite _____ in giving his comments.

   (A) reserved
   (B) melancholy
   (C) complicated
   (D) generous   (   )

9. Most viewers agreed that the movie _____ was not as good as the book.

   (A) routine
   (B) version
   (C) copy
   (D) issue   (   )

10. The native greeted the travelers in a _____ language which was strange to them.

    (A) contrary
    (B) relative
    (C) peculiar
    (D) spiral   (   )

TEST 42 詳解

1. (**C**) Because Mr. Chang has been busy these days, it's <u>doubtful</u> whether he will come to the party.
   張先生最近很忙，所以<u>不確定</u>他是否會參加這個宴會。
   (A) unlikely〔ʌn'laɪklɪ〕*adj.* 不可能的
   (B) impossible〔ɪm'pɑsəbḷ〕*adj.* 不可能的
   (C) *doubtful*〔'daʊtfəl〕*adj.* 不確定的；懷疑的
   (D) inevitable〔ɪn'ɛvətəbḷ〕*adj.* 無法避免的

2. (**D**) I'm quite <u>accustomed</u> to the weather in Taiwan, so I think I'll stay here for another year.
   我很<u>習慣</u>台灣的天氣，所以我想我會再待一年。
   (A) devoted〔dɪ'votɪd〕*adj.* 專心的；熱衷的
   (B) satisfied〔'sætɪs,faɪd〕*adj.* 滿意的
   (C) pleased〔plizd〕*adj.* 高興的
   (D) *accustomed*〔ə'kʌstəmd〕*adj.* 習慣的　　*be accustomed to* 習慣於

3. (**A**) Mr. Smith won't tolerate talking during class; he says it <u>disturbs</u> others. 史密斯先生不容許上課聊天；他說這樣會<u>打擾</u>別人。
   (A) *disturb*〔dɪ'stɝb〕*v.* 打擾　　(B) deserve〔dɪ'zɝv〕*v.* 應得
   (C) destroy〔dɪ'strɔɪ〕*v.* 破壞　　(D) dismiss〔dɪs'mɪs〕*v.* 解散；下 (課)
   * tolerate〔'tɑlə,ret〕*v.* 容忍

4. (**A**) On the basis of the clues, can you predict the <u>outcome</u> of the story? 根據這些線索，你能預測故事的<u>結局</u>嗎？
   (A) *outcome*〔'aʊt,kʌm〕*n.* 結果
   (B) headline〔'hɛd,laɪn〕*n.* 標題；頭條新聞
   (C) cause〔kɔz〕*n.* 原因
   (D) performance〔pɚ'fɔrməns〕*n.* 表演
   * *on the basis of* 根據　　predict〔prɪ'dɪkt〕*v.* 預測

5. (**B**) A good reader can often figure out what new words mean by using <u>context</u>. 高明的讀者，常可利用<u>上下文</u>了解生字的意義。
   (A) contact〔'kɑntækt〕*n.* 接觸
   (B) *context*〔'kɑntɛkst〕*n.* 上下文
   (C) content〔'kɑntɛnt〕*n.* 內容
   (D) contest〔'kɑntɛst〕*n.* 比賽
   * *figure out* 了解

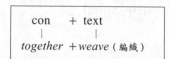

con　+ text
|　　　|
together +*weave*（編織）

6. (**C**) I wonder why she <u>deliberately</u> turned up the radio when I was studying.

我想知道她為什麼在我讀書時，<u>故意</u>把收音機開得很大聲。

(A) sympathetically〔ˌsɪmpə'θɛtɪklɪ〕*adv.* 同情地

(B) primarily〔'praɪˌmɛrəlɪ〕*adv.* 主要地

(C) ***deliberately***〔dɪ'lɪbərɪtlɪ〕*adv.* 故意地

(D) thoroughly〔'θɝolɪ〕*adv.* 徹底地

＊ ***turn up*** 開大聲

7. (**B**) It suddenly <u>struck</u> me that I had to get to the airport to meet a friend. 我突然<u>想到</u>，我得去機場接一位朋友。

(A) take〔tek〕*v.* 拿 　　　 (B) ***strike***〔straɪk〕*v.* 使想起

(C) occur〔ə'kɝ〕*v.* 發生（須改為：occur to~ 使~想起）

(D) surprise〔sə'praɪz〕*v.* 使驚訝

＊ meet〔mit〕*v.* 接

8. (**A**) Being a very careful person, he is quite <u>reserved</u> in giving his comments. 他為人謹慎，在評論時會<u>有所保留</u>。

(A) ***reserved***〔rɪ'zɝvd〕*adj.* 有所保留的

(B) melancholy〔'mɛlənˌkalɪ〕*adj.* 憂鬱的

(C) complicated〔'kampləˌketɪd〕*adj.* 複雜的

(D) generous〔'dʒɛnərəs〕*adj.* 慷慨的

＊ comment〔'kamɛnt〕*n.* 評論

9. (**B**) Most viewers agreed that the movie <u>version</u> was not as good as the book. 大部分觀眾都認為電影<u>版</u>沒有原著好。

(A) routine〔ru'tin〕*n.* 例行公事

(B) ***version***〔'vɝʒən〕*n.* 版本

(C) copy〔'kapɪ〕*n.* 影本；複製品

(D) issue〔'ɪʃu〕*n.* 問題

＊ viewer〔'vjuɚ〕*n.* 觀眾

10. (**C**) The native greeted the travelers in a <u>peculiar</u> language which was strange to them.

土著以遊客不熟悉的<u>奇特</u>語言來迎接他們。

(A) contrary〔'kantrɛrɪ〕*adj.* 相反的

(B) relative〔'rɛlətɪv〕*adj.* 相對的

(C) ***peculiar***〔pɪ'kjuljɚ〕*adj.* 奇特的

(D) spiral〔'spaɪrəl〕*adj.* 螺旋狀的

＊ native〔'netɪv〕*n.* 原住民；土著　　　 strange〔strendʒ〕*adj.* 陌生的

TEST 43

Directions: *Of the four words given after each sentence, choose the one most suitable for filling in the blank.*

1. The main _____ of this test is to find out how much you have learned in high school.
   - (A) countenance
   - (B) discipline
   - (C) objective
   - (D) procedure   ( )

2. I hope to live in a student dormitory when I am in college. I am tired of _____ to school in a crowded bus every day.
   - (A) commuting
   - (B) dropping
   - (C) swaying
   - (D) wandering   ( )

3. They were behind schedule and had to apply for _____ manpower to complete their project in time.
   - (A) basic
   - (B) extra
   - (C) introductory
   - (D) profound   ( )

4. Out of _____ and consideration, I always write a thank-you note when someone sends me a gift.
   - (A) concentration
   - (B) convenience
   - (C) courtesy
   - (D) courtship   ( )

5. The boy _____ to the teacher for his improper behavior.
   - (A) apologized
   - (B) appealed
   - (C) approached
   - (D) attached   ( )

6. The problem with Jane is that she tends to take criticism too _____ and gets angry easily.
   - (A) eventually
   - (B) positively
   - (C) intimately
   - (D) personally   (   )

7. Almost everybody is a _____ of many different "selves"; we show different faces to different people.
   - (A) combination
   - (B) communication
   - (C) competition
   - (D) complication   (   )

8. John has been working at the computer for twenty-four hours. He _____ needs a good rest.
   - (A) accidentally
   - (B) efficiently
   - (C) obviously
   - (D) previously   (   )

9. Nowadays students can _____ information from a variety of sources, such as computers, television, and compact discs.
   - (A) press
   - (B) express
   - (C) oppress
   - (D) access   (   )

10. Sorry for being late. Someone gave me _____ directions and I got totally lost.
    - (A) dreary
    - (B) faulty
    - (C) handy
    - (D) steady   (   )

TEST 43 詳解

1. (**C**) The main <u>objective</u> of this test is to find out how much you have learned in high school.
這項測驗主要的<u>目的</u>，是要知道你在高中學到了多少。
- (A) countenance〔'kauntənəns〕*n.* 面容
- (B) discipline〔'dɪsəplɪn〕*n.* 紀律
- (C) *objective*〔əb'dʒɛktɪv〕*n.* 目的
- (D) procedure〔prə'sidʒɚ〕*n.* 程序

2. (**A**) I hope to live in a student dormitory when I am in college. I am tired of <u>commuting</u> to school in a crowded bus every day. 上大學後我希望能住學生宿舍。我受夠了每天擠公車<u>通勤</u>。
- (A) *commute*〔kə'mjut〕*v.* 通勤
- (B) drop〔drɑp〕*v.* 掉落
- (C) sway〔swe〕*v.* 搖擺
- (D) wander〔'wɑndɚ〕*v.* 徘徊
- * dormitory〔'dɔrmə,torɪ〕*n.* 宿舍　　*be tired of* 對~感到厭煩

3. (**B**) They were behind schedule and had to apply for <u>extra</u> manpower to complete their project in time.
他們的進度落後，必須申請<u>額外的</u>人力，才能及時完成計畫。
- (A) basic〔'besɪk〕*adj.* 基本的
- (B) *extra*〔'ɛkstrə〕*adj.* 額外的
- (C) introductory〔,ɪntrə'dʌktərɪ〕*adj.* 介紹的
- (D) profound〔prə'faund〕*adj.* 深奧的
- * schedule〔'skɛdʒul〕*n.* 進度　　manpower〔'mæn,pauɚ〕*n.* 人力

4. (**C**) Out of <u>courtesy</u> and consideration, I always write a thank-you note when someone sends me a gift.
如果有人送禮，基於<u>禮貌</u>和尊重，我都會寫封感謝函。
- (A) concentration〔,kɑnsn'treʃən〕*n.* 集中；專心
- (B) convenience〔kən'vinjəns〕*n.* 便利
- (C) *courtesy*〔'kɝtəsɪ〕*n.* 禮貌
- (D) courtship〔'kort·ʃɪp〕*n.* 追求
- * *out of* 由於；出於　　consideration〔kən,sɪdə'reʃən〕*n.* 體諒；尊敬

5. (**A**) The boy <u>apologized</u> to the teacher for his improper behavior. 小男孩為自己不當的行為向老師<u>道歉</u>。
- (A) *apologize*〔ə'pɑlə,dʒaɪz〕*v.* 道歉
- (B) appeal〔ə'pil〕*v.* 吸引；懇求
- (C) approach〔ə'protʃ〕*v.* 接近
- (D) attach〔ə'tætʃ〕*v.* 貼上

```
apo +  log  +ize
 |      |     |
off +speak + v.
```

6. (**D**) The problem with Jane is that she tends to take criticism too <u>personally</u> and gets angry easily.
珍的問題在於，容易認為批評是針對她個人，而且容易生氣。

(A) eventually 〔 ɪˈvɛntʃʊəlɪ 〕 *adv.* 最後；終於
(B) positively 〔ˈpɑzətɪvlɪ 〕 *adv.* 正面地；積極地
(C) intimately 〔ˈɪntəmɪtlɪ 〕 *adv.* 親密地
(D) ***personally*** 〔ˈpɝsn̩lɪ 〕 *adv.* 就個人而言

* ***tend to*** 易於~　　take 〔 tek 〕 *v.* 看待

7. (**A**) Almost everybody is a <u>combination</u> of many different "selves"; we show different faces to different people.
幾乎每個人都是許多不同自我的結合體；面對不同的人，我們會表現出不同的面貌。

(A) ***combination*** 〔ˌkɑmbəˈneʃən 〕 *n.* 結合
(B) communication 〔 kəˌmjunəˈkeʃən 〕 *n.* 溝通
(C) competition 〔ˌkɑmpəˈtɪʃən 〕 *n.* 競爭
(D) complication 〔ˌkɑmpləˈkeʃən 〕 *n.* 複雜

* self 〔 sɛlf 〕 *n.* 自我

8. (**C**) John has been working at the computer for twenty-four hours. He <u>obviously</u> needs a good rest.
約翰已經在電腦前工作了二十四小時。顯然他需要好好休息一下。

(A) accidentally 〔ˌæksəˈdɛntl̩ɪ 〕 *adv.* 意外地
(B) efficiently 〔 əˈfɪʃəntlɪ 〕 *adv.* 有效率地
(C) ***obviously*** 〔ˈɑbvɪəslɪ 〕 *adv.* 明顯地
(D) previously 〔ˈprivɪəslɪ 〕 *adv.* 先前

9. (**D**) Nowadays students can <u>access</u> information from a variety of sources, such as computers, television, and compact discs. 現在學生可以從各種來源取得資訊，像是電腦、電視和光碟。

(A) press 〔 prɛs 〕 *v.* 壓　　(B) express 〔 ɪkˈsprɛs 〕 *v.* 表達
(C) oppress 〔 əˈprɛs 〕 *v.* 壓迫　　(D) ***access*** 〔ˈæksɛs 〕 *v.* 取得；存取

* variety 〔 vəˈraɪətɪ 〕 *n.* 多樣性　　***compact disc*** 光碟

10. (**B**) Sorry for being late. Someone gave me <u>faulty</u> directions and I got totally lost.
抱歉我來遲了。有人告訴我錯誤的方向，害我迷路了。

(A) dreary 〔ˈdrɪrɪ 〕 *adj.* 陰沈的　　(B) ***faulty*** 〔ˈfɔltɪ 〕 *adj.* 錯誤的
(C) handy 〔ˈhændɪ 〕 *adj.* 方便的　　(D) steady 〔ˈstɛdɪ 〕 *adj.* 穩定的

TEST 44

Directions: *Of the four words given after each sentence, choose the one most suitable for filling in the blank.*

1. Women should be aware of their _____ rather than limiting themselves to the traditional roles.
   - (A) shortcomings
   - (B) pressure
   - (C) origin
   - (D) potential   (   )

2. The girl has the great virtues of _____ and kindliness.
   - (A) humility
   - (B) humidity
   - (C) greed
   - (D) revenge   (   )

3. When supply _____ demand, the computer price drops.
   - (A) succeeds
   - (B) exceeds
   - (C) proceeds
   - (D) precedes   (   )

4. A child, when falling, will not cry if there is no one around to offer _____ .
   - (A) gratitude
   - (B) regret
   - (C) encourage
   - (D) sympathy   (   )

5. A man's _____ depends not upon his wealth or rank but upon his character.
   - (A) dignity
   - (B) privilege
   - (C) intellect
   - (D) eloquence   (   )

6. After retirement, he works as a(n) _____ social
   worker, which enriches his life.
   (A) enthusiasm
   (B) depressed
   (C) vicious
   (D) volunteer   (   )

7. Look at the pictures of those starved Africans. We should
   not be _____ to their sufferings any more.
   (A) relieved
   (B) ignorant
   (C) indifferent
   (D) concerned   (   )

8. When you go to a new country, you must _____
   yourself to new manners and customs.
   (A) transform
   (B) overcome
   (C) adapt
   (D) adopt   (   )

9. At the Olympic Games, our representatives are in _____
   with the best athletes from all over the world.
   (A) competent
   (B) competition
   (C) compliment
   (D) compare   (   )

10. All living things need _____ to grow and stay
    healthy.
    (A) nourish
    (B) nutrition
    (C) resolution
    (D) medicine   (   )

TEST 44 詳解

1. (**D**) Women should be aware of their <u>potential</u> rather than limiting themselves to the traditional roles.
女性應意識到自己的<u>潛力</u>，而不要把自己侷限在傳統的角色中。

(A) shortcoming〔'ʃɔrt,kʌmɪŋ〕*n.* 缺點
(B) pressure〔'prɛʃɚ〕*n.* 壓力
(C) origin〔'ɔrədʒɪn〕*n.* 起源
(D) *potential*〔pə'tɛnʃəl〕*n.* 潛力

* *be aware of* 知道；察覺　　*rather than* 而不是

2. (**A**) The girl has the great virtues of <u>humility</u> and kindliness.
這女孩有著<u>謙虛</u>和親切的美德。

(A) *humility*〔hju'mɪlətɪ〕*n.* 謙虛　　(B) humidity〔hju'mɪdətɪ〕*n.* 濕度
(C) greed〔grid〕*n.* 貪婪　　(D) revenge〔rɪ'vɛndʒ〕*n.* 報復

* virtue〔'vɝtʃʊ〕*n.* 美德　　kindliness〔'kaɪndlɪnɪs〕*n.* 親切；友善

3. (**B**) When supply <u>exceeds</u> demand, the computer price drops.
當供給<u>超過</u>需求時，電腦的售價就會下降。

(A) succeed〔sək'sid〕*v.* 成功
(B) *exceed*〔ɪk'sid〕*v.* 超過
(C) proceed〔prə'sid〕*v.* 進行
(D) precede〔prɪ'sid〕*v.* 在前

* demand〔dɪ'mænd〕*n.* 需求

4. (**D**) A child, when falling, will not cry if there is no one around to offer <u>sympathy</u>.
小孩跌倒時，如果周圍沒有人表示<u>同情</u>，他就不會哭。

(A) gratitude〔'grætə,tjud〕*n.* 感激　　(B) regret〔rɪ'grɛt〕*n.* 後悔
(C) encourage〔ɪn'kɝɪdʒ〕*v.* 鼓勵　　(D) *sympathy*〔'sɪmpəθɪ〕*n.* 同情

5. (**A**) A man's <u>dignity</u> depends not upon his wealth or rank but upon his character.
人的<u>尊嚴</u>不在於他的財富或地位，而在於他的品格。

(A) *dignity*〔'dɪgnətɪ〕*n.* 尊嚴　　(B) privilege〔'prɪvḷɪdʒ〕*n.* 特權
(C) intellect〔'ɪntḷ,ɛkt〕*n.* 智力
(D) eloquence〔'ɛləkwəns〕*n.* 口才

* *depend upon* 取決於；視～而定　　rank〔ræŋk〕*n.* 階級；地位

6. (**D**) After retirement, he works as a <u>volunteer</u> social worker, which enriches his life. 退休後，他擔任義工，生活過得十分充實。

    (A) enthusiasm〔ɪn'θjuzɪ‚æzəm〕*n.* 熱心

    (B) depressed〔dɪ'prɛst〕*adj.* 沮喪的

    (C) vicious〔'vɪʃəs〕*adj.* 邪惡的

    (D) ***volunteer***〔‚vɑlən'tɪr〕*adj.* 自願的

7. (**C**) Look at the pictures of those starved Africans. We should not be <u>indifferent</u> to their sufferings any more. 看看這些非洲飢民的照片。我們不應再<u>漠視</u>他們的苦難。

    (A) relieved〔rɪ'livd〕*adj.* 鬆了一口氣的

    (B) ignorant〔'ɪgnərənt〕*adj.* 無知的

    (C) ***indifferent***〔ɪn'dɪfərənt〕*adj.* 漠不關心的

    (D) concerned〔kən'sɜnd〕*adj.* 關心的

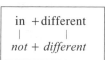

8. (**C**) When you go to a new country, you must <u>adapt</u> yourself to new manners and customs. 到一個陌生的國家，你要讓自己<u>適應</u>新的禮節和習俗。

    (A) transform〔træns'fɔrm〕*v.* 轉變

    (B) overcome〔‚ovə'kʌm〕*v.* 克服

    (C) ***adapt***〔ə'dæpt〕*v.* 使適應　***adapt oneself to*** 適應~

    (D) adopt〔ə'dɑpt〕*v.* 採用

    * manners〔'mænəz〕*n. pl.* 風俗；禮貌

9. (**B**) At the Olympic Games, our representatives are in <u>competition</u> with the best athletes from all over the world. 奧運會上，我們的代表與來自世界各地優秀的運動員<u>比賽</u>。

    (A) competent〔'kɑmpətənt〕*adj.* 能勝任的；能幹的

    (B) ***competition***〔‚kɑmpə'tɪʃən〕*n.* 比賽

    (C) compliment〔'kɑmpləmənt〕*n.* 稱讚

    (D) compare〔kəm'pɛr〕*v.* 比較

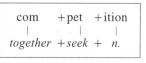

    * ***the Olympic Games*** 奧林匹克運動會

    representative〔‚rɛprɪ'zɛntətɪv〕*n.* 代表

    athlete〔'æθlit〕*n.* 運動員

10. (**B**) All living things need <u>nutrition</u> to grow and stay healthy. 所有生物都需要<u>營養</u>來成長與保持健康。

    (A) nourish〔'nɜʃ〕*v.* 滋養　　　(B) ***nutrition***〔nju'trɪʃən〕*n.* 營養

    (C) resolution〔‚rɛzə'luʃən〕*n.* 決心　(D) medicine〔'mɛdəsṇ〕*n.* 藥

    * ***living things*** 生物

TEST 45

Directions: *Of the four words given after each sentence, choose the one most suitable for filling in the blank.*

1. We should give children nutritious food, or malnutrition will _____ the growth of children.
   (A) promote
   (B) retard
   (C) advance
   (D) avoid   (   )

2. Americans traditionally have held independence and a closely related value, individualism, in high _____ .
   (A) privacy
   (B) autonomy
   (C) assertion
   (D) esteem   (   )

3. The government _____ new taxes on imported goods.
   (A) imposes
   (B) composes
   (C) disposes
   (D) supposes   (   )

4. We _____ a red ball for a blue one to see if the baby would notice the difference.
   (A) substituted
   (B) replaced
   (C) constituted
   (D) instituted   (   )

5. The old principal's address _____ strongly to the students.
   (A) concealed
   (B) appealed
   (C) attracted
   (D) contacted   (   )

6. The theater was filled to _____ ; there was standing room only.
   (A) publicity
   (B) simplicity
   (C) capacity
   (D) electricity   (   )

7. We are too busy to take a long holiday this year, not to _____ the fact that we can't afford it.
   (A) speak
   (B) tell
   (C) say
   (D) mention   (   )

8. Whatever happens, we ought to keep life in _____ .
   (A) pessimism
   (B) preparation
   (C) perspective
   (D) prevention   (   )

9. Our team _____ our opponents by a score of 3 to 0.
   (A) won
   (B) defeated
   (C) lost
   (D) defended   (   )

10. The _____ of world population has changed during the last two centuries. A lot of people have moved from the country to the cities.
    (A) contribution
    (B) construction
    (C) distribution
    (D) destruction   (   )

TEST 45 詳解

1.(**B**) We should give children nutritious food, or malnutrition will <u>retard</u> the growth of children.
我們應給孩子營養的食物，否則營養不良會<u>阻礙</u>孩子的成長。

(A) promote〔prəˋmot〕v. 促進
(B) *retard*〔rɪˋtard〕v. 阻礙
(C) advance〔ədˋvæns〕v. 使前進
(D) avoid〔əˋvɔɪd〕v. 避免

＊ nutritious〔njuˋtrɪʃəs〕adj. 營養的

2.(**D**) Americans traditionally have held independence and a closely related value, individualism, in high <u>esteem</u>.
傳統上，美國人相當<u>尊重</u>獨立性和另一個密切相關的價值——個人主義。

(A) privacy〔ˋpraɪvəsɪ〕n. 隱私　　(B) autonomy〔ɔˋtɑnəmɪ〕n. 自治
(C) assertion〔əˋsɝʃən〕n. 斷言
(D) *esteem*〔əˋstim〕n. 尊重　　*hold ~ in high esteem* 相當尊重~

3.(**A**) The government <u>imposes</u> new taxes on imported goods.
政府對進口貨品<u>課徵</u>新稅。

(A) *impose*〔ɪmˋpoz〕v. 課徵　　(B) compose〔kəmˋpoz〕v. 組成
(C) dispose〔dɪˋspoz〕v. 處置　　(D) suppose〔səˋpoz〕v. 以為

＊ tax〔tæks〕n. 稅　　imported〔ɪmˋportɪd〕adj. 進口的

4.(**A**) We <u>substituted</u> a red ball for a blue one to see if the baby would notice the difference.
我們用紅色球<u>代替</u>藍色球，看看嬰兒是否會注意到它們的不同。

(A) *substitute*〔ˋsʌbstəˏtjut〕v. 代替　　*substitute* A *for* B 用A代替B
(B) replace〔rɪˋples〕v. 取代　　*replace* A *with* B 用B代替A
(C) constitute〔ˋkɑnstəˏtjut〕v. 組成
(D) institute〔ˋɪnstəˏtjut〕v. 設立

5.(**B**) The old principal's address <u>appealed</u> strongly to the students.　老校長的演說，非常<u>吸引</u>學生。

(A) conceal〔kənˋsil〕v. 隱藏　　(B) *appeal*〔əˋpil〕v. 吸引
(C) attract〔əˋtrækt〕v. 吸引（為及物動詞，不加 to）
(D) contact〔ˋkɑntækt〕v. 接觸

＊ principal〔ˋprɪnsəpl̩〕n. 中小學校長
address〔əˋdrɛs , ˋædrɛs〕n. 演講

6. (**C**) The theater was filled to <u>capacity</u>; there was standing room only. 戲院客滿，只剩站票。

(A) publicity〔pʌb'lɪsətɪ〕*n.* 公開
(B) simplicity〔sɪm'plɪsətɪ〕*n.* 簡單
(C) *capacity*〔kə'pæsətɪ〕*n.* 容量　　***be filled to capacity*** 客滿
(D) electricity〔ɪ,lɛk'trɪsətɪ〕*n.* 電
＊ ***standing room*** 站位

7. (**D**) We are too busy to take a long holiday this year, not to <u>mention</u> the fact that we can't afford it.
今年我們太忙了，沒時間放長假，更別提我們負擔不起了。

(A) speak〔spik〕*v.* 說
(B) tell〔tɛl〕*v.* 告訴
(C) say〔se〕*v.* 說
(D) ***mention***〔'mɛnʃən〕*v.* 提到
＊ afford〔ə'fɔrd〕*v.* 負擔得起

8. (**C**) Whatever happens, we ought to keep life in <u>perspective</u>.
不論發生什麼事，我們都應該以<u>正確的眼光</u>看待人生。

(A) pessimism〔'pɛsə,mɪzəm〕*n.* 悲觀
(B) preparation〔,prɛpə'reʃən〕*n.* 準備
(C) *perspective*〔pə'spɛktɪv〕*n.* 正確的眼光
(D) prevention〔prɪ'vɛnʃən〕*n.* 防止

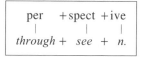

9. (**B**) Our team <u>defeated</u> our opponents by a score of 3 to 0.
我們隊伍以三比零的分數<u>擊敗</u>對手。

(A) win〔wɪn〕*v.* 贏（win 須接物當受詞，如 win a game「贏得比賽」，win a prize「贏得獎品」，不可接人當受詞。）
(B) *defeat*〔dɪ'fit〕*v.* 打敗
(C) lose〔luz〕*v.* 輸
(D) defend〔dɪ'fɛnd〕*v.* 防守
＊ team〔tim〕*n.* 隊伍　　opponent〔ə'ponənt〕*n.* 對手

10. (**C**) The <u>distribution</u> of world population has changed during the last two centuries. A lot of people have moved from the country to the cities.
過去兩個世紀以來，世界人口的<u>分布</u>情況已有所改變。許多人從鄉村移往都市。

(A) contribution〔,kɑntrə'bjuʃən〕*n.* 貢獻
(B) construction〔kən'strʌkʃən〕*n.* 建設
(C) *distribution*〔,dɪstrə'bjuʃən〕*n.* 分布
(D) destruction〔dɪ'strʌkʃən〕*n.* 破壞

TEST 46

Directions: *Of the four words given after each sentence, choose the one most suitable for filling in the blank.*

1. When we are ill, we should _____ a doctor instead of taking medicine ourselves.
   (A) diagnose
   (B) prescribe
   (C) consult
   (D) analyze   (   )

2. John's only _____ is to attend the needs of the living, not the glory of the dead.
   (A) desire
   (B) disease
   (C) deserve
   (D) decline   (   )

3. To convince our teacher, can you invent a _____ excuse for our being late?
   (A) clear
   (B) reasonable
   (C) complicated
   (D) experienced   (   )

4. _____ , there is a great improvement in the patient's condition. The doctor feels relieved.
   (A) Universally
   (B) Unfortunately
   (C) Undoubtedly
   (D) Unfaithfully   (   )

5. Although the children are _____ to death, they still enjoy skating on the pond.
   (A) pleasing
   (B) freezing
   (C) encouraged
   (D) defeated   (   )

6. At Christmas, Americans _____ their houses, stores, and public buildings with red and green.

(A) construct
(B) experiment
(C) decorate
(D) expand   (   )

7. Before you lay a carpet in a room, you have to _____ the size of the room.

(A) measure
(B) predict
(C) forerun
(D) meter   (   )

8. _____ man made tools and weapons from sharp stones and animal bones.

(A) Previous
(B) Modern
(C) Original
(D) Primitive   (   )

9. The children were clever, but their behavior showed that there was not much _____ in the school.

(A) discipline
(B) disciple
(C) decibel
(D) disagreement   (   )

10. Since noise pollution prevails in big cities, we have to enforce the antinoise laws more _____ .

(A) primarily
(B) invariably
(C) increasingly
(D) strictly   (   )

TEST 46 詳解

1. (**C**) When we are ill, we should <u>consult</u> a doctor instead of taking medicine ourselves. 生病時應該去看醫生，不要自行服藥。
   - (A) diagnose〔ˌdaɪəg'noz〕*v.* 診斷
   - (B) prescribe〔prɪ'skraɪb〕*v.* 開藥方
   - (C) ***consult***〔kən'sʌlt〕*v.* 請教；看（醫生）
   - (D) analyze〔'ænlˌaɪz〕*v.* 分析

2. (**A**) John's only <u>desire</u> is to attend the needs of the living, not the glory of the dead.
   約翰唯一的願望是滿足生者的需要，而非增添死者的榮耀。
   - (A) ***desire***〔dɪ'zaɪr〕*n.* 願望
   - (B) disease〔dɪ'ziz〕*n.* 疾病
   - (C) deserve〔dɪ'zɝv〕*v.* 應得
   - (D) decline〔dɪ'klaɪn〕*n.* 衰退；拒絕
   - * attend〔ə'tɛnd〕*v.* 照顧　***the living*** 生者

3. (**B**) To convince our teacher, can you invent a <u>reasonable</u> excuse for our being late?
   為了讓老師相信，你能不能為我們的遲到編一個合理的藉口？
   - (A) clear〔klɪr〕*adj.* 清楚的
   - (B) ***reasonable***〔'riznəbl̩〕*adj.* 合理的
   - (C) complicated〔'kɑmpləˌketɪd〕*adj.* 複雜的
   - (D) experienced〔ɪk'spɪrɪənst〕*adj.* 有經驗的

4. (**C**) <u>Undoubtedly</u>, there is a great improvement in the patient's condition. The doctor feels relieved.
   無疑地，病人的情況已大有改善。醫生覺得鬆了一口氣。
   - (A) universally〔ˌjunə'vɝslɪ〕*adv.* 普遍地
   - (B) unfortunately〔ʌn'fɔrtʃənɪtlɪ〕*adv.* 不幸地
   - (C) ***undoubtedly***〔ʌn'dautɪdlɪ〕*adv.* 無疑地
   - (D) unfaithfully〔ʌn'feθfəlɪ〕*adv.* 不忠實地

5. (**B**) Although the children are <u>freezing</u> to death, they still enjoy skating on the pond.
   儘管孩子們快冷死了，他們還是喜歡在池塘上溜冰。
   - (A) please〔pliz〕*v.* 使高興
   - (B) ***freeze***〔'friz〕*v.* 結冰；感覺寒冷　***be freezing to death*** 快冷死了
   - (C) encourage〔ɪn'kɝdʒ〕*v.* 鼓勵
   - (D) defeat〔dɪ'fit〕*v.* 打敗

6. (**C**) At Christmas, Americans <u>decorate</u> their houses, stores, and public buildings with red and green.
聖誕節時，美國人會用紅色和綠色來<u>裝飾</u>自己的房屋、商店和公共建築。

    (A) construct〔kən'strʌkt〕v. 建造
    (B) experiment〔ɪk'spɛrəmənt〕v. 實驗
    (C) ***decorate***〔'dɛkə,ret〕v. 裝飾
    (D) expand〔ɪk'spænd〕v. 擴大

7. (**A**) Before you lay a carpet in a room, you have to <u>measure</u> the size of the room. 舖地毯之前，要先<u>測量</u>房間的大小。

    (A) ***measure***〔'mɛʒɚ〕v. 測量   (B) predict〔prɪ'dɪkt〕v. 預測
    (C) forerun〔for'rʌn〕v. 預告；在～之前
    (D) meter〔'mitɚ〕v. 用儀器測量　*n.* 公尺

    * lay〔le〕v. 舖上；放　　carpet〔'kɑrpɪt〕n. 地毯

8. (**D**) <u>Primitive</u> man made tools and weapons from sharp stones and animal bones. <u>原始</u>人用尖石及獸骨製作工具及武器。

    (A) previous〔'privɪəs〕adj. 先前的
    (B) modern〔'mɑdɚn〕adj. 現代的
    (C) original〔ə'rɪdʒənḷ〕adj. 最初的；獨創的
    (D) ***primitive***〔'prɪmətɪv〕adj. 原始的

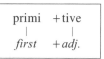

9. (**A**) The children were clever, but their behavior showed that there was not much <u>discipline</u> in the school.
孩子們很聰明，但是他們的行為顯示，在學校沒有什麼<u>紀律</u>。

    (A) ***discipline***〔'dɪsəplɪn〕n. 紀律；訓練
    (B) disciple〔dɪ'saɪpḷ〕n. 門徒
    (C) decibel〔'dɛsə,bɛl〕n. 分貝
    (D) disagreement〔,dɪsə'grimənt〕n. 意見不合

10. (**D**) Since noise pollution prevails in big cities, we have to enforce the antinoise laws more <u>strictly</u>.
由於大都市到處都有噪音污染，我們必須更<u>嚴格地</u>執行噪音防治法。

    (A) primarily〔'praɪ,mɛrəlɪ〕adv. 主要地
    (B) invariably〔ɪn'vɛrɪəbḷɪ〕adv. 不變地；必定
    (C) increasingly〔ɪn'krisɪŋlɪ〕adv. 逐漸地
    (D) ***strictly***〔'strɪktlɪ〕adv. 嚴格地

    * prevail〔prɪ'vel〕v. 盛行；普遍　　enforce〔ɪn'fors〕v. 強制執行
    antinoise〔'æntɪ,nɔɪz〕adj. 防止噪音的

TEST 47

Directions: *Of the four words given after each sentence, choose the one most suitable for filling in the blank.*

1. Diane is so diligent that she inspires her colleagues to work _____ .
   (A) industriously
   (B) miserably
   (C) potentially
   (D) ordinarily   (   )

2. We are particularly _____ to him for his timely help.
   (A) conscious
   (B) grateful
   (C) notorious
   (D) steady   (   )

3. The top of the 63-story skyscraper commands a _____ view of the city.
   (A) significant
   (B) spectacular
   (C) spontaneous
   (D) sufficient   (   )

4. Above his desk hung a _____ of his wife, which was painted by a famous artist.
   (A) decoration
   (B) manuscript
   (C) symmetry
   (D) portrait   (   )

5. It is expected that the accomplishment of the Taipei Rapid Transit System will _____ public transportation.
   (A) migrate
   (B) operate
   (C) facilitate
   (D) restrain   (   )

6. He does not fit the _____ of a used car salesperson. He is quiet and informative, not loud and pushy.

  (A) stereotype
  (B) scholar
  (C) vehicle
  (D) declaration   (   )

7. Her face was old and covered in _____ .

  (A) merriment
  (B) wrinkles
  (C) eyelashes
  (D) whistles   (   )

8. She likes to spend her afternoons sunbathing, so she has a tanned _____ .

  (A) complication
  (B) feature
  (C) repentance
  (D) complexion   (   )

9. Not a soul was seen in the _____ and bleak town.

  (A) cultivated
  (B) additional
  (C) deserted
  (D) fertile   (   )

10. Be sure to _____ your rooms before going traveling.

  (A) preserve
  (B) reserve
  (C) deserve
  (D) conserve   (   )

TEST 47 詳解

1. (**A**) Diane is so diligent that she inspires her colleagues to work <u>industriously</u>. 黛安非常勤勉，也激勵同事<u>勤奮地</u>工作。

   (A) ***industriously***〔ɪnˋdʌstrɪəslɪ〕*adv.* 勤奮地
   (B) miserably〔ˋmɪzərəblɪ〕*adv.* 悲慘地
   (C) potentially〔pəˋtɛnʃəlɪ〕*adv.* 潛在地
   (D) ordinarily〔ˋɔrdṇ͵ɛrɪlɪ〕*adv.* 平常地
   * diligent〔ˋdɪlədʒənt〕*adj.* 勤勉的   inspire〔ɪnˋspaɪr〕*v.* 激勵

2. (**B**) We are particularly <u>grateful</u> to him for his timely help.
   我們特別<u>感激</u>他及時的幫助。

   (A) conscious〔ˋkɑnʃəs〕*adj.* 知道的
   (B) ***grateful***〔ˋgretfəl〕*adj.* 感激的
   (C) notorious〔noˋtorɪəs〕*adj.* 惡名昭彰的
   (D) steady〔ˋstɛdɪ〕*adj.* 穩定的

3. (**B**) The top of the 63-story skyscraper commands a <u>spectacular</u> view of the city. 在六十三層摩天大樓的頂端，可俯瞰<u>壯觀的</u>市景。

   (A) significant〔sɪgˋnɪfəkənt〕*adj.* 意義重大的
   (B) ***spectacular***〔spɛkˋtækjələ〕*adj.* 壯觀的
   (C) spontaneous〔spɑnˋtenɪəs〕*adj.* 自然的
   (D) sufficient〔səˋfɪʃənt〕*adj.* 足夠的
   * story〔ˋstorɪ〕*n.* 層   skyscraper〔ˋskaɪ͵skrepə〕*n.* 摩天大樓

4. (**D**) Above his desk hung a <u>portrait</u> of his wife, which was painted by a famous artist.
   他書桌的上方，懸掛著一幅由名畫家幫他妻子所畫的<u>肖像</u>。

   (A) decoration〔͵dɛkəˋreʃən〕*n.* 裝飾
   (B) manuscript〔ˋmænjə͵skrɪpt〕*n.* 手稿
   (C) symmetry〔ˋsɪmɪtrɪ〕*n.* 對稱性   (D) ***portrait***〔ˋportret〕*n.* 肖像

5. (**C**) It is expected that the accomplishment of the Taipei Rapid Transit System will <u>facilitate</u> public transportation.
   一般認為台北捷運系統的完成，會<u>使</u>大眾運輸更為<u>便利</u>。

   (A) migrate〔ˋmaɪgret〕*v.* 遷移   (B) operate〔ˋɑpə͵ret〕*v.* 操作
   (C) ***facilitate***〔fəˋsɪlə͵tet〕*v.* 使便利   (D) restrain〔rɪˋstren〕*v.* 限制
   * accomplishment〔əˋkɑmplɪʃmənt〕*n.* 完成
   Rapid Transit System 捷運系統   ***public transportation*** 大眾運輸

6. (**A**) He does not fit the <u>stereotype</u> of a used car salesperson. He is quiet and informative, not loud and pushy.

他不符合二手車銷售員的<u>典型</u>。他很安靜、見聞廣博，不會吵鬧，也並不積極進取。

(A) ***stereotype*** (ˈstɪrɪəˌtaɪp) *n.* 典型；刻板印象
(B) scholar (ˈskɑləˋ) *n.* 學者
(C) vehicle (ˈviɪkḷ) *n.* 車輛
(D) declaration (ˌdɛkləˈreʃən) *n.* 宣告

* ***used car*** 二手車   informative (ɪnˈfɔrmətɪv) *adj.* 見聞廣博的
   pushy (ˈpʊʃɪ) *adj.* 進取的

7. (**B**) Her face was old and covered in <u>wrinkles</u>.

她的臉十分蒼老，而且滿是<u>皺紋</u>。

(A) merriment (ˈmɛrɪmənt) *n.* 歡樂　　(B) ***wrinkle*** (ˈrɪŋkḷ) *n.* 皺紋
(C) eyelash (ˈaɪˌlæʃ) *n.* 睫毛　　(D) whistle (ˈhwɪsḷ) *n.* 口哨

8. (**D**) She likes to spend her afternoons sunbathing, so she has a tanned <u>complexion</u>.

她喜歡利用下午時間做日光浴，所以才會有古銅色的<u>膚色</u>。

(A) complication (ˌkɑmpləˈkeʃən) *n.* 複雜
(B) feature (ˈfitʃəˋ) *n.* 特色
(C) repentance (rɪˈpɛntəns) *n.* 懊悔
(D) ***complexion*** (kəmˈplɛkʃən) *n.* 膚色

* sunbathe (ˈsʌnˌbeð) *v.* 作日光浴   tanned (tænd) *adj.* 曬成褐色的

9. (**C**) Not a soul was seen in the <u>deserted</u> and bleak town.

在這<u>荒涼的</u>城鎮裡，看不到半個人。

(A) cultivated (ˈkʌltəˌvetɪd) *adj.* 有教養的
(B) additional (əˈdɪʃənḷ) *adj.* 額外的
(C) ***deserted*** (dɪˈzɜtɪd) *adj.* 荒涼的
(D) fertile (ˈfɜtḷ) *adj.* 肥沃的

* soul (sol) *n.* 人   bleak (blik) *adj.* 荒涼的

10. (**B**) Be sure to <u>reserve</u> your rooms before going traveling.

旅行前一定要<u>預訂</u>房間。

(A) preserve (prɪˈzɜv) *v.* 保存　　(B) ***reserve*** (rɪˈzɜv) *v.* 預訂
(C) deserve (dɪˈzɜv) *v.* 應得
(D) conserve (kənˈsɜv) *v.* 節約

TEST 48

Directions: *Of the four words given after each sentence, choose the one most suitable for filling in the blank.*

1. All her teachers _____ Mary as she graduated with honors.
   (A) complimented
   (B) complemented
   (C) implemented
   (D) supplemented   ( )

2. She spent $10000 buying a coat; it was really a(n) _____ deed for a child to do so.
   (A) extraordinary
   (B) depressed
   (C) extravagant
   (D) fragrant   ( )

3. The fire must have _____ out after the staff had gone home.
   (A) started
   (B) broken
   (C) burnt
   (D) caught   ( )

4. He wouldn't tell them the outcome but kept them in _____ .
   (A) dispel
   (B) suspense
   (C) trespass
   (D) dreadful   ( )

5. It is _____ to say that since the poor have no bread to eat, they can live on steak.
   (A) delicious
   (B) gorgeous
   (C) paradox
   (D) ridiculous   ( )

6. The Shinkong Mitsukoshi Building is the highest building in Taipei and thus becomes the new _____ of Taipei.
   - (A) magnet
   - (B) pole
   - (C) landmark
   - (D) hypothesis   (   )

7. It is impolite to _____ people while they are talking.
   - (A) interpret
   - (B) interact
   - (C) intercept
   - (D) interrupt   (   )

8. I made some _____ sketches which would serve as guides when I made the actual portrait.
   - (A) preliminary
   - (B) primary
   - (C) elementary
   - (D) fundamental   (   )

9. The floods did not start to _____ until three days after the rain had stopped.
   - (A) recede
   - (B) retire
   - (C) retreat
   - (D) sink   (   )

10. This is our last semester in this school, and we hope our _____ classmates and our beloved teachers can help us tide over the hard time.
    - (A) imitate
    - (B) closed
    - (C) closely
    - (D) intimate   (   )

TEST 48 詳解

1. (**A**) All her teachers <u>complimented</u> Mary as she graduated with honors. 瑪麗以優異的成績畢業，所有的老師都<u>稱讚</u>她。

    (A) ***compliment*** 〔'kɑmpləmənt 〕 v. 稱讚

    (B) complement 〔'kɑmpləmənt 〕 v. 補充

    (C) implement 〔'ɪmpləmənt 〕 v. 實施

    (D) supplement 〔'sʌpləmənt 〕 v. 增補；補充

    * honors 〔'ɑnɚz 〕 n. pl. (在大學的) 優等成績

2. (**C**) She spent $10000 buying a coat; it was really an <u>extravagant</u> deed for a child to do so.
她花了一萬元買一件外套；這對小孩子來說是很<u>奢侈的</u>行為。

    (A) extraordinary 〔 ɪk'strɔrdn̩‚ɛrɪ 〕 adj. 不尋常的

    (B) depressed 〔 dɪ'prɛst 〕 adj. 沮喪的

    (C) ***extravagant*** 〔 ɪk'strævəgənt 〕 adj. 奢侈的

    (D) fragrant 〔'fregrənt 〕 adj. 芳香的

3. (**B**) The fire must have <u>broken</u> out after the staff had gone home. 一定是員工回家後，才<u>發生</u>火災。

    (A) start 〔 stɑrt 〕 v. 開始   (B) ***break out*** (火災、戰爭) 爆發

    (C) burn out 燒完   (D) catch 〔 kætʃ 〕 v. 捕捉

    * staff 〔 stæf 〕 n. 全體員工

4. (**B**) He wouldn't tell them the outcome but kept them in <u>suspense</u>. 他不告訴他們結果，讓他們很<u>緊張</u>。

    (A) dispel 〔 dɪ'spɛl 〕 v. 驅散

    (B) ***suspense*** 〔 sə'spɛns 〕 n. 緊張；懸疑

       keep sb. ***in suspense*** 使某人緊張

    (C) trespass 〔'trɛspəs 〕 v. 侵犯；侵入

    (D) dreadful 〔'drɛdfəl 〕 adj. 可怕的

5. (**D**) It is <u>ridiculous</u> to say that since the poor have no bread to eat, they can live on steak.
「窮人沒麵包吃，就可以牛排為食。」這種說法真<u>荒謬</u>。

    (A) delicious 〔 dɪ'lɪʃəs 〕 adj. 美味的

    (B) gorgeous 〔'gɔrdʒəs 〕 adj. 非常漂亮的

    (C) paradox 〔'pærə‚dɑks 〕 n. 自相矛盾的話

    (D) ***ridiculous*** 〔 rɪ'dɪkjələs 〕 adj. 荒謬的

6. (**C**) The Shinkong Mitsukoshi Building is the highest building in Taipei and thus becomes the new <u>landmark</u> of Taipei.
新光三越大樓是台北最高的建築物，因此變成台北的新<u>地標</u>。

    (A) magnet〔'mægnɪt〕*n.* 磁鐵
    (B) pole〔pol〕*n.* 竿；（南、北）極
    (C) ***landmark***〔'lænd,mɑrk〕*n.* 地標
    (D) hypothesis〔haɪ'pɑθəsɪs〕*n.* 假設

7. (**D**) It is impolite to <u>interrupt</u> people while they are talking.
<u>打斷</u>別人說話是很不禮貌的。

    (A) interpret〔ɪn'tɜprɪt〕*v.* 解釋   (B) interact〔,ɪntə'ækt〕*v.* 相互作用
    (C) intercept〔,ɪntə'sɛpt〕*v.* 攔截   (D) ***interrupt***〔,ɪntə'rʌpt〕*v.* 打斷

8. (**A**) I made some <u>preliminary</u> sketches which would serve as guides when I made the actual portrait.
我先畫好<u>初步的</u>草稿，眞正要畫的時候可以作爲參考。

    (A) ***preliminary***〔prɪ'lɪmə,nɛrɪ〕*adj.* 初步的
    (B) primary〔'praɪ,mɛrɪ〕*adj.* 主要的
    (C) elementary〔,ɛlə'mɛntərɪ〕*adj.* 初等的
    (D) fundamental〔,fʌndə'mɛntl̩〕*adj.* 基礎的
    * sketch〔skɛtʃ〕*n.* 草稿   guide〔gaɪd〕*n.* 指引

9. (**A**) The floods did not start to <u>recede</u> until three days after the rain had stopped. 雨停後三天，洪水才開始<u>消退</u>。

    (A) ***recede***〔rɪ'sid〕*v.* 後退
    (B) retire〔rɪ'taɪr〕*v.* 退休
    (C) retreat〔rɪ'trit〕*v.* 撤退
    (D) sink〔sɪŋk〕*v.* 沈沒

```
re   +cede
 |      |
back +  go
```

10. (**D**) This is our last semester in this school, and we hope our <u>intimate</u> classmates and our beloved teachers can help us tide over the hard time.
這是我們在學校的最後一個學期，我們希望<u>親愛的</u>同學和敬愛的老師能幫我們渡過這段艱難的時期。

    (A) imitate〔'ɪmə,tet〕*v.* 模仿   (B) closed〔klozd〕*adj.* 關閉的
    (C) closely〔'kloslɪ〕*adv.* 密切地   (D) ***intimate***〔'ɪntəmɪt〕*adj.* 親密的
    * beloved〔bɪ'lʌvd〕*adj.* 親愛的   ***tide over*** 渡過

TEST 49

Directions: *Of the four words given after each sentence, choose the one most suitable for filling in the blank.*

1. Teenagers need _____ ; it allows them to have a life of their own.
   - (A) privacy
   - (B) monotony
   - (C) excitement
   - (D) nutrition   (   )

2. The official supporter's club has appealed to fans to _____ from violence.
   - (A) awaken
   - (B) reconcile
   - (C) diminish
   - (D) refrain   (   )

3. The chairman had to intervene when the lecturer went an hour beyond _____ .
   - (A) instruction
   - (B) schedule
   - (C) concession
   - (D) tolerance   (   )

4. With no party holding a(n) _____ majority, it is likely that a coalition government will be formed.
   - (A) mutual
   - (B) efficient
   - (C) absolute
   - (D) accurate   (   )

5. Because of air pollution, the visibility in Taipei was _____ reduced this morning.
   - (A) spontaneously
   - (B) theoretically
   - (C) overwhelmingly
   - (D) invariably   (   )

6. The operation was successful, but the patient is still in
_____ condition.

   (A) critical
   (B) melancholy
   (C) excellent
   (D) sober   (   )

7. The anti-war rally was _____ by police with tear gas.

   (A) whacked
   (B) consoled
   (C) dispersed
   (D) stimulated   (   )

8. Opinion polls show that there has been a big _____
in favor of opposition parties.

   (A) swing
   (B) premium
   (C) diplomacy
   (D) sustenance   (   )

9. The U.N. Security Council passed a _____ condemning
the country's unilateral action.

   (A) suggestion
   (B) humiliation
   (C) association
   (D) resolution   (   )

10. According to the terms of the pact, a U.N. peace-keeping
force will _____ law and order.

   (A) retain
   (B) contain
   (C) maintain
   (D) sustain   (   )

TEST 49 詳解

1. (**A**) Teenagers need <u>privacy</u>; it allows them to have a life of their own. 青少年需要隱私權；如此他們才能擁有屬於自己的生活。
   (A) **privacy** (ˈpraɪvəsɪ) *n.* 隱私權　　(B) monotony (məˈnɑtnɪ) *n.* 單調
   (C) excitement (ɪkˈsaɪtmənt) *n.* 興奮
   (D) nutrition (njuˈtrɪʃən) *n.* 營養
   * teenager (ˈtinˌedʒə) *n.* (十幾歲的) 青少年

2. (**D**) The official supporter's club has appealed to fans to <u>refrain</u> from violence. 支持官方的社團吸引了一群反暴力的人。
   (A) awaken (əˈwekən) *v.* 喚起
   (B) reconcile (ˈrɛkənˌsaɪl) *v.* 使和解
   (C) diminish (dəˈmɪnɪʃ) *v.* 減少　　(D) **refrain** (rɪˈfren) *v.* 避免
   * **appeal to** 吸引　　fan (fæn) *n.* 迷

3. (**B**) The chairman had to intervene when the lecturer went an hour beyond <u>schedule</u>.
   若演講人的演說超過預定時間一小時，主席必須出面干涉。
   (A) instruction (ɪnˈstrʌkʃən) *n.* 指導
   (B) **schedule** (ˈskɛdʒul) *n.* 時間表
   (C) concession (kənˈsɛʃən) *n.* 讓步　(D) tolerance (ˈtɑlərəns) *n.* 容忍
   * chairman (ˈtʃɛrmən) *n.* 主席
     intervene (ˌɪntəˈvin) *v.* 干涉；介入　lecturer (ˈlɛktʃərə) *n.* 演講者

4. (**C**) With no party holding an <u>absolute</u> majority, it is likely that a coalition government will be formed.
   因為沒有政黨佔有絕對的多數，因此很可能會形成聯合政府。
   (A) mutual (ˈmjutʃuəl) *adj.* 互相的
   (B) efficient (əˈfɪʃənt) *adj.* 有效率的
   (C) **absolute** (ˈæbsəˌlut) *adj.* 絕對的
   (D) accurate (ˈækjərɪt) *adj.* 準確的
   * majority (məˈdʒɔrətɪ) *n.* 多數　　coalition (ˌkoəˈlɪʃən) *n.* 聯合

5. (**D**) Because of air pollution, the visibility in Taipei was <u>invariably</u> reduced this morning.
   因為空氣污染的緣故，今天早上台北的能見度一定會降低。
   (A) spontaneously (spɑnˈtenɪəslɪ) *adv.* 自然地
   (B) theoretically (ˌθiəˈrɛtɪklɪ) *adv.* 理論上
   (C) overwhelmingly (ˌovəˈhwɛlmɪŋlɪ) *adv.* 壓倒性地
   (D) **invariably** (ɪnˈvɛrɪəblɪ) *adv.* 不變地；必定
   * visibility (ˌvɪzəˈbɪlətɪ) *n.* 能見度

6. (**A**) The operation was successful, but the patient is still in
<u>critical</u> condition. 手術非常成功，但病人目前仍未脫離險境。

    (A) ***critical*** 〔ˋkrɪtɪkḷ 〕*adj.* 危急的

    (B) melancholy 〔ˋmɛlən͵kɑlɪ 〕*adj.* 憂鬱的

    (C) excellent 〔ˋɛksḷənt 〕*adj.* 優秀的   (D) sober 〔ˋsobɚ 〕*adj.* 清醒的

7. (**C**) The anti-war rally was <u>dispersed</u> by police with tear gas.
警方以催淚瓦斯驅散參加反戰集會的群眾。

    (A) whack 〔hwæk 〕*v.* 用力敲打   (B) console 〔kənˋsol 〕*v.* 安慰

    (C) ***disperse*** 〔dɪˋspɝs 〕*v.* 驅散   (D) stimulate 〔ˋstɪmjə͵let 〕*v.* 刺激

    * anti-war 〔͵æntɪˋwɔr 〕*adj.* 反戰的   rally 〔ˋrælɪ 〕*n.* 集會

8. (**A**) Opinion polls show that there has been a big <u>swing</u> in favor
of opposition parties. 民意調查顯示，反對黨的支持度大幅領先。

    (A) ***swing*** 〔swɪŋ 〕*n.* 振幅；擺動

    (B) premium 〔ˋprimɪəm 〕*n.* 重視；保險金

    (C) diplomacy 〔dɪˋploməsɪ 〕*n.* 外交；外交手腕

    (D) sustenance 〔ˋsʌstənəns 〕*n.* 食物；（生命等的）維持

    * poll 〔pol 〕*n.* 民意測驗   ***in favor of*** 支持

    opposition party 反對黨

9. (**D**) The U.N. Security Council passed a <u>resolution</u> condemning
the country's unilateral action.
聯合國安理會已通過一項決議案，譴責該國的單獨行動。

    (A) suggestion 〔səˋdʒɛstʃən 〕*n.* 建議

    (B) humiliation 〔hju͵mɪlɪˋeʃən 〕*n.* 屈辱

    (C) association 〔ə͵sosɪˋeʃən 〕*n.* 協會；公會

    (D) ***resolution*** 〔͵rɛzəˋluʃən 〕*n.* 決議案

    * ***U.N. Security Council*** 聯合國安理會

    condemn 〔kənˋdɛm 〕*v.* 譴責

    unilateral 〔͵junɪˋlætərəl 〕*adj.* 片面的；單獨的

10. (**C**) According to the terms of the pact, a U.N. peace-keeping
force will <u>maintain</u> law and order.
根據協定條款，聯合國和平部隊必須維持法治與秩序。

    (A) retain 〔rɪˋten 〕*v.* 保留   (B) contain 〔kənˋten 〕*v.* 包含

    (C) ***maintain*** 〔menˋten 〕*v.* 維持   (D) sustain 〔səˋsten 〕*v.* 支持

    * term 〔tɝm 〕*n.* 條款   ***U.N. peace-keeping force*** 聯合國和平部隊

TEST 50

Directions: *Of the four words given after each sentence, choose the one most suitable for filling in the blank.*

1. With his patience and efforts, none of us had any doubt that _____ he would succeed.
   (A) spontaneously
   (B) attentively
   (C) barely
   (D) eventually   (   )

2. The child was only adopted a year ago , but he has completely _____ into the family's life.
   (A) transformed
   (B) adapted
   (C) integrated
   (D) separated   (   )

3. We have regulations to follow here. Those who break them will be severely _____ .
   (A) disciplined
   (B) exalted
   (C) tolerated
   (D) suffered   (   )

4. Jane got this bike from someone else. She isn't its _____ owner.
   (A) potential
   (B) obvious
   (C) original
   (D) artificial   (   )

5. Thank you for your help. I really couldn't adequately express my _____ to you.
   (A) indifference
   (B) disposition
   (C) perspective
   (D) gratitude   (   )

6. Mary didn't want to go to school, so she ———— that she was sick.

(A) discovered
(B) pretended
(C) introduced
(D) permitted   (   )

7. She was showered with ———— on her excellent performance.

(A) compliments
(B) frustrations
(C) humiliations
(D) challenges   (   )

8. What you are saying is ————. Nobody would believe it.

(A) enchanting
(B) ridiculous
(C) credulous
(D) populous   (   )

9. The bridge isn't strong enough to allow the ———— of heavy trucks.

(A) passage
(B) sustenance
(C) inspection
(D) fracture   (   )

10. Since he has been selfish and mean, no one ———— with his misfortune now.

(A) apologizes
(B) appreciates
(C) sympathizes
(D) supplies   (   )

TEST 50 詳解

1. (**D**) With his patience and efforts, none of us had any doubt that <u>eventually</u> he would succeed.
   由於他的耐心和努力，我們都相信他<u>最後</u>會成功。
   - (A) spontaneously〔spɑn'tɛnɪəslɪ〕*adv.* 自然地
   - (B) attentively〔ə'tɛntɪvlɪ〕*adv.* 專心地
   - (C) barely〔'bɛrlɪ〕*adv.* 幾乎不
   - (D) *eventually*〔ɪ'vɛntʃʊəlɪ〕*adv.* 最後；終於

2. (**C**) The child was only adopted a year ago, but he has completely <u>integrated</u> into the family's life.
   這小孩一年前才被領養，但他已完全<u>融入</u>現在的家庭生活中。
   - (A) transform〔træns'fɔrm〕*v.* 轉變
   - (B) adapt〔ə'dæpt〕*v.* 使適應
   - (C) *integrate*〔'ɪntə,gret〕*v.* 融合
   - (D) separate〔'sɛpə,ret〕*v.* 使分開
   - * adopt〔ə'dɑpt〕*v.* 領養

3. (**A**) We have regulations to follow here. Those who break them will be severely <u>disciplined</u>.
   在此我們必須遵守規定。違反的人將遭受嚴厲的<u>處罰</u>。
   - (A) *discipline*〔'dɪsəplɪn〕*v.* 懲罰
   - (B) exalt〔ɪg'zɔlt〕*v.* 提高
   - (C) tolerate〔'tɑlə,ret〕*v.* 容忍
   - (D) suffer〔'sʌfə〕*v.* 受苦
   - * break〔brek〕*v.* 違反   severely〔sə'vɪrlɪ〕*adv.* 嚴格地

4. (**C**) Jane got this bike from someone else. She isn't its <u>original</u> owner. 珍從別人手中得到這輛腳踏車。她不是這輛腳踏車的<u>原主</u>。
   - (A) potential〔pə'tɛnʃəl〕*adj.* 有潛力的
   - (B) obvious〔'ɑbvɪəs〕*adj.* 明顯的
   - (C) *original*〔ə'rɪdʒən!〕*adj.* 原來的
   - (D) artificial〔,ɑrtə'fɪʃəl〕*adj.* 人造的

5. (**D**) Thank you for your help. I really couldn't adequately express my <u>gratitude</u> to you.
   謝謝你的幫助。我不知該如何適當地表達我的<u>感激</u>。
   - (A) indifference〔ɪn'dɪfərəns〕*n.* 漠不關心
   - (B) disposition〔,dɪspə'zɪʃən〕*n.* 性情；氣質
   - (C) perspective〔pə'spɛktɪv〕*n.* 正確的眼光
   - (D) *gratitude*〔'grætə,tjud〕*n.* 感激
   - * adequately〔'ædəkwɪtlɪ〕*adv.* 適當地

6. (**B**) Mary didn't want to go to school, so she <u>pretended</u> that she was sick. 瑪麗不想去上學，就<u>假裝</u>生病。

(A) discover〔dɪˈskʌvɚ〕*v.* 發現　　(B) ***pretend***〔prɪˈtɛnd〕*v.* 假裝
(C) introduce〔͵ɪntrəˈdjus〕*v.* 介紹　(D) permit〔pɚˈmɪt〕*v.* 准許

7. (**A**) She was showered with <u>compliments</u> on her excellent performance. 她優異的表現受到衆人的<u>讚賞</u>。

(A) ***compliment***〔ˈkɑmpləmənt〕*n.* 稱讚
(B) frustration〔frʌsˈtreʃən〕*n.* 挫折
(C) humiliation〔hju͵mɪlɪˈeʃən〕*n.* 屈辱
(D) challenge〔ˈtʃælɪndʒ〕*n.* 挑戰

* ***be showered with*** 被大量地給與~

8. (**B**) What you are saying is <u>ridiculous</u>. Nobody would believe it. 你說的話很<u>荒謬</u>。沒有人會相信。

(A) enchanting〔ɪnˈtʃæntɪŋ〕*adj.* 迷人的
(B) ***ridiculous***〔rɪˈdɪkjələs〕*adj.* 荒謬的
(C) credulous〔ˈkrɛdʒuləs〕*adj.* 容易相信別人的
(D) populous〔ˈpɑpjələs〕*adj.* 人口稠密的

9. (**A**) The bridge isn't strong enough to allow the <u>passage</u> of heavy trucks. 這座橋不夠堅固，大卡車無法<u>通行</u>。

(A) ***passage***〔ˈpæsɪdʒ〕*n.* 通行
(B) sustenance〔ˈsʌstənəns〕*n.* 食物；（生命等的）維持
(C) inspection〔ɪnˈspɛkʃən〕*n.* 檢查
(D) fracture〔ˈfræktʃɚ〕*n.* 裂縫

10. (**C**) Since he has been selfish and mean, no one <u>sympathizes</u> with his misfortune now.
因爲他旣自私又卑鄙，所以現在沒有人<u>同情</u>他的不幸。

(A) apologize〔əˈpɑlə͵dʒaɪz〕*v.* 道歉
(B) appreciate〔əˈpriʃɪ͵et〕*v.* 欣賞；感激
(C) ***sympathize***〔ˈsɪmpə͵θaɪz〕*v.* 同情
(D) supply〔səˈplaɪ〕*v.* 供給

* selfish〔ˈsɛlfɪʃ〕*adj.* 自私的　　mean〔min〕*adj.* 卑鄙的
misfortune〔mɪsˈfɔrtʃən〕*n.* 不幸

INDEX